# CAPE HENRY HOUSE

Jolly Walker Bittick

To America's veterans:

Thank you for your service.

The workday had been long, so when I pulled into my driveway, I was slow to get out of the pickup. A tune played on the radio that I hadn't heard in a long time, so I listened. It was a classic from the mid-2000's and it kicked up some old memories. I pictured myself driving the old beater for a car I had during that time, back when CDs were a mainstay, and you were considered cool if you had a cellphone with a camera. The tune ended, and the glimpse of a day passed faded.

When I got out of the pickup, I headed inside through the laundry room. I could smell a mild odor coming from the trash in the kitchen. I promptly emptied the can and ran the bag to the receptacle outside. Some fluids from the bag spilled onto the sleeve of my button up as I hurled it into the bin. I cursed, slamming the lid shut.

Inside, I replaced the bag, then got a beer out of the fridge. Through the kitchen window, I saw the lawn standing tall and in need of mowing. Sipping the beer, I retreated to the couch in the living room. After failing to wipe the stain off with cleaning wipes, I turned the TV on, kicked my feet up on the coffee table, and channel surfed. One channel featured a stupid reality show, another had a screaming politician, the third showcased a movie. As I watched, I realized the movie was a coming-of-age comedy about some young fools that end up at a wild party. It brought me back to the memory of my old car, one that everyone used to refer to as "Green Beater".

The movie continued to play, but I became swept away in memories. I remembered driving Green Beater to a place known as "Cape Henry House". I swerved up over the curb while making a U-turn in the middle of the street so I could get a premium parking spot out front. Inside the house, an unbelievable party raged. The movie vanished from consciousness, and there I was… *it was early 2008*.

# 1. Green Beater

I was a greaser on helicopters in the Navy. I turned
21 the previous summer, and I was still trying to
figure myself out. It was the neophyte phase of life;
too old to be a kid and too young to be considered
an adult. My first year in the military was tough, they
stationed me at a place far from everything I knew
around many people from different walks of life. I
was lucky by my second and third year to have a
good core group of friends, many of whom I
bonded with during a recent deployment. A lot of us
came of age together since we were in the same boat,
sometimes literally.

Overall, the military lifestyle was rocky. On
shore, the routine was cutthroat: work ridiculous
hours in the hangar or on the flight line and, if lucky,
make it out in time for last call at the local bar. At
sea, it was even simpler: 12 hours on and 12 hours
off. The only catch at sea, however, was that there
were only so many places to go on a ship, so
lounging in the berthing area was often the only
genuine option. In early 2008, I was back on shore
assigned to night shift (night check) at the command,
and unlike the day shift (day check) crew, they did

not set night check hours. We reported at 1400 and finished whenever the superiors released us. Day check worked a square shift from 0600 to 1500, and we knew that had a lot to do with the brass of the command working then as well. With that, came more freedom for night check to get work done, the caveat was the longer hours. Sometimes, the sun was rising as we were still wrenching away on the helicopters (or "helos" as we called them); a situation that we more or less dealt with and not one we ever got used to.

On one Friday shift in late January, night check finished up well early of the normal timeframe of 0200 - 0300 in the morning (Saturday). The Maintenance Chief, the senior most enlisted person in charge of the maintenance, summoned us all to muster up in the hangar. Muster was a formation three to four rows deep of shipmates standing at attention awaiting further instruction. As things were often more relaxed on night check, muster was more informal than those on day check. Chief called us to announce that we covered all the maintenance requests and were good to go for the night. Since it was only 0030 in the morning, we were thrilled. A few drinks at the local bar were in order.

We hurried to the locker room to change out of our Navy issue coveralls and back into our personal clothes, or "civies" as we called them. Most of the boys knew what was in order; change, hop in the car, and head down to "Greenies", the local bar. Greenies was five blocks off base along the bay shore, and they never closed early. I took my time getting changed out of my coveralls as some messy work done on a helo gearbox soiled them. We wore white under shirts with every uniform, including our coveralls. In the aviation maintenance line of work, white under shirts often stunk of jet fuel and hydraulic fluid. Even worse, the fuels and oils left brutal stains on clothing; nothing looked worse than the stains on white under shirts. I did my best to clean up, then made my way to Greenies.

In the winter months, it was always easier to find parking at Greenies. It was a ratty place, and we only frequented it during the early days because of its proximity to base. Over time, the place grew on us. It also helped that the bartenders knew us, we were favorites among the staff and the patrons, and in exchange for good tipping, they looked out for our group. Once inside, I looked for my pals. Only four were there——Paul "B-man" Blaine, Timothy Madzik, whom we called "Zick", Nathan Dolvar, and Johnny Kline. They sat up at the crowded corner of the bar where we often sat or stood.

When they saw me approaching, they all called out my name, "Bosner!" Their boisterous yelling drew attention from just about everyone in the establishment, to which I nodded and said "hi" in return. I ordered a beer and gave a cheer to my four shipmates, or members of what many at the command referred to as "the gang".

"So, what's good, guys?" I asked.

Zick and Kline looked over to B-man and Dolvar.

"Dolvar and I are moving into a place down the road from base."

"No shit?"

"Nope." Dolvar grinned.

He and B-man were two different men; B-man was tall and slim with a shaved head, while Dolvar was short and stalky with a crop haircut. They were both New Yorkers, however.

"Well, where's this place at?" I asked.

"Off the highway by the airport. Cape Henry Avenue, I think." B-man replied.

Kline laughed. "You're moving into a place without even knowing where it's at?"

B-man sipped his beer. "Hey asshole, I can show you. That's good enough for me."

"What kinda place we talking, a house or some apartment crap? Would be nice to have a place to do some grilling and chilling outside." Zick said.

Zick, the newest shipmate among the gang, was a hearty, mechanically inclined fellow from Michigan.

"You know Mark Penley? He and his wife were looking for a few roommates, and asked Dolvar and I if we were interested. The place is pretty good sized. Come out tomorrow and see for yourself." B-man replied.

Mark Penley was another shipmate, one who worked in the generator shop at the command. In terms of the gang, he was more of a "hang around".

He was a slim, unassuming guy from Ohio. He recently married his wife, Anne. While both shared the name "Penley", we only called him Penley since we served together; the gang always knew his wife as "Anne". That B-man and Dolvar, consummate partiers, were moving in with a married couple, seemed curious to me. A thought crossed my mind, which made me wonder how an arrangement with such roommates would pan out. Before I thought any deeper about the scenario, I took the news for what it was; good. As the gang saw it, we were about to have a house to relax at and unwind away from the cramped barracks.

"I say cheers to the new place." Dolvar said before shouting, "LETS DO SHOTS."

Taking his lead, we followed suit in taking shots. I didn't ask what it was they ordered, but it was dark, so I assumed it was whiskey. I gulped it down with the rest of the gang. Soon after, the night drifted into a blur like many other nights had at Greenies. The music blared, and the laughing increased until it dimmed out and things went into a daze. I remembered nothing after that.

A bright light glared in my eyes when I opened them, and then a moan sounded. For a moment, I couldn't figure out what the light or the sound was. The light soon dimmed enough for me to realize I made it to my room, and the moaning was coming from me. I cleared my throat, then licked my lips. *Damnit Dolvar*, I thought to myself. Feeling frail, I got up onto my feet and made a trip to the bathroom. My feet dragged as I tried walking straight, and my shoulders slouched because of the sheer exhaustion. I reached the bathroom, and after taking care of business, I looked into the mirror at the sink.

"Bosner..." I said aloud.

In the mirror was a reflection of a guy with bruises all over his lower neck and upper chest. I was in disbelief and somewhat scared that they may have come from someone undesirable. Upon review, there were dark bruises on my left shoulder and even on my upper back as well. They were hickeys, but from who? The night was a blur, and it was impossible to know. I could do nothing but shake my head and hope they came from at least a five or higher. I cleaned up, got dressed, and made my way outside. At that point it was almost Noon, and as I trudged out of my room into the barracks corridor, I saw the usual sights.

A few doors down from my room was Casello, a Massachusetts native dedicated to making it to Master Chief, the top enlisted rank. He sat in the hallway outside his room on his laptop. I nodded to him and he followed suit. Just before reaching the quarterdeck (the barracks lobby, but the Navy liked to use ship terms on everything) was the entryway to the laundry room. As I walked by, I saw Wilkins, a brother from Louisiana whom everybody knew as "Wilky". He was on his phone arguing with someone. We fist bumped as he continued arguing over the phone.

When I reached the quarterdeck, sitting watch as Officer on Deck (known better as "OOD") was Petty Officer Second Class Andrew Pickens, a person liked by nobody and whose only claim to fame was that he outranked everyone who lived in the barracks. He tried in pathetic fashion to be a bully, or an authoritarian, but it made us look at him in an even lesser way. On that day, he was with a Petty Officer First Class I had never seen before. The two were conversing until I attempted to pass unnoticed. With Pickens, a clean exit was impossible.

"Bosner." he called.

"What's up?"

He appeared to be offended. "That's no way to talk to a Second Class."

I tried not to laugh at all 150lbs of him, with unkept red hair that was almost beyond Navy regulations.

"Pickens, what do you want?"

"First, I want you to stand at attention when I speak to you. Second, I want you to meet Petty Officer Thompson. He will take over leadership at the barracks."

I stood at ease, and because Pickens was less than a fan favorite of everyone's at the barracks, I hoped that the new First Class would be an improvement.

"Good morning Petty Officer, I'm Bosner, I live in Room 129."

I reached out to shake his hand. Thompson was a tall, sharp dressed First Class, but he stood staring at me with my arm extended.

"Hello Bosner, what's your command?"

Since he rebuffed by attempted handshake, I answered over his question.

"I'm an aviation mechanic."

"What's your command?" he asked in robotic fashion.

I felt a rudeness from Thompson, so I was difficult back.

"What's your command?" I asked.

Pickens stood from behind the desk. "Bosner, that's enough of that, answer the question."

Thompson gave off a squinting smile as though he put me in my place. After a pause, I proceeded towards the door.

"You two have a nice day."

"Bosner! Bosner! You can't walk away like that!" Pickens shouted.

"I just did. Later."

I walked out the door.

"Bosner I'm not done with you! No women are allowed at the barracks! I heard about you last night!! You hear me?" he continued.

His last remarks at least explained what the bruises on my upper body were from. It tempted me to go back and ask him if the woman that I allowed into the barracks was at least a seven, but Pickens was bad news and the new First Class Thompson appeared little better. I continued towards the

parking lot to find my car, Green Beater. It was a
1995 clunker that I bought for low cost from a
distant uncle who once lived in the area. The rear
driver's side door gave off a creaking sound
whenever opened, the wheel alignment was less than
stellar, and mysterious stains riddled the back seat.
On some occasions, I called Green Beater home, as
I slept in it during the summer if I went out to a
party where "face vandals" lurked.

I found Green Beater parked in a place that
wasn't a legitimate parking spot. One of the biggest
advantages to having a compact car was the
additional parking options in congested places. I
turned on the ignition and was reminded that I had a
CD of hard rock in the stereo which made me flinch.
Still feeling rough, it took me a second to muster the
function necessary to lower the volume before
shutting off the stereo altogether. I left hungry, but I
knew a good greasy lunch (or breakfast) was the
right cure for the zinger of a headache I was dealing
with. I drove to a burger joint just outside of base to
get some recovery food. The magic of a triple patty
cheeseburger, and how it made headaches and
hangovers disappear, was stuff of legend.

Once I grabbed food, I remembered what was
on the schedule for the day; a trip to B-man and
Dolvar's new place. I called B-man to get directions,
but he didn't answer. As it was still early in the
afternoon, I drove to a nearby beach to eat my
hangover cure. There was plenty of parking since it
was winter, and only a few scattered people on the

sands braved the brisk temperatures. There was a clipping wind, but I thought that sitting outside and eating would help with the hangover. I settled for sitting on the roof of Green Beater, facing the ocean. As I ate and spilled ketchup on my lap, a couple walking a dog passed by.

"Cold, at all?" The man asked.

"I love it cold! Nice pup." I said.

The couple smiled and proceeded onward as the dog barked at me. The cold dining on the roof of Green Beater at least kept my headache from worsening. As I finished up eating, I tried my best to wipe the annoying ketchup stain off my lap. Inconveniently, the stain was in the crotch area of my pants. Once I gave up trying to rid myself of the stain, I opted to go for an impromptu drive around town. I returned to the confines of Green Beater and got back on the road. I cranked up the stereo and cruised around town with the windows down so that anyone within distance could hear me jamming out for no particular reason. After about an hour, and the disappointment that there were few if any pretty ladies out and about in downtown, I got a call from B-man.

"Top of the mornin to ya." I answered.

"Bro, what's up!"

"Just strolling around town. Had an interesting night."

B-man laughed. "Was she good?"

"Not to me, there are wounds."

He continued to laugh.

"So, where am I going?" I asked.

"Take the airport exit on the Interstate. From base take the westbound or opposite if you are coming from the other way."

There was a pause.

"And?"

"Yep." he replied.

"Dude, work with me here. So, airport exit—for me it will be eastbound side. Then...?"

"Bro, I'm still feeling last night. Airport exit, then a left. Turn right just before the railroad tracks."

"There ya go! Okay man, I'll be there soon. I'll just look for your car." I said.

"Yep. See you soon."

B-man was known for one-liners, at least when sober. He was more of a "show you" type, so we learned how to understand him when he gave vague directions. Maybe the most notable thing about B-man was that he and I were only a week apart in age. We both had shared notoriety among the gang and many at the command for us both turning 21 in Vietnam by virtue of the previous year's deployment. The two of us always got off on telling that to people who always thought we made it up. We didn't!

While I swerved Green Beater through traffic on the freeway, I thought about B-man and Dolvar's new house, and its potential. For the gang, being loud was another way of being comfortable with ourselves. I thought of all the times we had gathered at someone's apartment and partied. Often it seemed like neighbors complained and called the cops, or there was limited space to sprawl. I sprawled, which was how everyone described my penchant to drink and then take extended naps during a party. On over one occasion, I was moved while sprawling to an undesirable location such as a dog's bed or under a dining room table. Having a house to party at meant there was more of a chance to find good places to crash, and that alone made the prospects of the new place well worth it! In my mind, there wasn't much that we could do at the new house that we hadn't done already—except we could be louder.

As I cruised the Interstate crossing paths with a few unsavory drivers, one moron in a lifted pickup who was swerving around cars caught my attention. I was approaching the airport exit, but the truck served in the exit lane and sped up. They were trying to pass me, but in the process, they blocked me from getting over into the lane. I squeezed into the lane just in front of them and made for the exit. After, I made the left as B-man instructed, then kept straight, looking for the railroad tracks. As I continued, I wondered what type of neighborhood the house was in. On one hand, a terrible neighborhood might mean that we could party harder, on the other, it could also mean we would clash with neighbors who may bring bad habits to our parties. Either way, I had little doubt we could blare music and chill at the new place.

I fell into a sort of trance listening to a tune on the stereo when a railroad crossing appeared. Just before the crossing was a T-intersection with a street going to the right; it was Cape Henry Avenue. I swerved right to make the turn and almost struck a car stopped at the intersection. The driver honked at me in frustration as I waved at them to apologize. I saw a hub cap rolling with a bounce to my left; it was the final hub cap from Green Beater. The hub cap came to rest on the street after striking the curb. I watched it fall further in the distance through my rearview mirror as I shook my head. There was nothing out of the ordinary about Cape Henry Avenue; it was a street long and straight with houses on both the left and right. The houses looked similar to one another, so I looked out for B-Man's car—a silver four-door sedan with New York tags. Not much further down the street, I saw it parked on the left behind what I believed to be Penley's SUV. I passed by, making a U-turn in the middle of the street and running over the curb. When I returned to the house, I parked street side.

There was nothing about the house that stood out. It was a modest looking home that appeared to be older. It had brick siding with a decent sized porch and a small front lawn, shrubs lined the exterior beyond the porch. On the right was an attached one-car garage that appeared to be walled in providing additional floor space to the home. I sat in Green Beater for a moment looking at the house, then got out and proceeded to the front door. I approached the front door up the porch steps and then heard my name. Before I could react, the front door swung open.

"Welcome." B-man said.

"So this is the new castle!"

He ran his hand over his face. "Yea something like that. Still feeling last night."

"You gotta get some greasy, nasty grub to curb it!"

I walked into the house and saw it was as ordinary as the exterior. Just inside the front door was the living room, with the TV and sound system to the left, and couches on the right along the wall. Straight ahead was the kitchen and a sliding glass door to the back. A hallway to the left was presumably where the bathroom and bedrooms were. B-man was excited to show me the peculiar garage. I noticed on the outside that it was walled-in which showed that it was likely converted into a room. Indeed, it was a carpeted and insulated space.

"Pass out room!" he said.

"This alone makes the place an upgrade. Well done."

Inside the "pass out room" to the left was a makeshift wall concealing the laundry space just behind it.

"What do you think the max capacity is for this pass out room?" I asked.

B-man grabbed the back of his neck. "I don't know, bro. When you're drunk, who cares?"

With that, we proceeded to the fridge to begin the afternoon with a cold brew. He showed me the backyard, which was larger than the front with a patio and a charcoal grill. A fence lined the back, and beyond that were railroad tracks. We conversed outside for a bit before we went back in. When we went to get more beer from the fridge, a moan and footsteps sounded from the hallway. Feet dragging and looking like hell, there stood Dolvar.

"When was bedtime?" I asked.

"Bro, he was still up when I first got up."

"Bosner, get me a beer." Dolvar said.

Dolvar was the one in the gang who could out drink any of us. As a result, he was often the nasty drunk of the bunch. A mysterious person, none of us knew much about him except he was a New Yorker along with B-man. Among us, things were fine, except his ability to kill a rack of beers. He drank the one I gave him and then perked up.

"Bosner, what up clown!" he said.

I patted him. "Welcome back."

The three of us stayed in the kitchen drinking and gossiping until Penley walked through the front door.

"Bosner, I'm gonna kill you!" he said.

With a serious smirk, I wasn't sure what to make of him.

"He's fuckin with you, clown." Dolvar said.

Penley smiled. "Welcome to the new digs."

I was always a bit off. The gang was prone to sling insults back and forth as a way of showing "bromance", and I always reacted too slow to exhibit any form of wit. I think they liked that about me; I provided a unique character that stood out. The four of us stood around in the kitchen for a while, trading stories and drinking. In the back of my mind, I figured I would have a few more beers and then take a power nap on the couch. I was often the first in the group to retire for the night, as I had that "one last" beer a time or two too soon that would do me in. Since I often went to bed early, I would be up first thing to get coffee going and piss everyone off by waking them up for lunch. But on that night, B-man and Dolvar had ideas beyond our normal routine.

# 2. Party! A House

I relaxed into a pleasant buzz when the vibe of the evening changed on its head. A mostly quiet gathering at the new house turned into an invitation drive to get a party started. Penley went into his room while I kicked it on the couch and thought of inviting someone close to my heart, a woman named Maria. Unfortunately, she wasn't keen on being around the gang. She was 22 and mature; I was neither. Instead, I invited a fellow shipmate, Souza. It turned out that someone else already invited him and he was on his way.

I remained on the couch watching DVDs and sipping a beer while B-man and Dolvar went on a frenzy cleaning up. Afterwards, they went through their phone contacts inviting anyone and everyone to the house before they left. I was so relaxed watching TV that I didn't think to ask them where they were going. I was ready for another beer when the front door opened, and Anne came in. Short and red-headed, she was friendly but preferred to keep to herself.

"Glad you could find your way here." she said.

"How was your week?"

"Oh, just great. I'm looking forward to sleep."

"A beer might help you knock out." I said.

She waved her hand and headed straight to the hallway, lugging a backpack that was practically her size. As the bedroom door closed, it occurred to me that even if only a few people that B-man and Dolvar invited over showed up, Anne Penley would not get much sleep. I laughed at the realization, then grabbed another beer from the fridge. Just then, a voice sounded from outside the front door. Leaning back from the fridge, I saw Zick peering through the window. I grabbed an extra beer and proceeded to the door. Once near the door, it swung open, knocking one beer out of my hand and onto the floor; bottle broken, beer spilled.

"Asshole!" I said.

Zick stood in the doorway laughing. He took the lone beer in my hand and popped the cap.

"Got me a beer. Good man."

"Oh yea, you know it…"

We fist bumped.

"Hey, do you know Thayer?" he asked.

"I don't think so. Is he at the command?" I replied.

"No, no. He lives at my barracks. Big guy, never turns away food or drinks."

"Dude, that sounds like us. Except the 'big' part." I joked.

"Yea man, I invited him out. He might bring people, I vouch for 'em."

The door remained open, and then a gust whipped into the house. Zick grabbed a bag he placed on the porch and came inside. I closed the door, and we sat down. Penley came out of his room amidst the commotion. He gave a mean glare, then I remembered the spilled beer on the floor. Whenever he glared at me, I wasn't sure if it was him playing around or wanting to throw down. I cleaned up the spill and waited for him to boast. He didn't disappoint.

"That's right Bosner, clean that shit up. I'll kill you if you do it again."

Liquid courage had taken me by storm at that point.

"Oh yea?" I replied.

Zick spit up some beer. Penley turned to walk away, but after my response he slowly turned around. I finished cleaning up the glass on the floor.

"Finish that up and then we'll fight!" he said.

I glared back at him. "Cool."

Zick laughed. "Bosner, you look pretty good. The beer will break the fall."

I emptied the glass-filled dustpan in the trash and put the broom away. When I turned, Penley stood facing me, toe to toe.

"I heard you're scrappy shit." he said.

I assumed he was referring to a wrestling match I was recently in. My shop at the command had a very unceremonious way of settling beefs between shipmates. We called it "The Rat", slang for fight ring. It was nothing more than a bare spot on the concrete floor in the shop where two pissed off shipmates would throw down; often there was an audience. A few weeks prior, I went at it with Airman Aldman. Aldman took some of my equipment without telling me, which almost caused trouble when I couldn't account for it at the end of shift. When I confronted him, he challenged me to The Rat. I happily accepted and won.

"I can hold my own." I replied to Penley.

He laughed, then grabbed the collar of my shirt. I swung my right arm up under his left armpit and clutched the back of his right shoulder. We hit the floor, and then Anne screamed.

"What in the hell!"

Zick, standing above us, shook his head. "You call that a fight?"

Penley patted me on the back and started laughing.

"Fucker." I said.

Penley looked at Anne. "Honey, just testing the floor strength!"

She wasn't impressed. Just then, loud voices sounded out front. In came B-man, Dolvar, and a few others. B-man had groceries, Dolvar had some liquor. B-man looked at Penley and I as we remained on the floor.

"Are you making out?" he asked.

"I was beating Bosner's ass."

I scoffed. "Uh, no, I grabbed Penley and we—"

"Enough! Don't fight. Don't break stuff. I'm tired!" Anne said.

Zick pointed at her. "Great, let's get you a drink!"

She glared, then shook her head. Arms crossed, she stomped back down the hallway to the bedroom. Penley followed her.

"Pussy whipped clowns." Dolvar said.

After a pause, B-man threw one of the grocery bags at me. It was chips.

"I got a keg, bro. One of you come help me with it."

I handled the chips while Zick went out to help with the keg. Dolvar, myself, and three people I didn't know stood there awkwardly. There were two guys, one tall with a neck tattoo and another, shorter and tubby. The latter looked like he slept in a dumpster, his clothes looked disheveled, and he smelled. The third person was a girl, a solid six, maybe seven.

"So, this tall sexy bastard is an old friend of mine from A-School. Bill Richards, everyone calls him 'Billy'." Dolvar said.

I assumed the others were B-man's friends, since they seemed to have just met one another themselves. We shook hands.

"Hi Billy, I'm Bosner."

"Pleasure." he replied.

Dumpster dude nodded.

"Ian Thomas, fixed wing mech!"

"Bosner."

Lastly, the girl.

"Lana Lauridsen, but I go by 'Lorrie'."

She had dirty blonde hair with a fair complexion, expressive green eyes, and nice lips. She looked opposite of Thomas in every way; I kept my eye contact short and sweet.

"Hi Lorrie, I'm Bosner."

I went to get beers for everyone, but Dolvar reminded me about the keg. We stood around briefly, then went out front to check on B-man and Zick. As we approached the driveway, B-man stood up against his car laughing. At his feet lay Zick, the keg next to him on its side.

"Dude." I said.

B-man was laughing too hard to speak. Zick slowly got up.

"Hey." he gasped, trying to catch his breath. "Ever try bear hugging a fucking keg?"

I shook my head. "Nope. Glad to see you're okay though."

"I'm thirsty, clowns. Get up." Dolvar said.

We propped the keg upright and then Dolvar with B-man grabbed the handles and lugged it into the house. Inside, B-man re-introduced me to Thomas and Lorrie. Both were mutual friends of his who were at different commands on base; like Dolvar, he had met them through A-School. Navy A-School was specialized training that followed completion of boot camp. Interestingly, I joined the Navy in late summer 2005, when Hurricane Katrina tore through the gulf states and devastated New

Orleans. As a result, the traditional aviation-based A-Schools that are at Pensacola, Florida temporarily moved to naval bases across the country; mine was in Norfolk, Virginia. I was the only one in the gang who joined up during that time, and therefore my early days in the Navy were markedly different from everyone else's.

Billy emerged from the pass out room laughing at the concept.

"You have couches in the living room. A pass out room? Overkill don't ya think?" he asked.

B-man seemed irritated. "Bro—"

"Hey, it pays to be prepared. Where are the damned cups!" I interrupted.

Dolvar went tearing through the grocery bags to find them. Zick tapped my shoulder.

"Hey man. Dolvar is already in 'dick mode'. Might wanna keep the rum away." he whispered.

"It's your rum." I replied.

"I know, but last time that dude got ahold of it, he killed it. He woke up with the bottle in hand. He's crazy with the booze."

"Ah, aren't we all!" I said aloud.

Zick grinned. "Cheers. Let's get fucked up!"

They put the keg into a small tub filled with ice.      B-man got the tap set up, and in the kitchen, the games began. Zick and I raised our cups, then he wandered off to call his friend, Thayer. Already drunk, I watched as the night flowed into a steady rhythm. People, lots of them, began showing up. I knew almost none of them. A good balance of guys and girls made up the atmosphere, and among the girls there were a few good ones to look at. Music played on the TV with the speakers turned up. Anne came in and out of the bedroom; she was unhappy. The party chatter became loud to where I tried to cheer her up. I spoke words, but I can neither remember them, nor could I hear them at the time. For that matter, I couldn't hear her either. She threw her arms up in the air and stormed back into the room. *Bummer,* I thought.

Penley emerged from his bedroom and seemed to enjoy himself, but he was constantly in and out. Stuck between a rock and a hard place, he tried to enjoy the party while appeasing his not-so-happy wife. I noticed that my walking ability was declining, but I was still thirsty, so I went for cup number "I-lost-count" from the keg. B-man, Billy, and a few others stood nearby, I listened in to their conversation.

"Bro, Penley is cool and all, but he won't stop talking about throwing down. He says he's a semi pro fighter."     B-man said.

"Penley is the other roommate? Lanky guy?" Billy replied.

"Yea bro. Good dude, except the 'semi pro' talk. Gets annoying."

Billy, who looked drunk, had a sullen smirk. "Where's he from?"

"Ohio."

"Ha, there ya go. Probably a Buckeyes fan too."

I looked at Billy. "You're a Michigan guy, aren't ya?"

"Yea man, how'd you know?"

B-man smiled and shook his head. "Bosner."

"You scoffed at where he was from. That means you identify with a region of rivalry, and then the Buckeye's remark. Cherry on top of the cake."

Amidst the party chatter, there was a silence between the three of us.

"Wait, who are you?" Billy asked.

I smiled and raised my cup. As I walked away, I overheard B-man. "Bro, that's Bosner. Trivia machine. He'll probably knock out soon."

I stumbled around humming to whatever song was blaring, and then I saw three girls out on the front porch. I came up with the grand idea to introduce myself. When I opened the door, I felt a chilling gust. Outside, three girls, two on the right and one on the left, were smoking. As I tried to walk between them, my feet raced out from under me; I slipped on black ice. In slow motion, I watched one of them drop her cigarette and cover her face in shock. The other two simply turned and faced me as my rear struck the edge of the steps, then rattled down. It was quite painful.

"Oh my god! Honey are you okay?" one girl asked.

I initially stayed down and moaned, then I slowly raised my head and tried picking myself up. I felt stiff arms wrap around me from behind as I smelled a distinct combination of perfume, tobacco, and alcohol.

"Are you okay? That was a terrible fall." she asked.

The other two continued to laugh.

"Damnit. Lucky I don't sue..." I said.

The girl helped me up, and I looked at her. Slim, tall, wearing a white winter jacket, tight black pants, annoyingly white glitter boots, and with that very distinct tri-smell. She had highlights in her hair, to which I referred to her as "Ms. Highlights", and in my drunken state it seemed to matter for reasons unknown.

"Sue over the ice?" another girl asked.

I brushed myself off and laughed. "Nah... These guys are my friends. Just talking shit."

Ms. Highlights smiled. "Honey, you are drunk. Let's get you inside."

"I'm Bosner."

She laughed. "Yes, I'm sure you are."

Inside, the house was lit up. Loads of people jammed out to music, conversing, and getting drunk. B-man seemed fixated on staying near the keg. He leaned into somebody and lectured away about something; I couldn't quite make out what he was talking about. Zick was out back having a smoke with some others, notably a bigger dude I didn't previously see and whom I assumed was "Thayer". Dolvar was in the kitchen corner squinting, clearly drunk, and talking to some other people who didn't seem too interested in whatever it was he was saying.

Ms. Highlights was holding me and walking me towards the pass out room when a hand grabbed me from behind and spun me around. She flinched and stepped back.

"Whoa!" she gasped.

There stood Tom Souza.

"Bosner! Man, you gotta stop hustling women into coddling you. Step up your game, man. Really!" he said.

I hugged him. "Souza!"

"Hey who's the lady?"

She stared at him.

"Hi, I'm Tom Souza. You don't want Bosner, I know someone better!"

Ms. Highlights laughed and then walked back outside.

"You can do better, anyway." Souza said to me.

"Oh yea!" I drunkenly replied.

"Hey what was her name?"

"I don't fuckin know. Ms. Highlights. The ice is the real bitch."

Souza pointed outside at her. "You mean that wasn't the ice right there?"

I nudged him on the shoulder and laughed. We got a cup of beer and sat on the couch to catch up. Tom Souza was an interesting fella (as if the others weren't). He was a brash, opinionated dude from Missouri. The gang never got a good read on him, but if hell or high water came, you could always count on Souza. I zoned in and out of conversations we had because I was about done for the night. I tried my best to stay coherent, and I did well enough not to convince him otherwise. Finally, he got excited about the female partygoers and struck off to try his luck. Still not feeling ready to quit on the night, I slogged towards the keg. B-man was quite drunk as well, I couldn't understand anything he was saying. Dolvar discovered the rum and sat on the countertop in the kitchen. Right there with him was Zick and his friend.

"Bosner." Zick called out.

Sloppy as hell, I bobbed my head up and smiled. "Zick, Zick. Who beckons!"

His friend laughed. "So, you are Bosner."

"Sometimes."

"Hey Bosner, come here." Zick said.

Dolvar drunkenly waved his hand. "Clowns. You, him, all of you!"

I stumbled to the kitchen counter where they convened. Zick patted his friend on the back as he grinned nonstop, he was known within the gang for his drunken grin.

" This is Thayer."

Sure enough, his friend was big and boisterous. "Thayer, this time I'm Bosner."

We shook hands. "Right on. So, Zick says you like history and stuff…"

I perked up a little. "Actually, yes—"

"To a shot. Good answer, Bosner. Here you are." Zick interrupted, pouring shots of rum for the four of us.

Moronically, I took the shot. Blurred snapshot memories are all that remain of the rest of that night. Thayer and I back slapped. Dolvar tried to fight me, but he too slid on ice, how we ended up outside again, I don't know. B-man never left his unofficial post near the keg. I supposed that anyone who could understand him at the end deserved a free case of beer. Zick started singing loudly, but I didn't know the song. I pissed Thomas off after I called him "dumpster dude" to his face, but it made others laugh. Lorrie looked better and better, but she saw my "battle wounds" from the night before, and after that, all bets were off between her and I. Billy actually beat me to sleep. Lucky for him, he was the first one to christen the pass out room. Penley was in and out all night. He danced the high wire between drunken glory and marital fury. Souza disappeared with one of the girls. Everyone else, well, they were just "there."

# 3. Drool and Light

At some point, I kept hearing an annoying vibration. It sounded like a phone buzzing on a countertop or hard floor. Then came the sound of somebody turning over and licking their lips. I coughed, then opened my eyes. There I laid on the floor in the pass out room with my nose hurting. I blinked my eyes twice to get my vision straight, and then I felt a cool spot on the tip of my nose. Apparently, I had slept with my face up against the wall. I was the one turning over and licking my lips, naturally. I wiped curdled drool off the side of my face, some of which got on the carpet. When I rolled over to my right, in the dimmed room, I could see the outline of a few other people crashed out on the floor like me. *Shit,* I thought.

After running my hands over my face to gain composure, I got to my feet. I was heading for the bathroom, but halfway to the doorway out of the pass out room I tripped over something.

"What the fuck." a voice called.

I tripped over somebody, but I couldn't see them.

"Sorry." I whispered.

I focused harder on making sure I didn't trip over anyone else. When I got to the door, it was open just a crack. I entered the kitchen area to the blinding daylight and rubbed my eyes to get them adjusted. Heading down the hallway, I didn't know where the bathroom was. I recalled that the night before I was going outside and peeing behind shrubs.

In the hallway, there were two doors on the righthand side. Then, the hallway turned left, one of the rooms on that side was Penley and Anne's. It didn't seem too complicated to pick the right door and be off to races taking a leak; all I had to do was not bother anybody. Naturally, I tried the first door, which was a closet. I slowly opened the second door, but I couldn't keep it from creaking. Once opened enough, it revealed a bedroom with an air mattress and two or three people resting upon it. The covers on the mattress shifted, then long hair was visible as a female voice called out, "Blaine."

I chuckled quietly and slowly closed the door. Around the corner of the hallway were two final doors, one was on the left and the other on the right. The door on the left seemed most likely to be the bathroom, so I approached. Just before I put my hand on the knob, I had a change of thought. *Bosner, don't nuke it,* I thought to myself. I backed away and turned to the last door on the right, grabbing the knob and slowly turning it. As the door cracked open, I looked down hoping to see tile—the best indicator of the bathroom. *Linoleum!* I thought.

I saw linoleum and opened the door hastily all the way. Unfortunately, at eye level was a nightstand, dresser, TV, lamp, and a bed. On the bed was a vast blanket covering a large mound. In a flash, a head popped out of the covers. It was Penley!

"Bosner! You perverted fuck!"

"Bosner? Why?" Anne said.

They were having a moment and I had gotten in the way.

"Dumbass, the bathroom is the door behind you!" Penley added.

"Who has linoleum in a fucking bedroom! How was I supposed to know!" I replied.

"Dude, go."

I shut their bedroom door and shook my head. "Damnit."

Once in the bathroom, I forgot to close the door all the way because of the urgency to pee. Standing over the toilet for what seemed like minutes, I took a glorious leak while giving off a satisfying moan. Just then, I heard footsteps erratically filing down the hallway. The bathroom door flung all the way open, and in came Lorrie! She glanced before turning to the sink and vomiting.

"Hi Lorrie." I said.

A bottle of hand sanitizer stood on the windowsill near the toilet. Once I finished my business, I dabbed some on my hands and then helped her by holding her hair back.

"Clean hands. I promise."

She finished vomiting, then sipped some water from the faucet to gurgle. She looked up at me and patted me on the back. We both walked out into the hallway and into the living room. Zick was asleep on one couch while Ms. Highlights sat resting on the other with her head slouched.

"Yea, she's going to have a sore neck." Lorrie said.

"Definitely."

Zick opened one of his eyes. "What time is it?"

"I'm still trying to find my phone." I said.

As I turned to go back into the pass out room to search, I accidentally kicked a phone across the kitchen linoleum. The phone wasn't mine, but I picked it up and saw that it had 40 missed calls. It was likely the phone that caused the vibrating I heard when I woke up, so I placed it on the kitchen countertop. Once in the pass out room, the door remained wide open, pouring light into the dim space. A bunch of moans sounded. The one furthest from the door was Billy who was closest to where I awoke. I slowly stepped around everyone laid out on the floor to get to the back wall and search for my phone.

From the doorway, Lorrie laughed. "Oh my god. Welcome to Hotel Hangover."

I faced away, looking for my phone when a thud sounded from behind. It had come from the nook of the pass out room where the washer and dryer were. I jolted upright, startled by the noise as everyone on the floor woke up.

"Breakfast. Breakfast now!" a voice called.

From around the nook, Thayer walked out.

"Thayer, what the hell. You slept back there?" I asked.

He smiled. "Yup, I stole a couch pillow and crashed up on top of the washer and dryer. You should try it sometime."

"Weirdos." Lorrie said.

Billy laughed. "Well, where did you sleep?"

"On the mattress with Blaine, duh."

"What? Are you two—?" Thomas said.

Lorrie tilted her head and gazed at him.

"Of course," he stuttered. "Just a better place to sleep than in here."

Everyone who was resting got up. Some were people I didn't know and didn't see the night before, but hangover was prevalent. Curious why Thayer slept in the laundry area, we peered into the nook to see what the bed setup was. He had a pillow tucked up between the wall and the dryer, but there were no blankets. I figured the metal of the washer and dryer would be cold and hard compared to the carpet in the pass out room. I laughed. We began filing out into the living room and kitchen. Zick was up searching for food in the kitchen cabinets. There was little food in the house, just lots of alcohol. He reached into the fridge.

"Fuck it. Breakfast beer it is."

"Is the keg dead?" I asked.

"No idea."

Billy walked over and rocked it, it slogged in lumpy melted ice. "Still cold. Let's see."

He grabbed a random cup and rinsed it in the sink. Then he grabbed the tap and pumped. It made a gurgling sound, then foamy golden brew flowed. Everyone in the room gave off an "Oi!"

"No guys, we need to focus on food, not alcohol." Thayer said.

Zick sipped his beer and nodded. "Yea man, of course. We will figure something out."

Everyone who was going to leave began grabbing their belongings or searching for what they misplaced the night before. Ms. Highlights finally awoke from the couch. She yawned, then looked at me.

"Hi Bosner. How's your butt?"

Everyone stopped and looked, I wasn't sure what to say. I still didn't know Ms. Highlights actual name and her question even stopped Zick in his tracks when he was heading outside for a smoke. Lorrie laughed. The other girls who witnessed the previous night's fall laughed as well. I pointed at them.

"Wait, you know—"

"Uh huh yea. How is it, BOSNER?" they both said.

"All I did was fall...for real."

It was too late; I was had. I looked back at my new nemesis, Ms. Highlights. She smiled and winked as everyone resumed gathering their things. One of the random guests, a guy I didn't even see the night before, asked if anyone had seen his phone. *Aha,* I thought to myself. I went to the kitchen counter and grabbed it.

"Hey, this it?"

"Yep! Thanks." he said.

"No prob. By the way, lots of missed calls."

He snatched the phone from my grasp and peered at it. Then he put his hand on his forehead.

"Shit." he said.

One girl asked him if everything was okay. He didn't respond. Instead, he kept gazing at the phone and then made a call as he bolted out the front door. He ran to the street, but we heard the beginning of his phone conversation.

"Sweetheart, wait! No, no…I was busy I swear!"

Billy shook his head and laughed. "Bummer."

"So. Food?" Thayer asked.

Everyone scoffed, then Ms. Highlights and her two girlfriends made their goodbye rounds, as did a lot of others. Lorrie suggested the gang try a place down the street that none of us had heard of, a placed called "Johnny's". Zick came back in from his smoke break, and we waited a moment for B-man and Dolvar to get up. The two constantly slept longer than the rest of us, and it was likely that neither one was anywhere close to getting up. The gang decided to "politely" wake them, and it turned out that I was right about what I saw earlier in the first bedroom which was B-man's. Lorrie slept in there with him, along with a second girl who came to the party long after my coherence had died. For a guy that spent the entire night hovering around the keg, and who couldn't even talk when I last remembered, he scored a grand slam it seemed. Zick politely woke them by waltzing into the room, beating the wall and jumping on the mattress.

"Get up assholes, we're hungry!" he barked.

I stood in the hallway just outside the room. "Uh, yea so where is Dolvar?"

"In here, clown. I'm up. Just listening to you idiots." Dolvar said.

Lorrie opened the closet door. "Rise and shine!!!"

Dolvar mumbled something, then as Lorrie stepped away from the doorway, he emerged.

"A closet. How cute." I said.

Eyes red, face disheveled, he shook his head and tried to smile. "It's my crib.".

Beyond opening the closet earlier and not seeing Dolvar, I also failed to realize how big the closet was. Clothes hangers blocked vision beyond the entryway, concealing the space behind it from view. I stepped into the closet and saw that Dolvar had a small mattress along the back wall, and even a mini fridge. It was a nice setup for the drunken bachelor type, as Dolvar very much was.

"I'll be damned. You're here living in a closet." I said.

He smiled and nodded before grabbing his lower back. "What happened last night? My back and my ass hurt."

Lorrie's eyes opened wide, and she looked at us. "What the fuck?"

Thomas laughed. "What exactly went on last night?"

"Damnit, I fell outside, and I think Dolvar did too!" I said.

Billy grinned. "Yup, uh huh…that's exactly what happened. Or you two were—"

Just then, Zick, B-man, and the other girl came out of the room. B-man looked like he slept on a flight deck. The girl looked tired but presentable. I nodded to her and said "hi". She gave a brief smile as we converged in the living room.

"Or what?" I said to Billy.

He winked at me, and then I knew I had been had again! I faced B-man.

"Welcome to daytime!"

He rubbed his face and groaned. Dolvar got two cups of beer and tried giving the second one to B-man. In his waking state, he brushed his hand down at the beer. It fell out of Dolvar's grasp and spilled on the floor. Penley yelled and came running out of his room.

"What the fuck! It's too early for this shit." he said.

B-man cleared his throat. "I know it's too early. I don't want a beer."

"I have a machete; I can hack some fuckers. But I don't need it, I'm semi-pro—" Penley started.

Out of nowhere, B-man erupted. "Bro, it's early, I don't give a shit. Dolvar will clean up the beer!"

Penley smiled and pointed at him. "Oh, you and me tonight!"

"Bro, cool, whatever. I'm waking up. Not now." B-man said.

Penley kept smiling and shook his head as he walked back down the hallway to his room. Dolvar cleaned up the beer while Zick, B-man, and I looked at each other and started laughing.

"Sunday Funday!" Zick proclaimed.

We got ready to leave, having decided on Lorrie's place of choice for food. B-man and I agreed to drive everyone who was coming. As Zick was a freelance mechanic on the side, he went with B-man to check out a problem he had with the handling of his car. B-man, Zick, Thayer, and the girl went outside and stood by B-man's car. The rest of us stood inside as Thomas searched for his phone.

B-man popped the hood on his car while he, Zick, and Thayer looked at the engine; the girl stood by texting on her phone. As Thomas looked for his phone, he seemed not to care about the night before, when my dazed memory recounted how I had called him "dumpster dude". We helped look for the phone, and once we found it, we noticed that B-man, Zick, Thayer, and the other girl had left. Lorrie was worried that they didn't know where they were going, but I figured they left ahead of us to test out the driving of the car. We loaded up into Green Beater.

# 4. Diner Delight

B-man had a more spacious car than me, but he drove three people while I drove four. In Green Beater, Lorrie sat in the front seat while Dolvar, Billy, and Thomas sat in the back.

"Someone call B-man and make sure he knows where Johnny's is." I said.

Lorrie whipped out her phone. "On it."

She indicated that Johnny's was only a few miles away. I could tell by Lorrie's conversation that she was struggling to direct B-man. I thought about butting in and telling her to give him locations instead of street names, but she finally told him to put Zick, or "Melissa" on the phone. *Melissa it is!* I thought to myself. I took pride in my ability to figure out people's names through third parties or external means, especially since I was horrible at remembering names when a person introduced themselves.

As I drove down Cape Henry Avenue towards the T-intersection by the railroad crossing, Lorrie was finally able to direct B-man and company where to go. They already drove in that general direction, so they were going to get to Johnny's before us. As we got closer, I nearly missed a turn and when swerving to make sure I didn't, my tires screeched, and everyone grabbed ahold of something.

"What was that? A hub cap flying off?" Dolvar said.

Everyone laughed.

"Actually, I lost the last one yesterday."

Billy leaned in. "Drift racing are ya? Probably beats demo derby in this thing."

"Ah ha. Funny." I replied.

"If you miss enough turns like that, you'll swerve this car apart." Lorrie said.

"This is my baby. I've never wrecked it, I'm not hitting shit, so deal with it."

Dolvar leaned in and we fist bumped. Not long after, Johnny's appeared on the left, but a U-Turn was required to get there because of the road's divided median. It was a dumpy looking place but certainly of the diner variety. It had a rough exterior and the sign reading "Johnny's" looked like it was hand panted on a slab of tag board. Once I pulled into the parking lot, I saw B-man parked nearest the entrance, so I parked just to the right.

"Are you sure about this place?" I asked.

Lorrie laughed. "I wouldn't recommend it otherwise!"

Thomas gazed at the diner's sign. "How many times do they flip the food off the floor before they serve it?"

Lorrie turned in her seat and smirked.

"I don't care, I'm just hungry." Billy said.

"Who says food with floor seasoning isn't good? Salisbury steak is good off the sidewalk." Dolvar joked.

We got out of the car and I stopped to stretch and yawn. The exterior of the building was light blue with darker trim and in dire need of a new paint job. The windows were dirty, and the flimsy sign also looked ready to detach from the structure. I wasn't too excited.

"Bosner. You coming or not?" Lorrie said.

I realized I was the only one still outside. "Oh, yes, thanks!"

Johnny's had the vibe of a diner that probably had days; I could imagine how it looked in 1958, as opposed to 2008. It had an odd smell, but it was more distinct than it was bad. There were typical diner-style bar counters with chrome stools and stove tops visible just beyond. Two cooks worked the stove tops, both dressed in typical vintage white attire. Booths lined the windows, two of which we seated ourselves at as there was no server in sight. I sat next to Melissa at the second booth across from B-man, Zick, and Lorrie.

"Hi Melissa. I'm Bosner."

She smiled, and we shook hands. "How's your butt?"

I shook my head. Melissa had reddish brunette hair, brown eyes, a nice tan, and attractive figure. I wasn't sure how close either her or Lorrie were to B-man, so I played cool. She kept smiling, while both B-man and Zick gave me continuous hell about my butt. I eventually stopped trying to argue or explain "my butt" to kill the topic, and I grabbed the menu to ignore them. Johnny's menu was a one-pager, laminated and with a basic list of even more basic items. Only a few dishes were listed beneath "Breakfast", "Lunch", and "Dinner".

"Lorrie says this place is good. They must be really good considering the wide variety they have." I said.

"Bro, check out the 'Lunch' section. Is the 'Big Bacon Cheeseburger' underlined on your menu?"

Sure enough, it was.

"I guess I know what I'm getting." I said.

"Dude, you're letting 'Johnny' pick for you if you base your selection on that." Zick said.

I looked at him. "I saw the word bacon. That's good enough for me."

Melissa flipped the menu around. "Only one sided? No salad?"

"This is a Diner. Salad is foreign here." B-man replied.

"Yea but all the items on here are greasy and probably high calorie." she said.

Zick looked at her. "Did you not get shithouse last night? Greasy, high calorie food is the point!"

Melissa pushed her menu towards Lorrie. "What's good here? I don't like the selection."

"Patty Melt!" Thomas said.

"Corned beef hash!" Billy and Dolvar said in unison.

"All of it!" Thayer added.

Melissa rolled her eyes and ran her hand through her hair.

"I go with the Big Bacon Cheeseburger." Lorrie answered.

I pointed at Zick. "There ya go. Always bet on bacon!"

Dolvar reached over and patted me. "Bosner, I thought you were a corned beef hash guy!"

He was referring to the deployment the year prior. We were on a larger ship, which meant the food wasn't the best, so I relied heavily on the corned beef hash during breakfast in particular to get by. I was convinced the corned beef hash was good because it came from a can and not from disgruntled ship cooks, or as the Navy officially called them, Culinary Specialists. On a side note, I learned that smaller ships, or small boys as well called them, often had good food.

"Hey, corned beef hash is good stuff. So are grits. But bacon beats all!" I said.

Thomas laughed. "Grits in the Navy?"

"Bro, Bosner didn't know of grits until the Navy." B-man replied.

A server arrived. She was a petite, older woman with bleach blonde hair and a distinct tan. As it was January, I assumed it was fake. She was only missing the raspy voice of a chain smoker.

"Darlings, how y'all doing? Can I start you with drinks or are you ready to order?" she asked, with a sweet voice.

Everyone ordered coffee, water, or sweet tea. I opted for coffee.

"Excuse me. Why is the 'Big Bacon Cheeseburger' underlined?" I asked.

The waitress leaned in and looked at my menu. "Oh, it must be Johnny's special item."

Though unsure, I was all in on getting it.

"Okay cool. I'll take that. Fries and a pickle slice as well please."

She jotted down my order and continued with the others.

"You shoulda got the club sandwich. Letting the establishment pick for you is a bad deal." Zick said.

I winked at him. "Big bacon cheeseburger!"

When the waitress got to Melissa, she asked about healthy options. There was no salad on the menu, but after verbally jostling, she offered Melissa a cup of fruit. She ordered that, and we gave her hell.

"You all are assholes. I can't keep this figure if I eat that other junk." she said.

B-man laughed. "Hey eggs have protein. That works for me."

Zick pointed at Thayer. "Melissa, you could always order up…actually what all did you get Thayer?"

"This clown ordered two eggs, extra side bacon, corned beef hash, and asked for a special to go box of fries." Dolvar added.

Melissa made a gag face. "That's disgusting."

"Hey Melissa, I enjoy the taste of the grease as it oozes down the hatch." Thayer said.

Lorrie threw her menu at Thayer. "You are gross!"

The guys laughed, the girls didn't. We then sat there mostly quiet until the food came. The big bacon cheeseburger was a superb choice. I ate it so fast that I was sitting almost comatose as everyone else still sat precariously eating whatever they ordered. Zick picked at the club sandwich, barely eating half of it. He looked across at my empty plate with disdain. I winked at him and asked how much he enjoyed the non-underlined item. Melissa got her fruit cup which was small, and the fruit looked too ripe. As she stared at it with disappointment, B-man, Zick, and I laughed. She pushed it away.

"Maybe you could ask for a replacement?" I suggested.

"Bro, who orders a cup of fruit and then returns it? This place looks like a ma and pop joint. Would probably bankrupt them."

Melissa crossed her arms. "Whatever. I'm not hungry anyway."

Billy and Thomas offered some of their food, but it was all "greasy junk," as Melissa put it. We finished eating, and to cover for Melissa, I poured her fruit on my plate and covered it with a napkin. I glugged down the rest of my coffee and then we asked for the waitress' name. It was customary of our gang to get to know staff well at the places we visited and to tip generously barring really poor service. Her name was "Connie", but she became busy as we finished, so we spared her our routine and simply left her a modest tip of $50.00.

Everyone rode in the same vehicles. As we left the parking lot, Thayer realized he forgot his fries. I offered to turn around to go back since he had paid for them, but Lorrie wasn't having it. He pleaded with her, and I offered once more, but she grabbed my arm and demanded that I didn't. Dolvar suggested we grill for dinner, which resolved the dispute. Lorrie concluded that the forgotten fries served as punishment to Thayer for being gross to Melissa. *Women,* I thought to myself.

We returned to the house and everyone sat in the living room on the couches or on the few chairs available. As the sucker left standing, I settled for lying flat on the floor with my hands behind my head. It was "Sunday Funday", but the previous night (and frankly, Friday as well) took a lot out of everyone. We sat for a bit in silence, then Billy had a suggestion.

"Hey, I know Dolvar likes beer pong. I'm assuming you guys do too?"

Everyone perked up and looked at him.

"Yea bro. We like beer pong." B-man said.

Billy stared at the open space in the kitchen. "We gotta get a table. There's nothing in the kitchen. It's depressing."

Zick sat up and looked at Thayer. "We can donate one. A fold-up table."

Thayer nodded as Dolvar and B-man's faces lit up.

"What if Penley or Anne don't like it?" I asked.

Lorrie threw an empty cup at me. "Don't be a negative Nancy!"

"Hey, think democratic, a roommate vote!" Billy said.

Being my naïve self, I continued, "But what if both Penley and—"

"BOSNER!" Everyone shouted.

"Tell ya what. We're going to bring it, anyway. Worst case, just keep it outside." Zick said.

Everybody was back on their feet and the mood was upbeat. As it was a Sunday in late January, football playoffs were going on. Luckily for the two New Yorkers in the gang, the Giants were playing in the Conference Title game that evening against the Packers, everyone was invited to watch it. Thayer objected.

"Wait, Dolvar, you said we could grill."

Lorrie shook her head while B-man looked at Dolvar.

"Well, the Giants are playing. I'm not missing the game." he said.

"Neither am I." B-man added.

Zick put his hand on Thayer's back. "Look, next time. We gotta get going."

"Fine." he said, defeated.

Zick and Thayer gathered their things and got ready to leave, Thayer looked glum. Losing the fries at Johnny's and getting stiffed on grilling at the house served as a double rejection. When the two said their "goodbyes" and the door closed behind them, I laughed.

"Thayer's a trip." I said.

Dolvar glared. "Okay, who's catching the game with us?"

"Bosner, you're coming. No way out." B-man said.

Witlessly, I bowed my head. "I guess so."

# 5. Bar Blues

It was me, B-man, Dolvar, and of course, Lorrie and Melissa. The girls never said whether they wanted to watch the game with us, so we just corralled them into coming, regardless. B-man and Dolvar went to change into something they insisted was "more appropriate" for the game. Melissa went outside to talk on the phone, and Lorrie and I sat on the couches.

"So, do you have a girlfriend?" she asked.

"Well… not exactly."

"You don't. That was a giveaway."

I became defensive. "Actually, I do, well, did. She wants—"

"Wanted?" Lorrie interrupted.

"Whatever. I liked her, but it was between the gang and her."

Lorrie made a sad puppy face. "Oh, you picked your boys. Loyalty, Bosner."

"Hey, if I recall, you had to know this last night. I made a pass at you, didn't I?"

She laughed. "Honey, you were a drunk mess, and look at your fucking neck! It's chewed to hell. I'm surprised the others didn't notice!"

I thought she gave me a lifeline, a way to prove that I had a girlfriend and was just being naughty towards her last night. The neck was proof!

I patted my neck. "Hey, see, I'm seeing someone!"

"Your girlfriend or your ex didn't do that. Some random, sassy, bitch left those." she said.

"Damnit. Alright, you win."

She clinched her fists and smiled. We both sat silently until Dolvar and B-man emerged wearing New York Giants gear and the color blue, from head to toe.

"Hey, how did you two not see Bosner's neck?" Lorrie asked.

B-man grinned. "Oh, we knew. How could you not notice? Not sure if it was a whale or a tortoise that made them."

Dolvar laughed.

"Asshole, I told you! That's how you knew." I said.

"And B-man told me. What's it like to have your neck mauled by whales or tortoises?" Dolvar asked.

"Fuckers. I say she was a 6… I hope."

Melissa returned, impressed by the level of blue gear that B-man and Dolvar wore. They tried explaining who the New York Giants were, and what sport they played in. After trying to explain what a "football" was, they finally gave up and told her to get ready so we could all get going. As was typical, they made me the driver and everyone piled into Green Beater, B-man sat in the front, then Dolvar, Melissa, and Lorrie in the back. They wanted to go to a bar I never visited before, and B-man explained its location by trying to tell me what it was near. I didn't know what he was talking about, but I started driving anyway.

"B-man, did you know Bosner is such a shitty driver that he lost all his hub caps?" Dolvar said.

*Damnit, here we go,* I thought to myself.

"No bro, he didn't lose them. He traded them in for extra hash browns, remember?"

"What?" Melissa asked.

Lorrie shook her head. "Why does that not surprise me?"

B-man was referring to a true story, except for the hub cap part.

"A while back, we hung out and got shithouse drunk." I said.

"NOOOOOO." Everybody shouted.

"Yea, ha ha. So, we got really shithouse, and the next day we were all hungry and B-man insisted on getting hash browns. I drove us down to that fast food place by the base and we literally ordered $30 worth." I finished.

B-man and Dolvar snickered.

"That's retarded." Melissa said.

"No, it's fucking good. Real fucking good!" B-man replied.

"Clown, you forgot. You placed the order at the drive thru and they made us pull over in a parking spot to wait."

"I don't know. They prepare a lot of those in advance. If you order so many that they make you pull over and wait while they make the rest... that's..." Lorrie said.

"That's what? Retarded!" Melissa interrupted.

B-man turned around. "It's good. Greasy, fattening, and perfect for a fucking hangover."

Melissa made a sick face. The rest of us remained quiet for the rest of the drive. The gang wanted to go to a bar called "C.T. Slaters". It was only a few miles from the house, and it was on the infamous "Main Street". Main Street had a deep history revolving around sailors and drinking, my dad and grandpa both served in the Navy and were stationed elsewhere in the country, but even they knew about it. Synonymous with "sailors and sin" as the Navy brass would tell us, it remained a relatively dubious place. As a result, I was skeptical about C.T. Slaters and prepared for it to be a tavern version of Johnny's Diner, maybe on steroids.

As we turned onto rickety Main Street, I had my doubts about the quality of the venue we were going to. I worried it might be some smoke-filled basement style bar where the food was out of date and the drinks flat. We had been to places before where the French dip or buffalo wings made me sick to my stomach. Of course, when I thought harder, it might've had something to do with the dozen beers I also had. I continued down the street while everyone chatted, and then I saw the sign: a big low hanging board with elaborate lights silhouetting the name

"C.T. Slater's". I turned into the parking lot and found a spot in the very front because of Green Beater's compact magic.

We entered the bar, and to my surprise it was a nice place. It was well lit, smelled good, and even the staff was mostly attractive. It helped that the staff was mostly female and wore clothing that showcased certain body features particularly well. Looking at the females, I patted B-man on the chest.

"THIS is why you come here." I said.

"Yea bro. Let's get a table. The game is almost on."

We stood there for another minute or two, and I could see B-man tapping his foot, looking around anxiously for someone to seat us. Dolvar wandered off, and then the patrons clapped and cheered; kickoff began. We heard a loud whistle and then looked to our right. Dolvar was waving us down and signaling to a vacant booth. Luckily for us, the booth was fairly close to one of the projection screens.

"Yes, Dolvar!" B-man shouted.

We proceeded down the row. By then, people were leaning outward to get better views of the screen. The booth was spacious, but messy as the staff appeared too busy to clean up the table. Everyone sat down, avoiding a large section of the booth seat. Naturally, I didn't pay close enough attention and found out why. B-man and Dolvar were entranced by the game, Melissa was texting on her phone, and Lorrie stared at me and smiled.

"How's the seat, Bosner?"

I sat in a puddle of something, I hoped it was simply water. Out witted yet again, I shook my head.

"I hate you guys!"

"I figured the game would've distracted you." she said.

"Do I look like a Giants or Packers fan to you? You got your laugh earlier… and you get another one now."

She ran her hand down my back. "Bosner, we love you."

B-man and Dolvar were ranting and raving as each play unfolded in the game, and after some time a waitress finally approached us. She appeared to greet us, but all I could hear was the game audio and noisy patrons. Reading her lips, she was saying something other than "hello", or "how can I help you". Lorrie leaned forward to try listing to the waitress, but finally I stood and leaned in towards her to better hear.

"You were not seated here. You are going to have to get up and wait for an open table." she said.

Her voice was still difficult to hear over all the noise in the bar. Lorrie still leaned forward towards the waitress. "HUH?"

*Oh boy,* I thought to myself. The boys were glued to the game, in fact, they were so glued to the game they didn't even remember to order anything, including beer! Just then, fate intervened. The waitress, who's name tag read "Kelly", seemed to assume that I didn't hear her or was being nonresponsive, and so she tapped B-man's shoulder. He was sitting closest to the screen and the aisle. He reacted, and the waitress leaned towards his left ear presumably to repeat what I heard her say previously. B-man seemed to understand, nodding his head, but then he motioned for a pitcher of beer. The waitress then repeated herself, and      B-man motioned for five glasses to go with the pitcher. He signaled for menus as well.

"She wants us to move huh." Lorrie said.

"Yep, and I'll be damned if B-man can hear a thing she's saying."

Lorrie and I, now fascinated by the failure of the dialogue with the waitress, watched. B-man clearly thought his order was heard and turned to continue watching the game. Dolvar, sitting inside, hadn't even noticed the waitress there at all, and neither did the ever-texting Melissa. For a split second, the waitress stood up straight, looking confused and frustrated. Just then, the Giants committed a turnover. B-man, Dolvar, and roughly half of the people in the establishment roared with frustration, the other half, cheers. Once B-man's frustration cooled, the waitress leaned in again. Luckily for her, there was a commercial break and an almost odd silence in the place.

"Sir, you all need to get up. This table is not available. You were not seated here."

I was holding my breath, so was Lorrie.

Dolvar interjected. "Uh, we're ARE seated here now."

B-man stared at Kelly. The dim room made it hard to get a good look at her. She had darkish hair, a nose piercing, and what looked like a birthmark on her right cheek. Under better circumstances, she looked like someone I would get a phone number from.

"The game is on, nobody served us when we waited. What's the big deal?" B-man said.

Melissa finally looked up from her phone. "What's up guys?"

Kelly looked over at Melissa, then at Lorrie and me. She was clearly frustrated. She slowly closed her eyes, stood straight up, and walked away.

"Uh, okay." Lorrie said.

B-man and Dolvar seemed to forget about any of the conversation and became reglued to the screen. After a moment or two, Kelly returned with a manager, his name tag read "Tim". Conveniently, there was another commercial break and a silent period.

"Folks, we're going to have to ask you to leave." Tim announced.

Time seemed to stop. B-man and Dolvar both looked back from the screen to Tim and Kelly. Oddly, it seemed like even the noise level dropped in the place. Rarely was the gang kicked out of an establishment. We always saw ourselves as the good-barfly crusaders. We drank heavy, tipped even more heavily, and championed the hot, hardworking bartender/waitress, and the hardworking bartender/waiter. A long silence seemed to ensue in the cold war that sprung into motion at C.T. Slaters. Lorrie, sensing that things could go many directions, leaned against me. I just sat and stared at Tim and B-man.

"What the hell is this? We waited and waited, nobody served us, so we served ourselves to this booth." B-man said.

Tim nodded. "I see that, but this booth is reserved."

"Hey, we've been here before and never heard of that. Reservations? Since when?" Dolvar asked.

Kelly interjected. "Since the playoffs started, and we began exceeding capacity."

"Listen, we are sorry for the slow service at the door, but this booth is reserved, and I will ask you only once more to please get up."

At that point, I realized I was going to have to step in. B-man was turning red, and Dolvar looked to be in an argumentative mood. Melissa was "blah" and Lorrie was waiting for someone to do something.

"Okay, Tim, we are going now. This is a real disappointment." I said as I stood up. "Guys let's go. We can do Greenies or something."

"Well, is there another table or a reasonable wait time for a table?" Lorrie asked Tim.

Dolvar brushed past B-man to the aisle. "Fuck that. I'm done with these clowns. Let's go."

The place erupted in cheers, and we turned to face the screen. The Giants had scored a touchdown. Even Kelly and Tim were briefly distracted, but then they turned to face us again. I ran my hand over my butt to feel the moisture from the wet spot nobody told me about; I tried to keep my nerves in check.

"Come on guys, I'll take us to Greenies." I said.

Tim and Kelly stood back to allow B-man and Dolvar by. We began walking towards the door, and then B-man turned to face the staff.

"You all suck. I'm never coming back. Giants are playing and then you come up with this bullshit 'reservation' crap."

Dolvar turned around and went back to the booth. He said that he had left his hat. The rest of us proceeded towards the exit, and then to my astonishment there stood Pickens, accompanied by a less than attractive female. She was dark haired, the opposite of the red headed Pickens, and she was roughly double the size of his 150lb frame. Her many pimples served as the cherry on top of the cake for the bar experience from hell. I knew at that very moment, at least karmically speaking, Pickens was involved in the fiasco, somehow. Everything seemed to freeze again, and Dolvar remained at the now vacant booth looking under the table. At the front, as we neared, another waitress approached Pickens and his companion.

"Hello sir. Your booth will be ready in just a moment."

He smiled and nodded at her, then turned and saw me.

"Well, well... Bosner and the gang."

I looked the other way, shaking my head.

"Leaving? Why? The game just began." he quipped.

The girls didn't know Pickens, but B-man and Dolvar did.

"Bro, you aren't even a Giants or Packers fan."

Pickens grinned, then put his arm around his large companion. "Nope, but my baby is a Packers fan."

I was furious. It was bad enough that we couldn't get a seat, but to have the seating yanked out from under us by Pickens—to even be in a scenario where he could flaunt something like that over us—was outrageous. In the gang, there were two diehard Giants fans, and we were a party of five. We needed a sizeable booth for seating, and it looked as though that was denied to us by a party of two. I supposed that maybe with Pickens' girlfriend, they could be considered a party of "two and a half", but that was beside the point. Now officially mad, I looked at the waitress seating Pickens and his girl.

"You're really letting those two reserve a space that big? They just told us that reservations are now policy because of limited space!"

The waitress looked up at me and then looked to my right. Kelly and Tim were walking with Dolvar who had found his hat, and they motioned to Pickens' waitress.

"Don't listen to them, they are leaving." Tim declared.

I pointed at Pickens. "No. Listen to me. This is bullshit. And for this jackass?"

Lorrie covered her smile as Melissa put her hand on my back. "Bosner let's just go. It's okay."

I was getting heated. And as I stood there, even    B-man and Dolvar proceeded closer to the door. I shook my head and faced Pickens' and his woman. He had an obnoxious look on his face; in fact, his face was obnoxious, period.

"Kiss my ass Pickens." I said.

He flapped his hand, waving goodbye to the gang as we walked out of C.T. Slaters. Once outside, Kelly and Tim stood at the foot of the front door, just on the inside, glaring at us so to make sure we didn't come back in. There was no way we would go back in there.

"C.T. Slaters. C.T. HATERS!" I yelled.

We got into Green Beater, dead set on watching the game at Greenies.

"Bro, when you get angry it's like everything stops."

"Bosner, you are cute when you get angry." Lorrie added.

I looked at B-man and we swatted hands. "Now, on to Greenies. And damnit, go Giants!"

Greenies was not an ideal sports bar as it had horrible TVs. But, as I drove down the potholed roads of our home port city, we filled the ladies in on Pickens and why he was despised. B-man suggested that Pickens was one of the driving factors for him moving out of the barracks and into the house.

"He's annoying and talks crap, yet it's hard to hate him. He's such a weakling. I almost feel bad at the thought of fighting him. He's too much of a wimp to be worth hurting." he said.

"He seemed to have a chip on his shoulder at the bar." Melissa replied.

Lorrie laughed. "He's proud of his 'baby'."

"I don't know, it almost felt like he knew we would be there and reserved that table to ruin our evening." I said.

"Bosner, you're such a clown. It's like Pickens is in your head."

I looked in the rearview mirror at Dolvar. "Dude, he just gets under my skin. I don't know why. I'm with B-man though. It's not a hatred, it's just he knows exactly how to annoy the shit out of me."

"Give the guy a little slack. He finally has a woman. Not the prettiest, but hey, you gotta start somewhere."      B-man joked.

"You guys are mean!" Melissa said.

I laughed. "No, for real. That has to be his first. You should've seen him when there was a decent looking girl that checked into the barracks one time. He couldn't even talk. She said 'hello' and he practically pissed his pants!"

We continued chatting about Pickens, mostly small talk, and then we arrived at Greenies. I turned right into the dirt parking lot which faced the bay.

Everyone got out of the car quickly except for me. I had received a text from an unknown number. As they filed into the bar, I stood for a moment in the chilled air to read the text.

> "Hi, I hope you are doing well. I'm leaving town, but I just wanted you to know that I will never forget you. You are a good person, and someday you will find your happiness. This number will be offline, so don't bother contacting it. Take care xoxo."

I immediately dialed the number, but it wasn't in service. I tried texting back, and it failed to send. My heart froze for a second, as I knew who it was. *Maria.* The gang knew of her, but I never brought her around, and as I had explained briefly to Lorrie, Maria wanted more of me than I could give. She was a real beauty, and a girl I had feelings for, but whom I also feared. For me, the tragedy was that she didn't push me too hard; she was understanding, in fact, but our relationship cooled over the previous few months because she was looking to settle down, and I was looking to find myself.

Maria Ortega, 5'8, jet black hair, natural Latina tan. I never figured out how I attracted her, and maybe that was the reason things didn't work out between us. I lacked the confidence and the maturity to be with such a woman. Her father was an investor, and they came from money. "Bosner" was the well-meaning, fit, quirky kind of man that kept her on her toes, by her own admission. Bosner was also the 21-year-old who still hadn't really found himself yet, and the previous year's deployment and the extended time away from the states didn't help matters. My eyes swelled up with tears, and I finally put my phone back in my pocket and headed into Greenies.

As I entered, I quickly wiped away the last of the tears so not to appear sad. The place was packed, so I began looking for the gang. Ron, the bouncer, approached me. We had a good rapport with the entire staff.

"Hey bud, they are in the back. We got you a spot by the big TV."

"Thanks man!"

I proceeded past the main bar, past the hallway to the bathrooms, and past the backroom bar to the room in the corner. In the back, at a table by itself in a corner, was where everyone sat. Sure enough, they had the luxury of Greenie's largest but still small TV. B-man and Dolvar were glued to the game.

"Bosner, are you okay?" Lorrie asked.

"Yea…"

I was a terrible liar. My tone was so off that even    B-man and Dolvar turned and faced me.

"What's up bro?"

I paused, then sat down. Once I realized even Melissa was looking at me, I finally mustered a response.

"It's Maria. We've been over for a while, honestly, but she gave me closure."

Before anyone could respond, two pitchers of beer arrived, by virtue of Sarah, mother of three, and one of our favorite bartenders. We raised our empty glasses, and she filled them.

"Cheer up!" she said.

Everyone looked at her, then back at me. She knew something was up.

"Bosner, talk to me." Sarah insisted.

I was silent again, but then Lorrie nudged me. "Talk to us!"

"Maria is someone I had a thing with. It didn't work. I wasn't ready for what she wanted, and she let me off easy. I guess I thought I could have my cake and eat it too."

There was a brief silence, then Sarah ran her hand on my shoulder and sped off. She returned with a shot of whiskey, a routine when one of us was having the blues.

"It sounds like it's for the better. But it's okay to be sad, let it be something you remember and grow from!" Melissa suggested.

I was flattered by the input. Dolvar, sitting across from me, reached out and fist bumped me over my heart.

"Bosner, you know it's tough for now, but you're a stand-up guy, clown."

Even with compliments, he couldn't resist the 'clown' jab.

I smiled. "Asshole."

"Bro, she was a hottie. She's no hoe, but you chose the 'bros before hoes' route. Love you, man. Drink up a bit, root on these damned Giants, and let time heal the wound."

I raised my shot glass to B-man and gulped the whiskey down, chasing it with beer. My lifestyle wasn't suited for Maria. I knew it, so did the gang. I perked up a little, as did the Giants. Before I knew it, I was ordering water to ease up my sobriety and have us ready to head back. The night ended on a high note as the Giants beat the Packers in overtime, 23-20. To the joy of B-man and Dolvar, their boys were going to the Super Bowl; the rest of us were happy for them.

# 6. Command Demand

I woke up on Monday morning in my barracks room feeling spry. The previous night after Greenies, I dropped B-man, Dolvar, Lorrie, and Melissa off at the house on Cape Henry Avenue. They partied more in celebration of the Giants' victory, but I had duty section on Monday morning and wasn't sure enough of myself to risk partying late the night before. Lorrie and Melissa were new to the gang, and I wasn't certain who they were to us, B-man in particular. Lorrie was easygoing, there was a sort of loving sister mentality in her. Her affection was generous, but it didn't cross the line. Melissa had a hot streak in her appearance, but she seemed bubbleheaded, something I found particularly unattractive. In just a single weekend, I grew to not have a particular interest in either one of them. Whether or not they actually were, I saw them as part of the gang.

   The weekend was an experience. Unlike previous weekends where the gang was couped up at the barracks drinking in relative silence or spending ungodly sums of our already meager paychecks at a bar, we had a place to converge and be ourselves.

Even better, having a house to hangout, party, and crash at was more appealing to the ladies. I laughed at the prospect of Dolvar living in a closet, the oddity of B-man having a shag-pad air mattress, and the legitimately awkward incident when I mistook a bedroom "in session" for a bathroom. The thoughts replayed in my mind as I drove to the command.

Although I worked night check, duty section served as an exception to any sailor's normal schedule. Depending on the duty section schedule, some merely had to show up and report that they were fit for duty, but for others, they were assigned watch. On that Monday, I had the 0500 desk watch, which meant that I had to be in my dress blue uniform (some call them the "cracker jacks") and I had to sit at the front desk of the command for eight hours. It was normally a boring affair, as it required the person on duty to answer phone calls, direct personnel visiting the command from external places, and accept packages and supplies on behalf of the command. Duty section and watch, at least in the Navy, was a big deal. One of the easiest ways to get into trouble in the Navy was to not show up for duty section, or to fall asleep while on watch. Caffeine was always a best friend, and before a few negligent shipmates at the command ruined it for us all by falling asleep, bringing a laptop to play videos or movies was a self-provisional amenity.

Because I had watch during my normal off hours, I didn't have to report for night check that afternoon. Nothing on that Monday sitting watch happened, aside from seeing all the usual personnel shuffle in and out. I passed the time with mugs of coffee, junk food, and reading a book on the history of "The French Revolution." I was (and still am) a history nut, and I always enjoyed learning more and then showering it on people at the most inopportune times, especially when drinking incessantly. At 1300, my relief came to take over the post. I was tired, even after all the caffeine, so I went straight to the barracks, made a snack and went to bed. I was pretty wiped out from the past weekend and was going to be back on normal schedule starting Tuesday at 1400.

Not much happened on Tuesday, I awoke earlier than normal since I went to bed almost immediately after watch the day before, so I took the extra time and continued reading the history book. Afterwards, I did laundry, while waiting in the laundry room, I saw Wilky. He was on the phone arguing with someone about the greatest basketball player through their first few years in the pros. When he got off the phone, I said "hi" and then added to his over-the-phone argument.

"There's no argument over who's honestly the greatest." I said.

He laughed. "Man, we could go all day about that."

"I'm sure we could!"

"Aight Bosner, be real. Who was the lucky lady this weekend?"

Confused at first, it occurred to me that he was asking about the mysterious one-night stand.

"Oh, that. To be honest, I don't know. We were at Greenies, then I woke up in my room and my neck was all chewed up." I said.

Wilky opened his mouth but remained silent. I pulled my shirt collar out a little, revealing the marks.

"Still is." I added.

He slapped his knee and laughed. "Hoss, what the…!"

"How did you find out?" I asked.

"Dog, who doesn't know!"

Just then, the washer buzzed. I began putting laundry in the dryer.

"It's like my life is under a microscope at this place." I said.

"Nah, but for real. Pickens was rambling about it on the quarterdeck."

"That guy. If the answer is red, he says blue, if I caught a fish that was 10lbs, he says he caught one that was 15lbs. I don't know who the girl was, I keep my fingers crossed she was a six or better."

Wilky smiled and patted me on the back. "You're cool. She was probably fine."

I finished loading the dryer, then faced him.

"Bruh, let me tell you a little secret." he said.

"Yea?"

"That motherfucker is jealous of you. All he has is an extra chevron on his sleeve."

As he spoke, his face lit up; I saw him as the champion of encouragement.

"Besides, rather than waste time thinking about that goof, focus on your inside game on the hoops. I also heard that's shit too!" he joked.

I laughed. "Dude, I haven't played serious ball since like 8th grade! Cut the white boy some slack!"

Wilky pointed and winked. He gathered his laundry and we bro hugged. As he left, the OOD entered the laundry room on their roving rotation. I didn't recognize who it was, but they were a First Class and they nodded at me and continued on. After the dryer stopped, I went back to my room and folded laundry, then got dressed. The only notable thing about Tuesday night was the cold weather. There was nothing I hated more than being stuck on a helo near the seawall wrenching on gearboxes in the cold. Often, I had to take off my gloves to fit my hands into the tight spaces within the gearbox assembly shaft to be able to service it. Hydraulic fluid was colored red, and with bare hands in the cold it was common to lose feeling in them. To my great frustration, I pulled my hands out from the shaft, and they were red, not with hydraulic fluid, but blood. I ended up having to postpone the assigned work to get my hands cleaned up, and that made the shift much more frustrating. Nonetheless, night check finished at 0200, a decent hour.

Some maintainers on night check would stay up into the wee hours of dawn before going to bed, but I normally went straight to the barracks, cleaned up, then slept. There were occasional exceptions, such as meeting the gang at Greenies or somewhere else. I tended to regiment myself into only going out on select nights, the weekends were naturally preferable. As it turned out, Wednesday, and even Thursday came and went without a snag—and then Friday beckoned. Friday was always a tenuous day on the schedule, especially for night check. On the tick of 1500, day check would bail, leaving night check with a laundry list of tasks to complete on the helos.

The command brass often gave ultimatums to us that work left by day check had to be completed before anyone could leave. To our constant chagrin, it meant that we could be stuck at the command and on the flight line wrenching on the helos until 0400, 0500, and sometimes even sunrise itself. Though Fridays were hellacious, the gang found time to pass through and say "hi" and I would do the same, but we mostly kept to ourselves and got work done. Night check had chemistry that put day check to shame on a routine basis. Where day check found reasons why a maintenance task couldn't be done, night check found reasons why they could be.

On that Friday night, we got stuck with a "wash job". A wash job could be summed up best by imaging a carwash and multiplying it in scale by ten or twenty times. In the summer months, they weren't too bad, but in the winter, they were miserable. If the cold temperatures weren't bad enough, the soap used was incredibly powerful, and it burned when it got in your eyes or in any bodily cavities. In the cold, we wore our standard Navy issue coveralls, and foul weather jackets to keep warm. For me, there was nothing worse than getting the cold water down the back of my neck and having it seep under my jacket making my clothing damp and cold. Nothing put me in a bad mood faster! Sometimes we got stuck with a creampuff on a wash job who took a rag and hid in the cabin to avoid working. Depending on the Lead Petty Officer (we knew them as "LPO") of the shop, there were ways that such attitudes were addressed.

Through and through, we got the helo washed, and it was inspected and given a "thumbs up". Sometime around 0300, the Maintenance Chief came into our shop and called upon the LPO's to meet in the Maintenance Control room. Whenever that occurred it meant one of two things; we would be leaving soon, or we had more work to do. Thankfully on that night, the LPOs came back to the shop and told us to clean up and check in our tools for the night. We happily scrambled to get things turned in so we could skedaddle. In my case, I was simply exhausted. Whereas the previous Friday the gang was off early enough to make last call, things were more typical this time around. As I turned in my equipment, B-man gestured to me if I was going to come over after work. I gestured back that I would call him later.

At the end of a shift, when someone in the gang told the others that they would call them "later", it meant the next day. I wanted extra sleep so that I would have time early in the afternoon to get errands done. I did just that—at 1430 on Saturday I got my room cleaned up and put a full tank of gas in Green Beater. To my surprise, I received my paycheck! Being a sailor, and working at the kind of command I did, it wasn't hard to forget the basics of a work week. In a way, we had no schedule. Feeling giddy about getting paid, I called B-man. He picked up quickly, and without hesitation told me to come over.

"Bro, we're going to have a doozy tonight! A lot of people heard about our shit show last week and they want in! Invite some people if you know they're cool!"

I wasn't sure how to take his enthusiasm. I answered as best as I could.

"Okay."

# 7. Vanilla Dancer

I got off the phone with B-man and finished up the small errands around my room. Once I left and proceeded towards the quarterdeck, I decided that I would extend a party invite to Wilky. Unfortunately, there were no less than ten suites in the vicinity of the laundry room, the only place I really associated with Wilky. Guessing what room was his and ending up with another bathroom incident wasn't something I wanted to revisit, so I proceeded to the quarterdeck.

Luckily, the OOD wasn't Pickens, it was a Second Class named Anderson. She was someone who sat at the barracks quarterdeck a few times in the past, but not someone I knew well. Short, with tattoos all up and down her arms, and with a buzz cut, she was knocked by some for listening to death metal music with the volume up too high. Personally, I never minded, but I also had a room that was far down the corridor. When I approached her, she looked at me and smiled.

"Hi."

"Hi Anderson. Can you by chance tell me what room Wilkins is in?"

She nodded and pulled out the barracks tenant roster. Thumbing through the index pages towards the back, she took her index finger and ran it down the page to "W." There were two "Wilkins" in the barracks.

"Uh, Ashley Wilkins, or Raymond Wilkins?"

*Obviously, Raymond,* I thought to myself.

"Raymond, most likely."

She dragged her finger from the name right across to the room number. "241."

It seemed off. Room 241 was the second floor, and there was no way in my mind that Wilky was up there.

"Oh…it has to be Ashley Wilkins. Sorry about that." I said.

Anderson looked at the number. "118."

I was certain that Room 118 was correct as it was near the laundry room. I thanked Anderson and then proceeded to the corridor. I walked by the laundry room to the third door on the right; Room 118. I stood there until someone walked by staring at me. Finally, I cleared my throat and knocked on the door. After the third knock, I heard footsteps on the other side and then the door opened. A woman stood staring, her eyes were striking, olive in color. She had a soft, brown skin tone and hair braided in a weave. My eyes roamed down from her nice lips, to her necklace, to her pastel green nails. She was dressed like she was going out somewhere nice. Only the thought of how big of an idiot I was for picking the wrong room allowed me to proceed beyond silent staring.

"You must be Ashley Wilkins. I'm sorry I went to the wrong Wilkins room!" I said.

The silence was searing!

"I'll go, I didn't mean to bother you." I continued.

As I started to walk away, she spoke.

"Ashley is here. He's washing up. I'm Shanae."

*Bosner, you dufus!* I thought to myself. I turned back around with an embarrassed grin on my face.

"Oh, cool. Shanae, I'm Bosner. Didn't know Ashley's name was Ashley."

"Come in! Do you drink?" she replied.

The moment became pleasantly awkward.

"Sure. What do you have?"

The barracks rooms were all standardly similar. In the entry way was the common area or kitchen, then to the left and right were the rooms, the bathroom was shared. Males and females were not paired into a shared suite; therefore, Shanae came from elsewhere. Whomever shared the suite with Wilky remained a mystery. Shanae pulled up a chair and motioned for me to sit down.

"Do you like cognac?" she asked.

"Do I get a choice in this?"

She smiled, then grabbed a pair of glasses and a bottle of cognac. The glasses were topped off with ice.

"Ashley told me about you. Say's your cool. Different kind 'a cracker."

Different may as well been my middle name; there was nobody else who got tore up at parties and then rambled on about the "Spanish Inquisition". In the context of Shanae, I wasn't sure how to proceed.

"You could say that. Wilky thinks if he gives me enough shit I'll work on my inside game on the court."

"You play ball?" she asked.

"I did when I was a kid and I know a thing or two about it."

I took a big sip of cognac and winced. Shanae laughed.

"You don't drink much huh?"

"I drink, but I prefer beer. Cognac isn't normally on my menu." I said.

The door to the bathroom opened, and out came Wilky.

"Bosner! What up boy!"

I stood and we fist bumped.

"Ashley Wilkins, nice touch." I said.

"Hey, I don't be messin with your name." he replied.

He had a stern look on his face, then as I thought he was serious he busted up laughing.

"Hey man, came by to see what you were doing. I'm heading to a party. You're—actually both of you—are welcome." I said.

He looked at Shanae, she in turn looked at me.

"We're heading downtown to do some dancing. Do you like dancing? I'm thinking you can roll with us." he said.

I couldn't dance if my life depended on it. My grandma once attempted to teach me two-step, but even that was beyond my comprehension. More than that, I was too white to groove. On the other hand, I didn't turn down opportunities for a good time and though it was likely that Shanae was Wilky's girl, I liked her. A good vibe ruled the tone of the room between the three of us. I shook Wilky's hand and told him I was in. He poured himself a glass of cognac, and we sat talking while we drank. I texted B-man that I would be coming later to the party and suggested to Wilky and Shanae that they could stop by after dancing. We were going out early enough to fit time in for a party afterwards.

We finished our drinks, and then left. Wilky indicated he was going to drive, so I didn't bother asking where exactly in downtown we were going. He had a custom car, lowered and with racing tires. It was dark purple with a custom shark fin and white racing strips over the top from the trunk to the hood. I wondered how much it cost him, and how he afforded it on the low salary of an enlisted man.

"Nice wheels. This had to cost you a bit."

He looked at me and smiled.

"What do you drive, Bosner?" Shanae asked.

Unsure how to answer, I pointed at Green Beater instead. She shook her head.

"You're a very humble man."

"Ah, I'm just boring." I said.

She pinched me and laughed.

"You cool with the backseat? It's a bit tight." Wilky said.

Being ornery I looked at Shanae, she scoffed and pushed me.

"Fool, you know your ass is sitting back there."

Wilky's car had a nice leather interior and cologne smell. The seats looked so clean I felt like I was dirtying them simply by sitting. Dark lights provided the lighting from the front seat mirrors to the dome light. Wilky turned up the music so loud I lost my train of thought and could feel my head rattling from the bass. I was in awe of how much money he must've spent to customize the car to such an extent. We left the parking lot and proceeded for Main Street, I focused out the side window and noticed how quiet it was, midafternoon may as well been 0430 in the morning.

"Isn't it a little early for dancing? I figured clubs aren't open yet." I said.

"Nah hoss. Not where we're goin. We prefer earlier, it's less crowded."

Wilky enjoyed riding up close on other cars and running through yellow lights quickly. Watching through the window at the speeds we reached with the music volume so loud and bass that rattled everything in sight made for a spectacle. I imagined what the sight for a person outside must've been of me in the back seat as Wilky sped through town with loud music and bass booming, it had to be priceless. Shanae laughed when I tried bobbing my head in sync with the beat and failed miserably, her and Wilky constantly leaned towards each other to talk. What was said, I had no idea.

We eventually made it to downtown, where we turned onto a backstreet and then an alley I wasn't familiar with. I started to look around as I hoped to figure out where exactly we were, but then we came upon a neat parking area perfectly hidden from any streets. We were in what was considered a bad part of town, but all around us were nice cars, some nicer than Wilky's! There were some rough buildings, but between two of the rougher high rises was what I thought to be a nice brick townhouse. It had lime green double doors and leading to it was a lime green carpet lined by lanyards in matching color. I had no doubt that it was the dance club. The sign above the door was hard to read, as it looked like a graffiti style sign; to me it read "Sex lurs", but I didn't bother asking Wilky or Shanae. We got out.

"I'll be...I never knew this was back here." I said.

"Now you do. And you 'gon dance!" Wilky replied.

I cringed, then Shanae patted the back of my head.

"Bosner, it's okay. You got this!"

I wasn't assured in the least, but I also wasn't as shy as I appeared. I resolved myself to have a damn good time. We proceeded to the door, and I then realized there was likely to be a cover charge. I had grown familiar with clubs during my time spent overseas. From Hawaii, to Guam, to Singapore, I became quickly educated on the "club life" as it were. I mentioned "cover charge" to Wilky and Shanae, but they shook their heads and told me not to worry.

When we entered through the green doors, my eyes had to adjust to the dimness of the room. Through a short hallway we entered into a larger room through swinging double doors. On the left was a wall of mirrors, to the right was a bar lined with trim lights a bit like those at C.T. Slaters. Rhythm and blues blared, and very quickly, the patrons of the venue froze upon seeing me enter. *White guy invading the house*, I thought to myself. I nodded to everybody and continued to follow Wilky and Shanae. The two were well dressed for the venue while I was sporting a pair of jeans and a thermal top. I knew right away that it would either be a great time, or a horrible one—nothing in between seemed possible. We proceeded to the back, all eyes remained on me, and then we took a seat on the other side of a dance floor from the bar area.

The venue was nice. The mirrors were a bit much, but there was a great sound system, a disco ball, and neat lighting. Shanae kept looking at me and laughing, and I kept looking around at all the lights and mirrors. A waitress approached us wearing an incredibly tight, short skirt dress. She had golden hair, and her lips stood out in contrast to the dark lights in the room. Wilky placed an order, and when I tried to ask him about options for drinks, he waved me off. Shanae leaned over and said, "We got you." The waitress came back with a bottle of cognac. *Shit, I might not make it out of here!* I thought to myself. Liquor was never a strong suit of mine, but I was in a brother's venue and I felt it best to go with the flow and respect customs.

"You like to get some liquid courage before hitting the floor!?" I asked Wilky.

He slapped me on the back. "Hell yes. But you gettin your ass out there too. No choice cracker!"

*Heh.* I thought to myself.

We drank from the bottle, as it became obvious to me that Wilky had picked up the tab. I was getting a buzz, and I noticed the club was now filling with patrons. I was never sensitive to being alone in a room as far as skin color was concerned, but I was focused on making sure my body language was up to par—in my travels I always understood the importance of body language. It seemed my every move made Shanae laugh, and she soon began talking a lot with the waitress. As it was so loud and the lighting was dim in the club, it was hard to see or hear them; they had to lean towards each other to communicate.

To my astonishment, the bottle of cognac was quickly bottomed out, I certainly helped kill it. I was a bit worried about how long I would last, but then as I zoned out, I felt an arm grab me and pull me up on the dance floor. It was just me, then to my right Wilky. Shanae followed. They began dancing to the beat. I stood briefly and looked around; it was literally just Wilky, Shanae, and myself. All eyes were on the white boy standing there. I gulped, then began "moving". Things became a blur.

I continued moving my eyes around the crowd in the room, and I saw heads bobbing, hands clapping, and some feet stomping. I could hear a higher pitched laugh coming from Shanae, and almost in a subconscious way, I could hear "YOU GO BOSNER." from Wilky. For a period of time that could've been minutes or even an hour, I was moving. I don't know how it looked, and I don't know if it was good or bad, but I was moving. The beat was good, but whether or not my moves matched it well, I will forever wonder. The reaction from everybody in the club was one of sheer appreciation of my ability, or sheer laughter at my ineptitude. I felt myself grow tired, and then Wilky finally motioned for us to return to our table. He was smiling, laughing, and patting me. Shanae looked like she had seen an elf grow a rainbow out of its ass.

Everything slowed back down as I took my seat. I noticed that I was sweating, and that I had danced, or moved, or whatever for an extended period of time. I was certainly drunk, which was helpful because it gave me an edge so I could play off whatever it was that I'd just done on the dance floor. Wilky and Shanae could do nothing but smile and laugh. The waitress returned and told me someone had bought a drink for me, finally Wilky let me get what I always preferred, "a shitty, light beer". The music then quieted down for some sort of intermission.

"That was the most interesting set of moves I've ever seen." Shanae said.

I remained speechless. Sensing that I was feeling uneasy over my dance performance, Wilky reassured me.

"Bruh, you a weird dude, but I like you. You're a rock star up in here!"

I wiped the sweat off my forehead and remained silent.

"What exactly do you listen to?" he asked.

"Old shit."

In fact, that was the truth. I was a sucker for classic rock. Just then, the waitress returned and addressed me.

"Darlin, a young lady at a table over there thinks you are sexy."

She then pointed across the room to a table in the corner. I looked at the table, which was seating five people. Facing me was a woman with glasses, I could see her smiling as she waved. I waved back. It was hard to see in the room in general, but it was made more difficult by my sweating forehead which had the effect of fogging the lenses up on my glasses. I still couldn't make out what the woman looked like, but I never had a specific type when it came to women. I figured there was as good of a chance that I would be attracted to her as any other woman. I sipped my beer, then turned to Shanae.

"What do you think?" I asked.

She smiled, then got up and walked over to the table. I pleaded with her not to go, but it was too late. In a flash, she was at the table speaking to the woman, who stood up and then walked back to our table with Shanae.

Wilky clapped his hands and laughed. "Bosner, scoring already are ya!"

"I guess…"

As Shanae and the woman got closer, I could see her better. She wore thick heals, had tight fitted pants, and a polka dotted button up top that was hard to distinguish with the lighting in the room. She smiled and waved again as she approached. Shanae motioned her to take the seat next to me. She did. The woman had curly hair, thick framed glasses, and large neon-colored earrings. She was voluptuous as well.

I remained silent as the woman waved at me in close proximity. "Hi, you!"

"Hi, I'm Bosner."

Her smile grew. "I'm Latisha. You know you can't dance very well, but you are mmmmm."

I sensed myself blushing. I couldn't help but self-assess—here was an admirer. My awful dancing hadn't phased her negatively in the least. Acting on a whim, I decided to cast humor on the situation.

"The dancing was supposed to put you on notice!"

She burst out laughing and then grabbed my leg. "You better watch it little boy!"

Her aggressive impulses prompted me to sit up right, stiffly. From my peripheral vision, I saw Shanae covering her mouth in disbelief at the speed that the exchange between Latisha and I was unfolding. I felt like I was in a pressure cooker! I quickly concluded in my mind that Latisha was too much woman for me. *Shanae, you're evil!* I thought to myself. If I thought that the situation was going to diffuse itself, Latisha made clear that I was thinking wrongly.

"You're coming up there with me in just a bit. I'll show you some moves!" she said.

My eyes bugged out. Wilky was covering his mouth not to show laughter. Shanae, whom I would've much rather been wrapped up with, stepped away. I could see things with Latisha poised to unravel faster and faster; I didn't know what to do! I began to surveille the room, and that's when I saw a man walk into the club wheeling equipment. I quickly realized he was the disc jockey and that the club was getting ready to set up for the night's activities. Thankfully, Shanae returned and spoke into Wilky's ear. He then stood up and motioned to me to stand and come to him.

"We're gonna roll out. They're getting ready to charge cover." he said.

I felt saved and then remorseful. I was going to walk back to Latisha and let her know that we were leaving, but Wilky stopped me.

"Don't worry, Shanae is 'gon let her know that were rollin."

I patted Wilky on the back, and then looked over to Shanae. She smiled at me, then turned and walked over to Latisha. I didn't know what exactly she said but we proceeded to leave, and as we did, patrons at the bar whistled and cheered me on. I felt a brief sense of pride and pumped my fist into the air. I looked back at Shanae, who walked just behind Wilky and me. She covered her mouth while she laughed, as she had for much of the evening. I could only imagine how silly the scene must've looked. We exited the club, and after a few steps past the doors which closed, Wilky and Shanae broke out into hysterical laughter.

"Bosner!!! You're a trip. God, you're funny!" Wilky said.

"You're adorable in your own way, don't let anyone tell you otherwise!" Shanae added.

I blushed. I wasn't upset, and I didn't feel good or bad, I was just numb. I enjoyed the club, mainly because it was a spontaneous activity and I got free drinks, even some attention! We then got back into the car. As I got situated in the back seat, I leaned forward between the driver and passenger seats.

"So, do you guys wanna come out to the party?"

There was a pause, then Wilky and Shanae looked at each other. "Fuck it. Let's go!"

# CAPE HENRY HOUSE

I proceeded to direct them to Cape Henry Avenue.

# 8. Hungry Keg Stands

Wilky asked me about whose house the party was at, but sporting a buzz from the cognac, I muttered, "It's Cape Henry House!" Both he and Shanae laughed. It seemed that my sheer existence brought them a sizable level of joy and laughter. For that matter, I couldn't help but smile myself. The beats blared, and Wilky drove recklessly just as he had on our way to the club. I directed him accordingly, and soon enough we approached Cape Henry Avenue on the left, just after crossing the railroad tracks. As Wilky made the turn onto Cape Henry Avenue, he looked up at me through the rearview mirror.

"Bosner, it figures that you invite us to a house by the railroad tracks!" he said.

"Figured it's a good follow up." I replied.

Shanae turned in her seat and faced me, rolling her eyes and then laughing. I grinned back at her and shrugged my shoulders as we proceeded down the street towards the house. I directed Wilky to continue on, but shockingly as we approached the house, there was nowhere to park! In the back of my mind, I assumed that the party wouldn't be in full swing quite yet since I wasn't there. As we pulled up closer to the house, it was already a zoo! With nowhere to park, Wilky stopped in the middle of the street directly in front of the house. He and Shanae stared through the large window next to the front door. The place was mayhem.

"Uh, I think I may have to pass on this party, Bosner. If I get as wild as them motherfuckers, I be 'gon to jail!" he said.

Shanae stared in awe at the chaotic looking party, then faced me. "Is this it? You don't seem like the guy that belongs at a party like this!"

At that moment, in what seemed like sheer chance, B-man stumbled out the front door and barreled down the steps towards us. Wilky rolled his window down.

"Blaine? Bruh, what's up!"

B-man, clearly intoxicated, put his hand on the roof of the car and leaned towards Wilky.

"PIZZA GUY!" he barked.

There was a complete pause. Shanae looked back at me, and silently lipped, "Are you sure about this?"

I nodded. She then tapped Wilky's shoulder, who turned away from B-man and leaned towards her so she could whisper something. B-man looked into the car and saw me.

"BOSNER. YOU GOT PIZZA, RIGHT?"

I flinched initially at the decibel level of his voice, but then I laughed and waved.

"Hey buddy. No, but I'm sure the pizza is coming!"

Wilky looked at me.

"I forgot that we got other plans bruh, but if you want out here that's cool. Had a blast with you!"

I was aware that Wilky and Shanae had seen enough of the party. I understood though, and so I thanked them for a good time at the club and for helping me get out of the tight spot with Latisha. Wilky then motioned B-man to step back so that he could open the door for me to get out. Shanae looked at me and grabbed my hand.

"Bosner, you be careful, okay?"

I smiled and nodded. I got out of the car, and the two sped off, blaring the beats. At the foot of the front lawn by the sidewalk stood B-man and me. He put his arm around me.

"HUNGRY, BRO. WHERE'S THE PIZZA?"

I was nowhere near as toasted as B-man, and I tried not to laugh. As he had his arm around my shoulders, I put my arm across his back to steer him towards the house. We proceeded towards the front door, and I began trying to take mental note of just how many people were at the party. There were four people I didn't recognize standing at the foot of the steps smoking, and as I acknowledged them, I noticed tiny snowflakes flailing in the wind. The four nodded at B-man and I as I guided him up the steps and through the front door.

The first thing I noticed when B-man and I entered the house was the blaring music. I looked to my right and saw none other than Zick, screaming into a microphone singing karaoke. He had a female companion by his side singing along. She was slim, slightly shorter than him, with red hair and a big smile. They looked like the perfect pair if I had ever seen one! I waved at Zick, and he along with his companion waved back. I lip synced with the two as I guided B-man through the living room towards the kitchen. The music and the loud party voices were as loud as any I had ever experienced before.

Once we reached the kitchen, B-man stumbled towards a crowd that was gathered around a new addition to the house: a fold up table and beer pong enthusiasts. I then remembered that Zick and Thayer had said they were going to bring a table. Sure enough, there the table was, and people were passionately playing beer pong. I struggled to distinguish people at the party, and I settled on a rough estimate of thirty people in attendance. I stood there looking at the crowd and thought about how B-man and Dolvar outdid themselves with the party. B-man then walked in front of me towards the kitchen sink. He leaned in and began drinking water directly from the faucet.

"B-man! Did you order pizza!?" I asked.

"Bosner. Bro, what up."

I laughed. "Hey buddy, did you order pizza!? You were asking me when I got here."

He stood up from the sink and turned to face me. He then turned his ball cap around backwards, for reasons unknown.

"I'm fuckin hungry bro."

I stood there for a minute and looked around. By chance, I saw Anne sitting in a chair in the corner between the beer pong table and the sliding glass door. I motioned to B-man to hold on a minute while I asked Anne if there was food coming. She was always the most sober of anyone when there was partying, so I figured she would be the best person to ask. I walked over to her, and then she saw me.

"Hi Bosner! I didn't think you were going to come!" she said.

"Me? Miss a party here? Hell no!"

Just then, a game of beer pong finished, and the crowd huddled around the table was going nuts. I leaned closer to Anne so she could hear me.

"Did anyone here order food? B-man said something about pizza, but nobody else seems to know, and he didn't seem to know either."

With the beer pong crowd continuing to be loud, she leaned towards me. Anne tried to speak twice, then the third time she leaned as close as she could.

"I doubt it, but even so, there's so many people here! If you can, maybe you and someone else can go!"

In truth, I hadn't eaten yet. I wasn't hungry, but after all the cognac I had earlier I figured food was probably a wise choice. As I had finished speaking to Anne, I looked outside through the sliding glass door and saw two people waving at me. When I looked closer, it was Bomber and Tee!

Bomber and Tee were an inseparable couple who heard about the previous week's wild party and decided to come see for themselves. Bomber, whose real name was Ken Williams, was from Arizona, and his girlfriend Tee, real name Rose Osborne, was from Regency, Illinois (she always drilled that into anybody who asked). They were part of our command, but they worked in other maintenance divisions. Both were known partiers, and Tee was legendary for beating everyone at the keg stand challenge. As soon as they saw me and waved, I was pulled into the competition to do a keg stand—the sheer act of being spotted by them drew their aggressive nature to pressure whomever into doing a keg stand for competition's sake. Unfortunately for me, I was one of the worst at it.

When I stepped outside, Bomber smacked me on the shoulders with both hands.

"Bosner, Bosner, Bosner! This just wouldn't have been a party without you!"

We fist bumped.

"I heard you were coming so I had to make a cameo appearance at least!" I said.

Just then, I was slugged in the arm by Tee.

"Give us a fact, Jack!"

We hugged.

"The approximate height of Mount Rainier is 14,411 feet. That makes it the fourth highest peak in the lower 48."

She was intrigued, or maybe not. "Yea, cool, now get your ass up her and do a keg stand!"

Everyone outside heard Tee mention "keg stand" and rushed to us. Tee pointed at me, and then a few of the partiers grabbed me. I hadn't even located the keg, so when they began lifting me up face down, I looked at Tee.

"Where's the fucking keg!?"

She laughed. Then, two random dudes slid out a keg in the tub with ice from behind the picnic table.

With my head down, and facing the concrete of the patio, I began cursing.

"You've got to be kidding me! Damnit! I'm trying to figure out the food situation!"

Bomber patted me on my back as I was being held in the air.

"No you aren't. You're trying to figure out how to do a keg stand properly!"

Tee then started yelling, "CHUG!" as she held the tap and put the nozzle up to my mouth. *Sonofabitch,* I thought to myself. I glugged and chugged as best I could, but as was usually the case for me, it was a five to seven second evolution. After about six seconds, the golden foam started flowing out my nose. I choked and gurgled, then they put me down to my feet as everyone declared me a "wuss". Tee flexed her arms and taunted me. I felt like I was going to vomit, so I ran off the patio towards the fence along the railroad tracks. I gagged twice but nothing came up. I did, however, get the best of Tee. She had one weakness: she couldn't witness someone in the act of vomiting without herself getting the bodily urge to vomit. Luckily for me, I made her queasy.

"Good one, Bosner!" Bomber said.

Tee bolted away from me and around the house gagging. I returned inside, and the beer pong games continued. The house was a complete ruckus. I motioned to Anne that I was going to get food, and at that moment Penley emerged from the hallway and at her direction, approached me.

"Bosner! Good to see you. How you feeling?"

"What up! I'm hanging in there. Looking to get food! What's the deal?"

Penley handed me some cash. "Take this. See if someone is good enough to drive you to get some grub.      B-man looks gone. It may be too late for him."

"Cool, I'll throw in on this too. B-man will be fine. If nothing else, he just needs a nap."

Penley grinned and patted me on the back. I then headed for the front door to figure out what I was going to do, but at that moment Zick had taken a break from blaring karaoke and grabbed me. He was lit, just like everyone else, but he had his signature grin. We fist bumped, and then he introduced me to his lady friend.

"This is Joanne Lewis! Joanne, this is Bosner!"

I shook Joanne's hand. "How'd you find this stud!"

She smiled as Zick playfully slugged my shoulder. "He made me sing. I liked it!"

Joanne seemed quite timid, but I wasn't sure if that was because she actually was, or if Zick's very loving but drunk introduction of us made things awkward. She too was drunk, but like Zick she had a seemingly permanent smile. I couldn't help but smile back and assure her that Zick was the man. In a lot of ways, among the gang, he was!

At that point, I was politely trying to step away from Zick and Joanne so I could resume my expedition to find food. Conveniently for me, the two resumed singing and romanticizing, so I made my way out front. On the front porch were more people I didn't know, and then the girls from the previous weekend, Ms. Highlights among them. She walked down the steps to the lawn to have a smoke. On that night, she was wearing duck boots, jeans, a thick brown jacket, and of course the highlights in her hair. Cute, no doubt.

"Bosner. We meet again."

"Indeed, we do." I replied.

"You look better this time. Taking it easy tonight?"

"You could say that. Hey, do you know someone who can drive me to the store? I'm trying to get food for the party."

She puffed on her cigarette and shook her head. "My one friend with wheels already left."

Just then, there was a commotion between the cars parked in the driveway. We both looked and saw two people in the dark cursing and disagreeing over something. One of them growled out, "motherfucker" while the other one pushed off. The scuffle intensified, and then they both tumbled towards us. Everyone but Ms. Highlights and I went inside. Once the two came into the porch light, I could tell that one of them was Dolvar, but they both continued to tussle on the lawn. Finally, they stopped, and the other person stood up and faced us. It was Sammy! I looked at Ms. Highlights.

"It's Sammy!"

She looked back at me. "And who's that?"

"OH MAN! Bosner!" he shouted.

"Good to see you at Cape Henry House!"

Sammy and I bro hugged as Dolvar and Ms. Highlights stood there confused.

"Cape what?" she asked.

Sammy laughed. "That's what you're calling it?"

"Has a nice ring to it." I said.

Ms. Highlights took one more puff off her cigarette and then headed inside. "You boys have fun out here."

"Fucking clowns." Dolvar said.

He too walked up the steps and went into the house. Outside in the porchlight, it was only Sammy and me. When I asked him what the fight was all about, he drunkenly replied, "I don't know. Just felt like fighting I guess."

I couldn't figure out what was going on with the party except that everyone was somehow drunker than me. Sammy at least seemed in good spirits. He was a thick guy from Wyoming; his full name was Ted Samuelson, a name bland enough to make "Sammy" seem more appealing. He had a penchant for yelling "OH MAN", particularly when he was drunk. Other than that, he was one of the mellower partiers we knew and in my mind he was a teddy bear (no pun intended!) to Dolvar's big bad wolf. As we both stood there in the on-and-off snowfall, I realized Sammy wasn't going to be much help getting food. Then again, at that point I knew that practically nobody at the party was going to be much help. With that, I asked Sammy if he was interested in coming with me.

"I need you to come with me so we can get food. Are you down?"

He turned and faced the window, then back at me. "OH MAN. Yep. Let's go!"

Sammy followed me into the house. Inside, Zick and Joanne continued singing passionately, B-man napped in the pass out room, Anne went back to her bedroom, and everyone else played beer pong or socialized. Sammy asked me when we were going to get food, but I didn't have a specific plan, and the two people who wanted me to get food were either in their room or out of commission, at least temporarily. Sammy grabbed and shook me.

"You tell me we're getting food, then you don't know?"

"Hey, everyone put this bullshit in my lap. I don't have a plan so I guess we will just walk to the corner store."

I turned around to walk back out the front door, but Sammy objected. He waved towards the sliding glass door.

"NO! Let's go this way! I know a short cut."

I followed him towards the door, but at that moment, Bomber, Tee, and others stepped inside. Sammy continued to wave towards the door while facing me, which led Bomber, Tee, and company to look at me and assume something that wasn't.

"Keg stand!?" Bomber asked.

I tried to immediately decline, but Bomber had sealed my fate. Those two words triggered a strong response from the party. Everyone in the kitchen and living room—including Zick and Joanne in the middle of their duet—repeatedly shouted "keg stand!"

Sammy looked at me with sympathy before he shrugged. "Keg stand?"

"Bomber, you bastard!" I said.

Tee pushed through and grabbed Sammy and me.

"Alright boys. Keg stand! Bosner must be thirsty for number two!" she said.

Bomber turned around and followed us, as did others. I tried resisting Tee, who kept pushing me towards the keg. Desperate to get out of the situation, I rambled off reasons why I couldn't do another keg stand; nothing worked. Unfortunately for Tee, I knew of the one surefire way to stop her, so I did the asshole thing and made gagging sounds. Tee immediately let go of Sammy and I, then ran towards the side of the house vomiting. Bomber laughed.

"You're a crafty little shit, Bosner."

I pushed Sammy off the patio and on to the back lawn.

"Sammy let's do it! Short cut, short cut!" I yelled.

"OH MAN! Go time!"

The two of us bolted across the lawn to the fence lining the railroad tracks. We leapt up and hurdled the fence, landing onto the gravel of the track bed and parts unknown. Off, we were!

# 9. Mission: 3 Beers Standing

Sammy and I sprinted across the railroad tracks and over an adjacent fence into the dark. It was hard to see, but we landed in some garden bushes that gave off a loud rustling noise. We both hit the ground hard and were slow to get up. After a second, a porch light came on and a dog began barking from inside a house. We laughed, but once the house lit up and we heard a voice, we quickly rose to our feet. Sammy almost tripped, but I held him up and pushed him forward. A woman stood at the front door and began opening a screen door that was keeping the barking dog from chasing us. I smacked Sammy on the back as we both ran.

Luckily, we scaled another fence, keeping the dog from reaching us. The woman's voice and the dog's bark faded into the distance. We cut through two more yards, and soon we could see the road just beyond one last lot. We climbed another fence into the final yard but greeting us was a dark mass about waist high. I could barely see, but a vicious growl and bark revealed it to be a big damn dog! It stood still in front of Sammy and I, so I took my chances and sprinted ahead as Sammy followed suit. Once we started running, the dog pursued us, and lights on the neighboring houses collectively lit up. Sammy and I focused squarely on the last fence separating us from the road, sprinting as fast as we could while we laughed. I reached the fence first and hurdled it with reckless abandon. I quickly rose to my feet from the other side to the sound of laughter and barking. I glanced back, and to my relief, Sammy had scaled the fence.

In our drunken stupor, we became so focused on escaping the dog and the yard that we bolted out into the road. Sammy was right behind me, and to our terror bright lights and a loud horn sounded. Sammy froze like a deer, so I ruthlessly grabbed him, and we stumbled to the shoulder of the road. He lost his balance and fell towards the grassy median. I looked back at the vehicle that almost hit us; it was a utility truck, and with that I realized how bad things could've gone. As for Sammy, a puddle in the median broke his fall and soaked him. Once on his feet, he cursed and laughed at the predicament as I put my arm around him.

"Hey, hey, let's cross the other lanes more carefully bud, what do you say?"

He nodded. "Works for me."

Fortunately, there was no traffic approaching from the other lanes, and we easily crossed in the dark. On the other side, we turned right and walked the 150 yards to the mini mart. As we approached its illuminated sign, I worried about the food selection such a small store may have. Besides chips and dip, I couldn't think of anything that a mini mart sold that would suffice for a party as big as ours.

"What is here that we can get for the party? Chips?" Sammy asked.

On the same page, I laughed. "I guess man. I can't think of anything else."

We entered the mini mart to the glare of the clerk. It was an older gentleman with reading glasses slouched over the counter doing crossword puzzles. He acknowledged us by nodding, and we followed suit. Sammy went to the chips aisle, and I went to the jerky section, a bit discouraged. I was certain that there would not be enough of anything at the mini mart to satisfy the party. As I circled around the aisle and returned to the front counter, I realized there was an entire rack of hot dogs cooking on the heat rollers just behind the front counter. *BINGO!* I thought to myself. From the cooler section, Sammy shouted my name, startling the clerk.

"Yep?" I replied.

"Do we need beer!?"

The clerk reacted negatively to his drunken speech. I gestured to him to quiet down before responding. "I don't think so."

Sammy smiled. "Cool. I'll get a box."

I looked at the clerk as he shook his head. I tried to appease Sammy. "Sure, why not?"

Sammy fumbled the beer, as evidenced by the excessive clanging sounds; the clerk grew suspicious. I did my best to disregard Sammy and focus on engaging the clerk about the hot dogs. At first, I attempted counting just how many hot dogs there were, but I gave up and ordered all of them; it seemed easier that way. The clerk stared at me for a moment and adjusted his glasses. The clanging noises continued as Sammy came around from the back with two boxes of beer. He plopped them at the register as he glared at the clerk.

"These too, good sir! Hey, would you like a beer?" Sammy asked.

The clerk stood straight up and gazed at us both. "I think I'm going to have to ask you two to leave."

We stood in disbelief. My mind raced while I tried to come up with a response, but then my impulses took over. I pulled out all the money in my wallet, and all the wadded cash in my pockets, putting it on the counter by the register.

"Take this and let us have the beer and the hot dogs." I said.

The clerk's mouth opened a bit while he stared. I stared straight back. He then looked at Sammy, as did I. To his credit, Sammy remained cool, just grinning and nodding. The clerk looked back at me and smirked as he began retrieving the hot dogs. I smiled. Sammy had two boxes of beer, and I had two bags full of hot dogs, though I didn't bother to count how many there were. We grabbed as many packets of ketchup and mustard as we could; I stuffed packets into the bags with the hot dogs, in my jacket pockets, and in my pant pockets. Off we were!

We had a much easier time crossing the road on the way back, but on the other side from the mini mart, we agreed to find a better way back to the party. We cut through yards that were further up the road and appeared more auspicious. Unfortunately, the first yard we snuck through had a fence that was tough to scale with boxes of beer. We tried anyway, and after I tied the bags of hot dogs and condiment packets through the belt loops on my pants and scaled it, Sammy and I found the beer-over-the-fence operation quite tough to manage.

As I had an easier time scaling fences with my lighter load, I planned to scale first, then help Sammy with passing the boxes of beer over. It worked until we ended up in another yard with a hostile pet—a dog, naturally. Just like before, the dog barked and house lights came on, but carrying bags of food and lugging boxes of beer made for a difficult escape. Sammy dropped one box of beer upon hearing the dog bark, which clanged loudly enough to set off house lights all around. I waved at him to hurry and forget the beer. There were now neighbors exiting their homes to investigate.

With an ecstatic fury, we ran towards the old wooden fence along the railroad tracks; we were home-free once we scaled it. Once we reached that fence, we scaled it with no regard, and as I landed on the gravel of the track bed and got up to run, Sammy yelled. I turned and met him at the base of the fence. His left hand was bleeding, but it appeared to be a cut from the fence wood and not bottle glass. In his cut hand, he clutched a shred of cardboard from the box of beer left behind. He still held the other box of beer in his right hand. I helped him to his feet, impressed we still had one box remaining. We proceeded on the tracks towards the lights and noise of the party. Some saw us from the other side of the fence.

"Hey check it out! Who is that?" someone asked.

"It's us!" Sammy said.

"Who's us!?" The voice replied.

I shook my head. "Oh fuck, whatever. See you in a second!"

Sammy scaled the fence into the yard first as I helped him with the beer. When I handed him the box, he grabbed it with both hands. The weight of the box in his wounded hand made him wince, then he dropped it. Everybody heard breaking glass.

"Son of a bitch!!!" I yelled.

"OH MAN!"

I scaled the fence and fell into the yard as people clapped and laughed. I leapt to my feet and gave an impromptu bow.

"We're back!"

I looked to Sammy, who shook the box of broken beer bottles, then peered into its partially torn-open side. He raised his hand and signaled "three". The great irony was that we didn't need the beer, we had a keg! It was a formality, food was not. It was at that moment that realized I was missing the hot dogs. As Sammy and I approached the patio, a random person looked at us.

"Dude, where's the food?"

Sammy laughed and then pointed at me. "He has the food."

"Fuck!" I said.

The bags were empty, both had gaping holes in the bottoms. Making matters worse, my pants were stained with ketchup and mustard. I charged towards the fence while Sammy and the others laughed and cursed about the humor and frustration of the wasted expedition. I leaped over the fence onto the tracks, running to where we escaped the yards. Nothing. Someone's yard, and possibly someone's dog, was the lucky recipient of a pile of hotdogs. Furious, I kicked the old wood fence, prompting the dogs to sound. I returned to the house, both disappointed and dejected. Once back, Lorrie was outside smoking.

"Bosner, what's up?"

"I'm a fuckin idiot. That's what's up."

She brushed debris off my sleeves. "You're a mess! You fell?"

"Went to get food. Got chased by dogs and wasted everyone's money instead. Oh, and almost got creamed by a fuckin truck."

She giggled. "Get your chin up, silly. You made it back. That's all that matters."

As she glared at me, she began to full-on laugh, I laughed as well. Snow fell harder, so we went inside. As I closed the sliding glass door behind me, everyone stopped and applauded. Sammy chugged one of the three beers from the trek back and tossed me another, it nearly hit me in the face. Luckily, I caught it. Everyone cheered and pumped their fists as I chugged. Bomber put his arm around me.

"You go out for food and you come back with empty bags, messy pants, and broken bottles?"

"Seemed like a good idea." I said.

Billy fixed my shirt collar. "Looks like the yards you cut through ate and drank well."

"The mission wasn't a total flop. There were three beers standing!" Sammy added.

I looked at Bomber. "Yea, three beers made it."

"Hello? We already had beer!" Melissa said.

I put my hand on her cheek. "Oh, but the three that came back were special!"

I grabbed the last beer and looked for Thomas, who was sitting on the couch half-asleep. Zick and Joanne sat next to him, romantically infatuated with one another as the karaoke background music played on the TV. I approached Thomas, he slowly acknowledged me.

"What's up?"

I handed him the beer. "Have this. It's for last week. Plus, you look a helluva lot better this time!"

"There's keg beer." he said.

"Sammy and I went on a mission to get food and came back with three beers instead. This is the last one. Take it."

Thomas smiled, then took the beer. As he sipped on it, Sammy was in the background bragging to everyone about the wild trip to the mini mart. Somebody coined the name "Mission: Three Beers Standing". On the couch, Zick raised his fist to us as he kissed Joanne.

# 10. The Great Hole

The night calmed down, and I was feeling better despite the wild trek to the mini mart. Sammy called his shot and stumbled into the pass out room for some shuteye. He was quite the trooper that night— sure; we wasted money on beer when we had a keg, and we pulled an "0-fer" on getting any food, but the doomed trek made for a great story. Best of all, three beers made it back with us! I sat down on the couch next to Thomas, Zick, and Joanne. The karaoke background music and my intoxicated state of mind soothed me. I zoned out into a calm, detached demeanor. I was staring at the lights above the beer pong table and listening to the chatter from everyone still partying; in my current state, everything sounded dull and distant.

Soon thereafter, the beer pong games wound down; Billy was on a roll, having defeated everyone. Bomber and Tee competed against him and Thayer hoping to snap his win streak. I noticed that beer pong was one thing that kept Thayer from mentioning food or hunger. I was curious whether B-man was going to wake back up and party more. Having forgotten that he was last seen entering the pass out room, I proceeded to his room to check on him. His bedroom door was slightly open, so I entered. With the limited hallway light shining into his room, I saw somebody sit up on the air mattress. A female voice asked who I was, I apologized for disturbing them and I closed the door; I assumed it was Melissa.

I proceeded to the pass out room, where I stood at the entryway. Instead of turning on the lights and pissing everyone off, I gazed at the dark figures resting on the floor, hoping to notice B-man. Unfortunately, I couldn't tell who the people resting were. The music and chatter of the party was loud, so I entered. I closed the door enough to provide some light into the room. As I tiptoed towards the back, the door swung open.

"B-man. Get your ass up!" Dolvar said.

I plead with him to quiet down. Drunk as I ever saw him, he brushed by me. Oddly, he seemed to know exactly where B-man was, and upon approaching the third figure laying down, he kicked them brazenly.

"Get the fuck up."

I grabbed Dolvar from behind. "Dude, cut that out."

He turned and pushed me; I stumbled backwards over someone resting on the floor. They quickly sat up.

"What the fuck! Asshole." they snapped.

I apologized, then turned back to Dolvar who kicked the third person again. Then, they sounded. It was B-man.

"I'm good, bro. Let me rest."

"No, clown. Get the fuck up. Party time."

He kicked B-man again.

"Dolvar—"

"Fuck you, Bosner." he replied.

I prepared to pull him out of the room as the person I tripped over, a random dude, was on his feet asking me who I was. Dolvar kicked B-man again.

"BRO. I'M GOOD. GO AWAY."

I again grabbed Dolvar, but he turned and swung at me. He missed, but I drunkenly stumbled backward getting caught by the random dude who proceeded to shoved me. My impulse was to get in the dude's face, but I felt it best to focus on getting Dolvar out of the room. He was unquestionably in one of his warpath moods, and I knew a fight was about to occur. By now Lorrie, Bomber and Tee entered. Making matters worse, a random person wanted to fight me. Bomber calmed the dude down, then asked about the situation with Dolvar.

Before I could respond, Dolvar kicked B-man for the final time. In a flash, B-man got up and grabbed him. The rest of us stood idle, unsure of what was going to happen next. Dolvar appeared dazed and stood limp in B-man's grasp. There was a strange pause that ceased when B-man grumbled loudly. His furious sound prompted Lorrie, Bomber, and I to step in to try stopping him from beating the hell out of Dolvar. Instead, B-man drove him back while we got out of the way. We watched as the two sped towards the wall separating the laundry space; it gave way, and with it came an awful sound. They fell through the drywall and damaged wall studs, Dolvar's head missed the dryer unit on the other side by mere inches.

The sight of the man-sized hole in the wall affected everyone differently. Lorrie stood dumbstruck, covering her mouth in disbelief. The random dude grabbed the back of his head and yelled obscenities. Zick and Joanne ran up to the doorway wondering what happened, Billy and Thomas stood behind them. Bomber, Tee, and I immediately approached the New York duo laying through the wall gap while both seemed stunned themselves. I plucked pieces of dangling drywall and tried straightening out the wall studs as Bomber and Tee helped the two up. Luckily, Dolvar was so drunk that he neither felt nor realized what he got himself into. B-man was tired enough (and probably drunk too) that running Dolvar through the wall was enough to cool him off.

The ruckus prompted Penley and Anne to come storming to the scene. Both nudged their way through the group huddled at the doorway to investigate. Anne mimicked Lorrie in covering her mouth in silence as Penley also covered his mouth to conceal laughter. Bomber and I walked Dolvar to the living room while Lorrie and Tee dealt with   B-man. They made their way into the kitchen where they got B-man a beer and kept him calm, Dolvar pointed at him and mumbled something. We watched him carefully, and when he walked towards the kitchen, Bomber grabbed him as the rest of us held our breath. B-man approached Bomber and Dolvar, tapping on Bomber's shoulder to get him to let Dolvar go. Bomber relented, then Dolvar hugged B-man.

I found humor in what had occurred. It was funny that Sammy remained asleep in the pass out room; apparently, we weren't loud enough. Even funnier, B-man and Dolvar put a man-sized hole in a wall after only a week in their new place. But it was funniest that Penley and Anne sought B-man and Dolvar to be their roommates, then stood and watched them throw outrageous parties as though they didn't see such an outcome on the horizon. As it was, Penley calmed Anne enough to keep her from throwing a fit that we could see festering in her eyes. He wasn't happy about what unfolded, but he had an admirable sense of humor and kept his cool. After they retreated to their room and we heard the bedroom door shut, we stood for a moment and looked at each other. We couldn't even muster a laugh, but Billy broke the silence.

"Shit. Let's keep 'er goin!" he said.

The rest of us responded with "Oi!"

Keep it going, we did. I snatched the karaoke microphone and sang as best I could to whatever came on the screen. It was not pretty, but nobody was coherent enough to tell me otherwise. Zick and Joanne were busy on the couch doing things, and Thomas returned to his comfy spot on the adjoining couch. Thayer lectured me about how terrible it was that I couldn't save even a single hot dog from the Mission: Three Beers Standing ordeal. The random dude decided he had enough and gave up on the pass out room, opting instead to call a cab and get a ride home.

"You guys are too much; I'm going to stick to video games." he said.

The hours on the clock rolled by, and I continued to gaze at the words rolling up the screen on karaoke mode, mumbling them as best I could. Through my peripheral vision, I saw maybe four people, then three, two, then maybe one... then blackout.

# 11. Clownfucks and Dildos

A dog barked in the far distance. Kissing, moaning, even a fart sounded. My eyes opened, and I saw white. I blinked a few times and rolled to my left side. The couch was bare, and the blinds were closed on the window behind it. The white outline on the blinds showed that daylight arrived, I rolled to my other side. I saw the beer pong table with some cups still on it. Wrapped in a small blanket under the table was Zick and Joanne. I found it odd, but I had seen weirder things before. I tossed and turned a few times before I rose to my feet. Behind me on the other couch was Thomas, whom I assumed was the farting culprit.

I yawned loudly and then stumbled down the hall towards the bathroom. It compelled me to knock on Penley and Anne's door just as a bathroom joke, but I refrained. In the bathroom, I ran water over my face from the sink before taking a long pee. After that, I stumbled back out to the living room. Since I ate almost nothing the night before, I was starving. I sat on the vacant couch for a moment and scrolled through my phone. I had no texts or calls, so I laid on the couch and nodded in and out of sleep. Thomas was snoring, still on the couch next to me, Zick and Joanne remained asleep under the beer pong table and I could hear snoring from the pass out room. Footsteps sounded from the hallway, then Lorrie emerged.

"Top of the mornin to ya." I said.

She rubbed her eyes and waved at me.

"You kinda disappeared last night." I continued.

"Yea, back to the air mattress."

"Is B-man in there?" I asked.

Lorrie nodded. "He stumbled in at some point and fell like a board."

Sammy sounded from the pass out room. "OH MAN!"

Lorrie flinched as I got up and greeted him.

"What the hell happened?" he asked.

"Do you remember anything?"

Someone lying next to Sammy rolled over. "Please, shush…"

I lowered my voice. "Do you remember going to get food?"

Sammy rubbed his face and scratched his head. "Uh, yea, the fence. My hand."

He got up, and we sat on the couches in the living room.

"Okay. What happened?" he asked.

"We went to get food, but we made it back with only three bottles of beer."

He looked dazed. "What?"

"You don't remember at all?"

He stared at me as I grew disappointed.

"Never mind. How's your hand?"

He stuck his hand out and turned it slowly. "It hurts a little, but I think it's okay. What the hell did I do?"

Lorrie laughed. "You were a trip. Running through yards, dodging dogs, spilling shit everywhere!"

Sammy was in disbelief. "Heh?"

I smiled and shook my head. "Nothing. Go get your hand cleaned up. Peroxide might help."

As Sammy walked toward the hallway, Zick sounded. "Mission: Three Beers Standing!"

Sammy saw Zick and Joanne under the table. "Wait, why the hell are they on the floor like that?"

Zick gave the middle finger salute.

"Getting lucky counts wherever." I said.

Zick laughed. "Who goes with a stack of cash to the store and returns with three bottles of beer and messy pants?"

Sammy shook his head and walked to the bathroom.

"I got here and everyone was hungry. I tried to get food; it just didn't work out." I said.

"Dogs chasing you and stealing it did though." Zick replied.

"I love you Zick but go fuck yourself."

Joanne giggled, then Zick responded, "Love you too."

"Okay lovers, so Johnny's for breakfast?" Lorrie asked.

Thayer sounded from the pass out room. "Breakfast!"

Zick rose to his feet. "Bastards, avoid certain words with him. Now he's triggered."

"But you tempered him down last week." Lorrie said.

"It was just luck!" Joanne replied.

Everyone perked up. Lorrie smiled and clapped.

"Zick has a lady now!"

"Sure does. I think he did well." I said.

Thomas rubbed his eyes and yawned. "Food sounds good."

"FOOD!" Thayer said, as he leaped into the kitchen.

We shook our heads, Thayer was Thayer, and that was that. He walked into the living room and reached down his pants to scratch his rear. He seemed to enjoy playing into the stereotype of a slob. I went to the kitchen sink to pour a cup of water, and as I drank, the sound of a door swinging open and clothes rustling caught my attention. Around the corner came Dolvar, who was putting on a sweatshirt. Looking predictably beat, an additional layer of rough showed on his forehead: it came as "CLOWNFUCK" written in permanent marker. Amazingly, as everyone looked at him, nobody said a thing.

Dolvar walked up to me, patted my back as he said "Oi", and poured himself a cup of water. I looked at Lorrie and gave a blank grin while she shrugged.

"Dolvar, what time did you crash?" I asked.

He cleared his throat and wiped his face. "How should I know? I made it to bed at least."

"Who drew last night?" Thomas asked.

Everyone held their breath, not sure if Dolvar would pick up on the question. He looked at Thomas, confused.

"I don't remember there being a marker." Thomas continued.

Thayer, who was rummaging through cabinets looking for a snack, retrieved a permanent marker from his pocket. His eyes lit up. "Check out the beer pong table. There was an art-fest going on last night."

Everyone converged at the table, and sure enough, writing covered its surface. There were phrases, names, and some small sketches. Lorrie began reading:

> "Billy-bitch…I'm wet, let's make a bet…Shocker and shots…Bomber and Tee keg stand champs…(Weird symbol I don't understand)…Go Giants…Zick 'hearts' Joanne…Where's the fucking food Bosner?...Wisconsin became a state in 1848."

She stopped, and everyone looked at me.

"Yea, Bosner that last one definitely wasn't you." Thayer said.

Lorrie rolled her eyes, then continued:

> "Thomas was here…OH MAN…Love you guys!…B-man vs. Penley upcoming…Someone has a secret admirer…Keg beer tastes like ass…Fuck you clowns…Cocks, balls, and clits."

"I'm inspired guys. This is quality!" Sammy said.

Thomas looked at one line in particular. "I wonder who has a secret admirer?"

"You. And you." Dolvar said.

"Okay, clownfuck." he replied.

Dolvar remained oblivious to Thomas' remarks, and so the charade continued. Joanne got up and stood with Zick as everyone stood around the table. Thayer found bread in the cabinet and began snacking while Lorrie retrieved the marker from him and returned to the table. She drew three hearts, and under them wrote her name in cursive. Billy crept into the living room, having emerged from his slumber. On his left cheek, a dildo was sketched in permanent marker. He rubbed his face as he tried to wake up and noticed an ink smear on his hand. He cursed under his breath and stormed past everyone down the hallway to the bathroom. The door slammed. Everybody laughed.

"People were really feeling artistic last night, eh?" Zick asked.

I shook my head. "The stakes get higher at each party. Next week there will be live music!"

Eventually, Billy came out of the bathroom looking defeated. His cheek was red. He tried vigorously to scrub the marker off his face, but the dildo faintly remained. We patted him out of sympathy.

"Who did it?" he asked.

"Hun, I don't think anyone here did." Lorrie replied.

Dolvar walked into the pass out room. His feud with B-man was still fresh on everyone's minds.

"Wake up clowns!" he said.

Lorrie ran into the room, then came out as she pulled Dolvar by the arm. He still looked drunk, and after Lorrie seated him on the couch, he got back up and went out for a smoke. Zick and Joanne followed him, then Billy too. I went through the DVDs in a case near the TV to put some entertainment on. Thomas joined me, and as we looked for something appealing, he kept selecting chick flicks I refused as I laughed at him. Finally, we agreed on some strange blooper movie about college kids doing stunts for cash. Everyone converged in the living room and watched. After a while, Penley emerged from his room. He looked at what was playing and then glared at us.

"Who the fuck is playing my DVDs?"

Lorrie sneered. "Who do you think you're talking to?"

"That's my DVD!"

Thomas stuttered. "Well, we just wanted to—"

Penley gestured to Thomas by closing his fingers and thumb together. "Shut it!"

"You shut it, asshole!" I said.

Penley smiled and charged at me as I sat on the couch. He put me in a hold, but I grabbed his thigh from behind. We both fell to the floor, and everyone reacted by laughing or screaming. As we tussled, Anne aggressively emerged from the hallway.

"For God's sake! Stop! Why are you fighting?"

"Dicks and testosterone. What do you expect?" Lorrie said.

Thomas remained glued to the TV. "Hey check it out, skanks kissing!"

Penley and I stopped and looked. In the movie, two girls made out as the host handed them cash.

"You two were on a roll! Why stop?" Zick asked.

Joanne looked at him. "Dicks and testosterone. What do you expect?"

Penley and I laughed as we rose to our feet. Anne remained irritated. He pointed at me before returning to his room with Anne.

"If we want Penley to leave the room, just have Joanne speak." I said.

I sat back down on the couch and we continued to watch the movie. We had to contest with Thayer once the movie ended. Though he snacked, he demanded breakfast. We told him to get breakfast and bring it back, but he insisted he wasn't going anywhere without Zick and Joanne, and they wanted to stay with the gang. Melissa eventually emerged from B-man's room and also wanted breakfast. The remaining people who crashed out in the pass out room left, it comprised three guys and four girls.

"Four to three girl-guy ratio in the pass out room. Nobody pounced!" Billy said.

"Those chicks weren't desirable." I replied.

Lorrie gave a mean look.

"Hey, they didn't catch my attention!" I added.

Dolvar patted me on the shoulder. "Nah clown. You prefer whales. Those were slim ladies."

Everyone laughed.

"Bosner, It's okay. Beauty comes in all shapes and sizes." Zick said.

"It's what's on the inside that counts!" Billy added.

Thomas smiled. "Bosner's big babes. Has a nice ring to it."

I bobbed my shoulders up and down as a mockery to the insults, which made everyone laugh more, except for Sammy.

"For real, someone get B-man's ass up. I'm hungry." he said.

Thayer pointed at Sammy and winked while Lorrie shook her head. Zick held Joanne's hand as they both entered B-man's room. She didn't seem the least bit interested, but Zick was the gang "waker-upper" everyone joked from time to time. A loud knock sounded on the wall.

"B-MAN! BREAKFAST! GET THERE!" Zick barked.

In a fainter voice, Joanne dissented Zick's technique.

"Where are we going to eat?" Melissa asked.

Everyone gazed at her.

"No, not Johnny's… the food selection—"

"Is greasy and fucking delicious!" Thayer interrupted.

Melissa threw a couch pillow at him.

"Hey, maybe the fruit cup will be more appetizing this time." I said.

She gave a middle finger salute. Sammy looked confused. "Uh, Johnny's?"

I looked at Lorrie.

"It's a diner down the road. Good food, Melissa just doesn't like hangover meals." she said.

Sammy nodded. "Can't drink like idiots and not have a landing spot for good diner food!"

Everyone except Melissa sounded, "Oi!!!"

B-man waved as he, Zick, and Joanne emerged from the room to everyone's applause.

"Alright, someone tell me what happened last night." he said.

"You got drunk. Clown."

B-man stared at Dolvar for a moment. "Clownfuck?"

Dolvar shook his head. "Why's everyone calling me that?"

"Why not?" Billy said.

"None of you fuckers ever say 'clown' let alone 'clownfuck'. What am I missing?"

Dolvar grew more frustrated as Melissa noticed his forehead.

"Wait, Dolvar look at your—"

Everyone shouted, "NO!"

Dolvar realized something was up. He marched down the hallway to the bathroom.

"Damnit! We were going to let it fly!" Lorrie said.

Melissa appeared confused. "I didn't even see what it said! He didn't know?"

"I was gonna let it ride." B-man added.

Lorrie looked at him. "I know, right!?"

"He's enough of a dick to have some embarrassment for a day." Sammy said.

Billy laughed. "Take a number."

Dolvar stomped out of the bathroom down the hallway. Like Billy, he was semi successful in getting the artwork scrubbed, but in its place was a red patch and a faint sign of permanent marker. He entered the kitchen, shaking his head as he flung open cabinets.

"Bro, what are you looking for?"

"Something to get this bullshit off of my head."

Thayer tried steering the conversation elsewhere. "Guys, food?"

"I'm not fucking going anywhere with this on my forehead." Dolvar said.

Billy walked up and spun him around by the shoulder. "Yes, you are. I'm going with this shit on my cheek."

Dolvar stared at Billy's cheek for a moment and grinned. He patted his cheek as Billy nodded. Both came back into the living room. Finally, everyone got ready to go. B-man and I drove again, Penley agreed to let me use his vehicle. Thayer agreed to be a third driver for the eleven of us, Sammy and Dolvar rode with me. We drove in a line, B-man was the first car, I was second, then Thayer behind us. The first part of the drive to Johnny's was silent, but Dolvar's remained frustrated.

"So, who wrote this shit on my forehead?"

"Honestly don't know. Not even sure where the marker came from." I said.

Sammy, sitting in the back seat, leaned towards us. "I didn't get a good look at it. Is it male or female handwriting?"

Dolvar pulled down the visor mirror. "I really can't tell. Probably female because it's legible."

"Bosner has good handwriting." Sammy said.

I glared at him through the rearview mirror. I was sure that I didn't write it.

"Whatever the fuck. They got Billy too. Hopefully nobody else notices it."

Once we reached Johnny's, we took the same booths as last time. Connie was there and quickly finished serving another table to come greet us.

"Welcome back! Seems you brought extras this time?"

B-man glanced at Sammy and Joanne. "Yea, well Johnny's is the spot!"

"I'll be right back with you." Connie said.

The seating was packed on that day. I sat at the second booth up against the window with Thomas and Dolvar, across was B-man and Lorrie.

"Look who's sitting at the same booth: Melissa and Thayer!" Thomas said.

Melissa sat facing away, Thayer sat across from her facing our booth. She swung around and gave us the middle finger salute as everyone laughed.

"Looks like you and Billy lucked out so far, Dolvar." Lorrie said, alluding to the facial artwork.

Dolvar sulked. "Hopefully it stays that way. This shit is terrible."

"Bro, I totally blacked out last night. I don't remember anything. Nobody wrote on me, did they?" B-man asked.

We looked at him; there didn't appear to be markings visible.

"What's the last thing you remember?" I asked.

He held the back of his neck. "I played beer pong with Billy against Bomber and Tee."

Lorrie looked at him, likely thinking the same thing as everyone. B-man didn't seem to recall running Dolvar through the wall in the pass out room. Dolvar didn't seem to remember either. I thought about it and realized that neither one saw the hole in the wall while sober. Lorrie and I looked at each other and kept quiet. B-man hummed as he kept trying to remember the night.

"I'll tell you what—my head hurts, and I don't think it's a hangover." Dolvar said.

B-man's face lit up. "Oh, there's a hole in the wall in the pass out room isn't there!"

Lorrie frowned sarcastically and nodded.

"You weren't going to tell me? It's not like I wasn't going to remember once I saw it." he said.

"Hey, I think it's amazing that it took you that long to remember." I replied.

Dolvar stared at B-man and laughed. "Clown… I kicked you and then you got pissed and put me through the wall."

Lorrie started laughing as well. "We were amazed that you two were totally cool after it happened. Bomber and Tee got B-man a beer to cool him off and you came running out to hug him."

I nodded at Dolvar and B-man.

"I still can't believe it. I don't even know what to say." Thomas said.

"I know what to say. Don't wake me the fuck up!" B-man replied.

From the other booth, Zick laughed. "I will, every time!"

"Zick, you pick when you wake him up wisely." I said.

Connie returned to take our order. She started with the first booth. I wasn't paying too much attention until I heard "dildo". I peered across to the other booth.

"…yea, we had a complicated night." Billy explained to Connie as she laughed hysterically.

"Honey, how much worse could it get than having that on your face?" she asked.

Billy grinned, then bobbed his head forward in Dolvar's direction. Connie looked and saw his head. Her face turned plain. "Oh my."

Dolvar looked angry, and Connie resumed taking the orders. When she got to us, I ordered the same thing as last time, the big bacon cheeseburger with fries, a pickle slice, and a cup of coffee. Dolvar faced downward with his arms crossed. He was hesitant to respond to Connie, but finally ordered a club sandwich. We tried not to laugh, but Dolvar's bad mood made it tempting to poke even more fun; after all, he did that towards us. Thomas ordered breakfast items, same as B-man, and Lorrie followed suit with me and got the burger.

"Bro, I'm not mad about last night. I hope you know."

Dolvar nodded. "I know. It's all good. You were sleeping."

"I just hope that Anne doesn't get too mad about it." Lorrie said.

"Honestly, she seems in denial about the place." I added.

"What do you mean, bro?"

"I get the vibe that she's getting pissy about the partying."

"How well does she know you guys?" Lorrie asked.

"I've known them for a bit, they used to invite me out to drink." Dolvar said.

"Don't get me wrong. It's not like you guys were one way and then changed when you moved in." I added.

Just then, Thayer interrupted. "Hey guys, guess what!"

He was so loud it disrupted other patrons. Lorrie shrank in her seat.

"Melissa likes the corned beef hash!"

Zick and Billy clapped. The rest of us followed suit. A random patron clapped as well.

Melissa covered her face. "I hate you guys!"

Connie, from behind the counter, looked at us and smiled. We finished the meals, then settled up on the check. On that occasion, we threw in $100 for the tip. As we exited, the door swung open behind us.

"Wait, you guys." Connie said.

As I was in the back of the group, I faced her. "What's up?"

"I can't, I can't take this."

B-man looked at her. "Yes, yes you can."

She gazed back. I took her hand that held the tip and turned it over, kissing it. She blushed as her eyes filled with tears.

"Just sayin, but that's our cap amount." I said.

She waved goodbye. "Bless you all!"

Melissa, Zick, and Joanne rode with me on the way to the house; Melissa sat in front. As I turned onto the highway, I started a conversation.

"So, Joanne, how did you and Zick...you know?"

She smiled and looked at Zick.

"Thayer. We were together at the smoke deck by the barracks. Thayer's the boisterous one and started talking to her." he explained.

Melissa shrieked, then turned and faced them. "Thayer?"

"No, no. He struck up a conversation with Joanne to invite her to the party. I was just chillin, would've probably said hi and then went on." Zick said.

Melissa gave a gushy smile. "That's so sweet. You two are really cute together."

I looked up at them through the rearview mirror. "Yea, who knew a party could bring a helluva couple together?"

Joanne kissed Zick on the cheek as he looked out the window, smiling.

"What about you Melissa?" I asked.

She perked up in her seat and looked at me. "What about?"

"Well, I mean, you and my man?"

Joanne looked at the rearview mirror, facing me. "Bosner, I didn't think you—"

Zick laughed and held her. "No, no, he's talking about B-man."

I scoffed sarcastically.

Melissa looked straight ahead. "He doesn't seem interested. I like him, but…"

Her response surprised me, but I wasn't sure if B-man was interested in either her or Lorrie, or both. He played close to the vest on such matters.

She continued. "I mean, there's no game or anything but it's Lorrie and me. I can't tell if he's just having fun or if he's actually into one of us or something…or not."

"Boys." Joanne said.

Zick looked at her. "Excuse me?"

They both smiled and held hands. Melissa looked at me, and I glanced at her for a moment. We both were in weird spots with the love thing. She was unsure about my good friend, and I was unsure about what I wanted or didn't want, if I wanted anything at all! For the rest of the drive, we remained quiet and at ease.

# 12. Things Get Awkward

When we returned to the house, Penley and Anne were in the pass out room looking at the gaping hole in the wall.    B-man and Dolvar approached them. Anne faced them, shaking her head.

"We will get it fixed." Dolvar said.

Penley stood still as if he didn't really care.

B-man lifted his ball cap and ran his hand over his head. "Shit's messed up. I wasn't trying to break anything."

Penley walked past them, then patted B-man on the back and continued on. Anne stood at the wall for a moment longer, then glared at B-man and Dolvar again before following Penley to the room. Sammy approached the wall.

"OH MAN."

I followed him and examined the wall again for myself. I laughed, then they did as well. Dolvar then went into the kitchen and got cups.

"Let's see if there's anything left in the keg. Whaddya say?" he asked.

I looked at B-man and Sammy. "Fuck it. Let's go!"

We stepped out onto the back patio. The keg remained in the tub, but the ice turned into lumpy water. Written near the tap in permanent marker was, "BOMBER AND TEE KEG STAND CHAMPS."

"Bro, is there anyone that can beat them at the keg stand?"

"Not me. I'm probably the worst one here." I said.

Dolvar plunged the tap down and up and we watched as golden brew flowed. We chanted "Oi." Dolvar handed everyone a cup. Sammy raised his.

"Well boys, Bosner and I went on a helluva trek last night and came back empty-handed."

"No, no. You succeeded." Dolvar said.

I laughed. "Mission: Three Beers Standing!"

B-man shook his head and raised his cup.

"I was out when you guys went on the adventure. Sounds like it went well. Cheers to broken shit." he said.

Zick and Joanne came out for a smoke, followed by Lorrie.

"Oh no, drinking again are you?" she asked.

B-man pointed at Sammy and me. "These two seriously went out and got nothing?"

Lorrie laughed. "Oh yes. Left for food, came back with torn boxes, broken bottles, and empty bags."

"Don't forget the hints of ketchup and mustard!" Dolvar said.

I shook my head as I thought hard about a good comeback line. By chance, I patted my left pant pocket and felt something. I reached in and pulled out an unopened mustard packet. Everyone's eyes opened wider.

"What about this! Motherfuckers! Get Thayer!" I said.

Everyone laughed hysterically. I chugged my beer and Dolvar took my cup to refill it. Thomas, Thayer, and Billy came outside in response to the loud laughter.

"Alright, what did we miss?" Thomas asked.

I looked at Thayer and threw the packet at him. "No hotdog but got ya dessert!"

Everyone continued to laugh. "Aight clowns. We're killing this keg!" Dolvar said.

He went to pour the first cup for the entire group, then the tap spurted foam; keg killed. Everybody gave off an "OHHH".

"For real bro, I was going to be pissed if there was much left in that keg. I'm surprised we didn't kill it all last night."

"I guess those three beers that Bosner and I brought back went a long way." Sammy joked.

"Actually, Bomber and Tee brought beer. It should be in the fridge." Lorrie said.

B-man looked at her, surprised. "Huh? I didn't see beer in there."

He went inside, and after a moment he came back out. "Nothing in there."

Lorrie insisted there was more beer. Just then, Dolvar gave off a smirk then ran inside. He came out with two boxes of beer. One had a hole in the side with a few missing.

"Get the fuck outta here, bro."

Lorrie laughed. "You did not sleep with them in the closet!"

"I know why I'm 'Clownfuck'. Last night, I fucked up a keg stand, and Bomber gave me shit. I think I tried to fight him, and he shoved me down hard. I got pissed and swiped their beer. Looks like I drank a few of them too."

"Must be why Bomber texted me saying that the party was very thirsty last night." B-man added.

"Dolvar you were on everyone's shit list last night." Thomas said.

Zick shook his head. "Breaking walls, fucking up keg stands, swiping beers. On a fucking roll Dolvar."

"Hey, hey, B-man conspired to break the wall with me."

"Bomber didn't draw the dildo too, did he?" Billy asked.

"I don't think it's possible for you to piss someone off, you're too cool." I said.

Lorrie walked up to Billy to inspect the artwork. "Does anyone think they can guess whose drawing style this is?"

Billy stepped back from Lorrie. "You know what, it's okay. Next time I'll break necks."

146

Everyone retrieved a beer from the boxes, then the afternoon took off. When I went inside to use the bathroom, I saw Melissa, Anne, and Penley sitting on the couches watching TV. After I finished my business, I returned and sat next to Melissa.

"How's it going?"

"It's okay. Just chillin." she said.

I knew better. She sat with her legs crossed, staring through the sliding glass door at everyone, B-man in particular.

"Is there anything I can say or do?"

She glanced at me, then faced outside. "I mean, I don't know what more I should do... how do I win him?"

Penley and Anne remained glued to the TV, trying to remain oblivious to the conversation. It was an awkward moment.

"Well. You don't even like football." I said.

She snapped. "I know enough! There's a game coming on tonight. I'm surprised he doesn't seem to notice that."

Unfortunately, she didn't realize a bye week followed the conference championships. Penley and Anne faced us.

"Yea... no game tonight. Super Bowl comes on next Sunday." Penley said.

Anne patted his leg, and they both retreated to their room. The moment grew cold.

Melissa shook her head. "Fine, I get it. So what should I do?"

"I mean, I'm in a tough spot with my shit... I say do what you think is best for yourself."

She stared at me. Her olive complexion and brown eyes really stood out. I felt something coming on, but I wasn't sure what. In the strangest way, she looked beautiful, but as she continued to stare, I felt a bad vibe, as though something wasn't right about our connection. I attempted to continue on with the discussion, but then she leaned in and put her lips against mine. She pressed me back as she put her arm around me. Young Bosner was beyond startled. The moment was all sorts of wrong in my mind. I neither had the swag nor the prick in me to do anything except push her back.

"Melissa, I can't do this with you..."

She flopped back, tears swelling in her eyes. She swiped her hair back. Attractive, she was, but I couldn't in a million years mess with Melissa, something in my gut wouldn't let me. I wasn't sure if it was loyalty to my brother in arms; I wasn't sure if it was that she wasn't the right person. It was probably both. I didn't think, I simply reacted. It was the right move. She sat looking at me for a long, long second. Tears fell down her cheeks before she covered her face to hide her weep.

"I have to go. I'll call my friend to come get me." she said.

I sat facing her, frozen. She whipped out her phone, got up, and headed for the front door. As I stood up, she waved me off and went outside. I remained still with a numbness feeling in my stomach. Finally, I peered out the window through the half open blinds. She was well on her way down the street. Part of me thought it would be best to see if she was okay, but the other part of me thought I should let things be, and just explain to B-man what happened. I had no idea of her motive, or what the point was of her actions. I wasn't a guy equipped to handle such a situation. Looking back on it, I'm not sure who else would've been. A few minutes passed, and I finally got up to get a beer. Lorrie entered from the back patio.

"Where's Melissa?"

At first, I couldn't speak. "Uh…yea, she said she had to leave. A friend came to get her."

For a second, I wasn't sure if Lorrie would buy my explanation. Then she slowly nodded. "That's strange. But okay."

She walked past me, down the hallway. I stood for a second to regain my composure, then went outside to join the rest of the gang. When asked about where Melissa went, I simply repeated what I told Lorrie. Luckily, everyone was fine with that explanation. After a while, Billy and Thomas left. Thayer lobbied to get some steaks and grill, but everyone felt too buzzed to drive. Determined, Thayer insisted we spot him some cash and he would drive to the store himself to get food. We accepted and pitched in some money.

Penley and Anne joined the rest of the gang outside. They pitched in for food as well. We commingled out on the patio, then back inside once it got dark and colder out. In   B-man's presence, I was too anxious to tell him about what happened with Melissa. The situation confused me; I couldn't understand why she would put me in such a weird spot. My mind continued to replay the incident, and it couldn't comprehend how a girl could go from being upset over not having a guy she wanted to macking on the guy's good buddy—all in one conversation! I had a bad feeling that it might come back to haunt me if I didn't get out in front of the problem sooner rather than later. B-man and Dolvar lit the grill, and soon thereafter Thayer returned with loads of food.

"Steaks, hot dogs, potato salad, chips, dips!" he shouted, as he juggled grocery bags and kicked the front door shut behind him.

"What, did you buy the entire store?" Penley asked.

Thayer smiled. "No, thought about it though. I'd need to win the lottery to pull that off."

Dolvar came inside to get a beer from the fridge. "Oi! Bring the meat out back!"

Zick looked at me. "He should've brought shit for a big bacon cheeseburger!"

We fist bumped. "Zick, it's not underlined here. This is a control-free environment."

I got another beer out of the fridge, then went outside. Thayer opened the wrapping on the steaks while   B-man tended to the grill. I faced the back towards the fence and railroad tracks with my right foot propped on the picnic table bench. Still in deep thought about what happened earlier, a hand smacked me on the back. I turned around; it was Sammy.

"Trying to retrace our footsteps from last night are ya?" he said.

"Oh. Yea. Which yards did we run through again?"

"Who knows... Hey, at least the dog didn't get us."

"Shit, I think there were a few dogs, Sammy. No bites or nothing."

"Yea, well them hot dogs were good decoys to keep them occupied." he said.

We stood there and laughed. Everyone went inside except for B-man, Sammy, Thayer, and I. B-man grew irritated by Thayer's obsession with the food on the grill.

"Yea B-man, back home, we make this seasoning and we put it in bags and put the meat in the bag and..."

"Bro, I need another beer. How about you go get me one?"

A look of disappointment came over Thayer's face. Penley came out as Thayer went inside.

"B-man. We gotta talk."

B-man turned the steaks, then looked up. "What's up bro?"

Penley glanced at us. "So, the partying. It's hard on Anne."

Sammy and I looked at each other and started for the door.

"No guys, stay. It's all of us." Penley said.

B-man shook his head. "I mean, yea the party last night was bomb, we don't usually go that hard. You know that."

Penley slowly closed his eyes. "I. I know. Anne… just."

We looked at Penley. Thayer and Dolvar came outside in the middle of the epic stare down. Thayer tossed a beer to B-man, who caught it while continuing to stare at Penley. Dolvar realized what was occurring and nudged Thayer to return inside with him.

"Bro, we paid you for the month and helped with the first month's rent. I get that the partying is—"

Penley put his hand up. "I'll try talking to her, but I'm having a hard time convincing her otherwise."

B-man shook his head. His face was flush. Sammy and I approached. Penley opened the sliding glass door to go back inside. While he stood in the doorway, he stopped and faced B-man.

"Still gotta face off, fucker!" he said.

B-man aggressively flipped the steaks on the grill as Sammy walked to the other side and faced B-man.

"Hey, let's just let the night play out. We have your back." Sammy said.

"Bro, Dolvar is paying them to live in a fuckin closet!"

It sounded tenuous, but then again, for Dolvar, anywhere he could drink cheaply worked for him. I thought about cracking a joke, but the time seemed inappropriate.

"B-man. Maybe this blows over. That party last night was unusual. Holes in walls aren't normally our style." I said.

"We paid them for the month, plus part on the fuckin deposit. If shit hits the fan, I'm at least staying here until I've gotten my money's worth." he replied.

In an ominous fashion, a cold gust stirred up. Late January kicked back in, it seemed. We helped B-man get the food on plates and brought it inside. The rest of the gang seated themselves in the living room and watched DVDs. B-man was mostly silent for the rest of the evening. Everyone noticed his mood and reacted accordingly—with a silent sort of psychic understanding that something not worth discussing occurred. Naturally, Thayer was the only one not to notice. He was happy about the meal and chatting on and on to the silent gang about how to make the steaks next time.

After everyone ate, Thayer noticed two steaks still on the main plate. To his disappointment, B-man told him they were for Penley and Anne. Everyone remained quiet in the living room, yet nobody seemed interested in the DVD playing. Lorrie eventually got B-man's attention, and they went into his room; a sign she wanted to discuss what made him so quiet. Zick, Sammy, Joanne and I sat on the couches as Dolvar and Thayer talked in the kitchen.

"Yea, so I sense some shit went down." Zick said.

"Might have to find a new party spot." Sammy added.

Witty as ever, Joanne took the news in stride. She playfully backhanded Zick across his chest.

"See? I knew we should've slept in the pass out room. Look at what we did!"

Everyone laughed. The gang mostly understood that the dynamic of the partying at the house was not workable for the long haul. Most understood that enjoying the times for what they were was probably best. Of course, nobody but B-man and Dolvar paid to live there; it was easy for everyone to take the rocky situation casually. B-man and Lorrie came out and sat in the chairs next to the couches and watched the DVD with the rest of the gang. Silence remained the tune of the night. Penley eventually emerged from the hallway and smirked as he walked over to the counter. He prepared the sides and plopped the steaks on two plates. B-man glared at him, but Penley faced away.

"Those steaks gotta be cold by now!" Thayer said.

"No shit, fucker." Penley replied as he walked back to his room with the food.

When the bedroom door closed, B-man glanced across at everyone in the living room and shook his head.

"Might have to move the operation elsewhere."

"Say what?" Dolvar replied.

"Don't worry about it. It might work out. Blaine. Stop. Let's enjoy the evening." Lorrie said.

Dolvar scoffed. "No. I know them."

He stood up and proceeded towards the hallway. I got up from the couch and ran up to him. B-man followed. I grabbed him from behind.

"No." I said.

"Bro, I'm pissed, but it's whatever. Lorrie is right. We will work this out or figure out something better."

Dolvar stood still, facing down the hallway as though he was still intent on confronting Penley and Anne. Finally, he turned around and came back to the couch, dejected. The rest of the evening was quiet except for a few obnoxious "food" remarks by Thayer. At around 2200, Thayer, Zick, and Joanne left, giving me a ride to base as well. B-man told me he would call sometime tomorrow, or maybe after. I figured he was going to strategize what to do about the house situation. Either way, sleep sounded better than anything else, so I left.

# 13. The New Addition

Monday arrived at the sound of an obnoxious alarm; obnoxious, because that's what it took to be awakened sometimes. I washed up for work, but I did so distressed. The situation with Melissa and the news of the rocky situation between the boys and Penley and Anne made for a low point in the good times at the newly christened Cape Henry House. I finished getting dressed, then proceeded to the corridor towards the quarterdeck. The corridor appeared unusually quiet and dim. Once I rounded the corner to the quarterdeck, Pickens greeted me. I attempted to walk by and pretend that I didn't notice him.

"Neck inspection, Bosner!"

I cringed. "Screw off, Pickens."

I continued walking past him and out the door.

"Hey, heard there was a wild party at Blaine's. I better not find out about illegal substances used by you or any of your shipmates!" he said as his voice faded in the distance.

I walked aggressively towards Green Beater. I was in a bad mood. My uneasy thoughts about the

Melissa incident, then having Pickens annoy me; it was putting me on edge! I flung open the car door and slammed it shut. I sped out of the parking spot and screeched through the lot on my way to the command. The day would've been best if it ended before it began, I was intent on avoiding as many people as possible. Unfortunately, when I entered the command, Senior Chief Walt Beaumont greeted me, he was best known as "Senior".

"Bosner!" he barked.

I couldn't help but think I was being karmically punished somehow.

"Yes, Senior!"

He had a trusting gleam in his eyes. "We have some newbies to the command. Trainees for your shop! I want you to be their peer on night check. You know the ins and outs!"

*Not today, damnit.* I thought to myself.

Senior stood at 6'2 and was from Barstow, California. We served on the previous year's deployment and I knew him as well as anyone at the command. His size made him good at out drinking most of us, and his temper when he lost a game of spades reminded us never to mess with him, as if we ever thought we could.

"Great. Are they in the shop? I'd be happy to take them under my wing!"

He smiled as he walked with me towards the shop. "Did you enjoy your weekend?"

I wasn't into small talk considering the mood I was in, but Senior wasn't someone I could blow off. "Oh yes. Grilled yesterday."

He chuckled. "I'm jealous. The wife made me take the Christmas lights down. I was hoping I could let it slide for a few more weeks. But, as they say— happy wife, happy life."

With my best effort, I laughed along and maintained interest in the otherwise pointless conversation.

"Say, you aren't married, are you?" he continued.

"Nope, not this guy."

He put his arm around me. "Bosner, you are a smart man. NEVER do it."

There was a brief pause, then I looked up at him.

"Na Bosner. When the time is right. When the time is right." he finished.

We entered the hangar. Dolvar and Zick were atop a helo towards the far end. They were working on a rebuild, and gearbox parts lined the hangar deck. They looked and gave a slight nod, not to distract me from my conversation with Senior as we continued through the hangar. When we entered the shop, everyone quickly turned and faced us, standing at attention.

Senior waved everyone off. "At ease. I hope everyone is having a good afternoon!"

The LPO's nodded. "You know it Senior!"

I glanced around the shop to see who the new shipmates were. The shop was a plain, mostly dull place. From the hangar, a person entered and to the right was a work counter up against the wall. At the end of the counter in the wall's corner was a computer for placing orders and requests for maintenance and parts on the helos. A cabinet stood in the middle of the shop facing away, behind it was a makeshift office. A bench seat lined the back of the cabinet in front. Straight ahead was a doorway out to the back where there were tow tractors, tow bars, and crates of all sizes. To the left was a doorway to the shop tool room, and beyond that was the LPO's office.

Only regulars lounged in the shop, but from behind the cabinets in the office space came five freshly pressed sailors. Crisp, clean coveralls served as the biggest giveaway of a newbie to the command. As everyone who worked in the hangar or out on the flight line would attest, a newbie's coveralls were "clean enough to eat off of, and worthy enough to be broken in." There were three men, two women; all looked timid, except for one. The untimid one was the tallest, his name was McCord. He stood relaxed as the other four stood petrified in the presence of Senior.

"At ease. Welcome to the command! This is Bosner, he's one of our best. He will be the one to show you around the aircraft. If you have questions, he can answer them. I will leave you all to him, and to our fine LPO's. Welcome aboard!" he said.

Senior winked at me, then left. The new sailors glared at me as I reviewed them. McCord stood on the left, but to his right was Tompkins, Uller, Sadina, and Franklin. I introduced myself, and at the LPO's insistence took them out to the flight line for an introduction to the helos. I felt better; having new sailors to train uplifted me. The new sailors, or trainees, were mostly shy.

McCord had a natural ability for working on the aircraft, and when I told the trainees to take 30 minutes for lunch, McCord insisted on coming with me. He was officially Jason H. McCord III, a few years older than me, married, and from Georgia with the southern drawl to match. We went to get a snack from the Gedunk, a Navy term for "snack shop" used on ships as well as shore commands. When we entered, Zick, B-man, and Dolvar sat at a table in the corner. They all greeted.

"Hey guys. What's up!" I asked.

"Bro, they have Zick and Dolvar on that beater in the hangar. They might be here all night!"

Zick and Dolvar didn't look pleased.

"Who's the new guy?" Zick asked.

McCord nodded, then reached out to shake hands. "McCord, how ya'll doin?"

"He's one of our guys. Good on the helos already." I added.

They shook hands and chatted while I got a microwavable snack. Zick and Dolvar received an extended break because of their task on the helo while B-man waited for his helo to return from its flight. Since I had paperwork to fill out, I told McCord to kick it for a bit with the boys; he was a natural fit for the gang. The evening rolled into the night, and luckily it was easy going with little to do. The LPOs let us go at around 2330. Zick and Dolvar remained with their maintenance crew on the fixer-upper in the hangar. We quietly taunted them on our way out, they returned with middle finger salutes.

B-man was nowhere to be found when the LPOs let us leave, and feeling tired, I went straight to the barracks to get rest. Having new shipmates to train helped me escape the Melissa situation for the time being, but as I drove towards the barracks, it ate at me again. I kept visualizing her staring at me, her eyes filled with tears. B-man came to mind as well. How was he going to react when he found out? I needed to speak up. As I walked into the barracks past the quarterdeck and onward to my room, I decided I would speak up. *Tomorrow maybe,* I thought.

I rested well that Monday night, and I was lucky to have a rather uneventful Tuesday. It rained heavily outside, and the Maintenance Chief that day only requested night check ready two helos for flying the following morning. McCord was learning the ins and outs on the aircraft quickly, and I was able to delegate a lot of the tasks to him so that I could focus on helping the other trainees with nomenclature and standard operating procedures. McCord also seemed to develop a good rapport with Zick, and after their discussion in the gedunk on

Monday, they were already discussing cars and wheeled "pet projects". He was a practical shoo-in for the next function at Cape Henry House.

Wednesday came, and I got out of maintenance work because the LPOs tasked me with driving the trainees to their respective barracks to retrieve important documents that the command needed immediately. Naturally, they failed to tell anyone until the last minute how important the papers were. We used one of the command vehicles, an old white van with chipped paint and a bad wheel alignment. Rumors around the command swirled about one of the duty drivers taking the van joyriding, which led to its condition. Of note during the evening, Uller misplaced some of her paperwork and we had to scramble to find it. Luckily, the OOD at the quarterdeck of Uller's barracks found it on the floor. We ate dinner off base at a local pizzeria, then returned to the command with the documents. Lucky for us, we were all released early for the night. I again slipped out quietly and enjoyed a good night's rest.

A phone call woke me late Thursday morning. A bit startled, I glared at the buzzing phone. I wiped my dreary eyes and saw it was B-man, I answered.

"Bro. You there?"

I cleared my throat. "Yep. Just got up. What's going on?"

"Lots of shit. I'm not going to be in today."

"Uh... so, what's up?"

He was silent at first, then he laughed. "So, Penley and Anne want us to move out, then the command announced that there's a det mobilizing. I'm going on det. I went in for my paperwork and they gave us the day off."

I snapped upwards from bed. "Det" was short for detachment, and that meant our command was sending some helos abroad to support a ship's deployment.

"Dude, for real? Where to?" I asked.

"Central and South America, Pacific side. We apparently ship out in three to four weeks." he said.

"Okay, who else is going?"

"I heard Souza and Kline were on the list. I didn't hear anything about you, bro."

"Damn, lots of moving parts. I'm assuming you'll move out of the house just before you leave?" I asked.

"That's what I'm planning on. I don't know what Dolvar will do. Anne and Penley want us both out. Still bullshit, but I figure the time left there will make up for what we paid them already."

"Double whammy for sure, but hey, that det might be quite an experience!" I said.

"Greenies tonight when you get out?"

"Yea man, IF I get off in time!"

We finished the conversation, then I put on some clothes and got something to eat. It was early enough that I lounged in my room and read. Two things dominated my mind while I lay in my room, I didn't muster the nerve to tell B-man about Melissa, and Cape Henry House seemed to be an experience that was ending as soon as it began. A part of me felt bad, because the gang was so excited about having a place off base to call our own, and it was a shame that things went south so quickly that Anne and Penley were not willing to let B-man and Dolvar stay. I continued to wonder as I slowly got ready for work. Once I left my room and walked down the corridor towards the quarterdeck, I saw Wilky. He was on his phone, but when he saw me coming, he covered the receiver and grinned at me.

"There's my man. Hey, did you pick up Latisha after we left?"

I frowned, then shook my head. "Man, really?"

"Dog, I thought you would've hit her up for a good time." he started laughing as he smacked his knee. "Hey, got Shanae on the phone now. I'll tell her the good news!"

I flailed my hand at him in disapproval and kept walking, my head drooped. Just before I rounded the corner for the quarterdeck, he called back out.

"Bosner, what's going on this weekend?"

I faced him. "Probably just hanging out with B-man and the gang."

"Aight cool, we'll stop by!"

I gave him a thumbs up and proceeded to the quarterdeck. Anderson was on duty and kindly waved as I waved back. At the command, there was a lot of commotion about the impending det. Some were excited to be on the list and others were anxious. It was common for shipmates on det lists who had families to be on guard because of the natural obstacles that came with being sent far away for long periods of time; I had no such obstacles. In my case, I couldn't help but feel a little envious that a handful of our personnel were going to be sailing down in the tropics of the Pacific while I remained up north in the wonderful winter weather at home port.

The buzz around the shop, and the command at large over the det took a lot of the attention, and so the night was slow on the flight line. I took the trainees onto aircraft to go over some terminology. Afterwards, I let them take a break. McCord and I went to the gedunk for a snack and sat down with Zick and Dolvar.

"Did you hear about the det list?" Zick asked.

"Oh yea, B-man called me. Heard that Souza and Kline are going as well. What about you guys?"

Dolvar, eating a sandwich, shook his head.

"Nah, me neither." Zick said.

"So, how do these 'dets' work around here?" McCord asked.

"Pretty much we are a shore-based command with sea duty personnel. The Air Wing can call our command up to detach and deploy with a ship. It's almost random. Sometimes the dets are work-intensive and rewarding and sometimes they are just tough." I explained.

"Bosner and I went on one last year that was quite a trip. It can depend though." Dolvar added.

Zick couldn't help himself. "Didn't Penley go on that det too?"

I knew exactly where the conversation was going. As Dolvar took another bite of his sandwich, I went to get a freezer item.

"Yep. And he had one helluva time, too…" I said.

Dolvar smacked his hand on the table, and while still chewing, mumbled, "The whole thing is dumb. They asked us to move in. We didn't go to them."

"Housing blues, eh? I'm in a barracks room, but tomorrow the wife arrives and we're gonna sign a lease on a place." McCord said.

Dolvar laughed. "Got room for me?"

"What are you guys doing after work? I'm meeting B-man at Greenies. Come out." I said.

Zick and Dolvar nodded as McCord and I stood. We left for the shop.

"Is Greenies that big old bar down the street?"

"Yep. On the water. It's the go-to joint. Smells of cigarettes, spilled beer, and shitty food."

He grinned. "Count me in!"

In the shop, we sorted through toolboxes to account for all items. Ensuring tool accountability was a staple of Navy aviation, a missing tool in the wrong place could bring down an aircraft with its crew. The det buzz wasn't going anywhere, so the

LPOs had little trouble releasing everyone at the generous time of 0030. Since they were scrambling to get rosters adjusted for the det, they spared us from an end of the night speech about "integrity" or "effort" on the job. I met McCord outside the command entrance and told him to follow me. Zick left just as I got into Green Beater, Dolvar rode with him.

# 14. The Iconic Drinking Institution

A light rain fell with a good gust, enough to rock Green Beater. I turned up the volume on the stereo and jammed out to some hair metal as I drove the five blocks to Greenies. The layout of Greenies was interesting, it seemed to be a building that once housed something other than a bar, but along with its rough exterior and its rougher interior, the place had a level of character beyond any other drinking establishment any of us had ever known. While it was a place we started going to because of its locational convenience to base, that changed with the camaraderie formed by many of us spending what little free time we had getting drunk or back slapping one another about the trials of a sailor's life.

Beyond just being our bar, we had a sort of VIP status with the staff. Though the TVs were terrible, we knew they would accommodate us in other ways; we always accommodated them with handsome tips. The gang never got violent or aggressive, at least not unless provoked. The gang's worst crimes were vomiting at the bar—or in my case, I once vomited over the railing outside—spilling drinks, or getting into a push and shove with the occasional drunkard who started it. While it may have been bad taste, the staff loyally had our backs. Among venues in the area, what truly set Greenies apart from the rest were the horse trough pissers in the men's room. It was common to see cash thrown into the troughs as a sort of novelty-like gesture by drunkards or whoever. I once found a $100 bill in one, and I'm not afraid to admit that I retrieved it! Odd things like that made the place iconic, Greenies was impossible to hate.

As I reached the parking area of the bar, I remembered Melissa. I reassured myself that I could simply bring the incident up later. Zick and McCord parked across from me, and they along with Dolvar entered at once. Inside, there was a modest crowd, but the jukebox was blasting, and B-man sat at the left corner of the main bar. Johnny Kline was with him; his det buddy.

"Oi!" Dolvar called out.

B-man and Klein acknowledged by raising their glasses.

"Shit, where's Souza? You dropped his name as being on the list!" I said.

"Fucker is in the back shooting pool with some heifers." Klein replied.

Zick and McCord both laughed. B-man shook his head.

"Bro, he had the good one but he liked the other two better."

Sarah approached our corner of the bar and waved. She eyed McCord as I pointed at him.

"Sarah! Here's a new addition, Jason McCord." I said.

She slid beers down to us and pointed at him while winking.

"Welcome. First one's on me."

McCord raised his beer, and we gave cheers.

"B-MAN, WE'RE GOIN ON FUCKIN DET!" Kline barked.

B-man barked back, but it was noise, not words. We stood there for a moment, then I went to find Souza. As I walked away from the gang, I could hear McCord and Zick talking about cars, and B-man telling Kline and Dolvar about why Souza was screwing up with the ladies at the pool table. I laughed aloud as I walked across to the billiards room. When I approached the pool tables, my face became engulfed in cigar smoke. I choked uncontrollably as I hastily walked onward to get clear. When I came to, I looked right and standing there was an older, smug man with long hair and a good three inches of height on me. Unsure why he blew the smoke in my face, I stood there glaring at him.

"Can I fucking help you?" he asked.

"Yea, blow your fucking smoke elsewhere."

The man remained still, so I walked away. Souza was at the furthest table on the right. He was with three women. Two were heavyset, the other was modest in figure. I couldn't see well from where

I stood because of the dimness and smoke in the room. Souza didn't see me approach him, and as he leaned down to make his shot on the table, I smacked him on the back. He made a scoffing sound, and his billiard stick scraped the table surface and struck the cue ball low. The ball arched upward and left the table, rolling into the bar area. The three women gasped, and Souza, likely out of reflex, spun around and grabbed me by my shirt, driving me into the wall.

He angrily gazed, then his complexion lightened as he realized who I was. I looked past him into the bar area where the cue ball rolled. It lodged up under an occupied barstool. Nobody saw it but me.

"Fucker! Good to see you. Trying to cock block me on a game of pool huh?" Souza said.

He released his grip on my shirt and hugged me. I looked at the women, then at Souza to give him the impression they did not impress me. He shook his head and playfully smacked me on the back.

"Good to see you too, Souza." I said.

I proceeded back to the bar area to retrieve the rogue cue ball. Unfortunately, the occupied barstool over top of the cue ball held a large, older woman. She sat facing the bar, and she conversed with another older albeit more petite woman to her right. Both smoked and appeared deep in conversation; unaware I was standing behind them readying to get the ball. Feeling awkward, I tried clearing my throat before politely letting them know I needed to get beneath the stool to retrieve it.

"Excuse me." I said.

Neither one heard me. The music in the bar seemed inconveniently louder than it had been, and so I tried once again to voice out. I had no better luck. Finally, I tapped the woman on her shoulder. It did not go well.

"We don't need a menu." The woman proclaimed.

The response baffled me.

"Um, no ma'am, I need to get a cue ball out from under you." I shyly replied.

The woman on the right finished a big puff off her cigarette and coughed out the smoke.

"What did you say to her?" she asked.

Almost trembling, I leaned between the two women.

"I need to get a cue ball out from under the stool."

Both women shrieked and faced the bar to get the bartender's attention. Worried at first, I sighed when I saw Sarah. I knew things would pan out.

"Excuse us, bartender!" The bigger woman called out.

Sarah approached them. "Yes ladies?"

They both spun around and pointed at me.

"This young creep is harassing us." The smaller one said.

For a split second everything stopped, and Sarah's baby blue eyes locked on me. She seemed frozen. My face went numb, but then Sarah busted out in laughter.

"Ladies, I know this young man. What exactly is he doing?" she asked.

They both sat still, then looked at each other. I began scratching the back of my head incessantly.

"I came over here to get a cue ball that rolled under your stool. It was struck off the pool tables by accident." I explained.

The two women again looked at each other, then began laughing. Sarah slowly nodded, then grinned before walking away. The bigger woman turned in her seat to face me. Her face lit up.

"I thought you were talking about something else." she said.

It was exactly the response I was afraid of.

"Nope. Just here to get a cue ball. I apologize."

Both women continued smoking, and I stood there momentarily. I assumed she would stand up so I could get around her, but she expected me to reach through the legs of the stool while she remained seated. It was quite awkward, and after she motioned for me to get the cue ball, I got on my hands and knees and reached through the legs of the stool. I closed my eyes and hoped to grab the cue ball and be back up on my feet and at the pool table with no one noticing. With my eyes closed, I reached back until my hand touched the foot of the bar. Lowering my hand, I ran it along the floor until I felt it—the cold, round surface of the cue ball. I clutched it, then pulled my arm out and stood up. I stood and looked at the two women, and they glanced at me before looking beyond. I turned around, and there stood Souza and his two female companions.

"Hi ladies. He's getting better. We took the pads and diapers off him just last week!" Souza said to the two older women.

They both laughed hysterically, I was had yet again. Before I could lower my head, or even snap back with something of measurable wit, Klein sounded from across the bar.

"Bosner, you're supposed to go younger and over, not older and under." he cracked.

Zick, McCord, Dolvar, B-man and some other bar patrons laughed. I shook my head and excused myself to take a piss break. When I returned to the bar, the boys settled back down while Souza remained occupied with the ladies. B-man and Dolvar resolved to have one last party weekend at Cape Henry House. They came up with three good reasons as B-man raised his glass.

"Penley and Anne will be out of town, Giants Superbowl on Sunday, and I'm getting my money's worth out of the place!"

"Cape Henry House!" I replied.

"GO GIANTS." Dolvar added.

Klein laughed. "I haven't been to one of the Cape Henry benders yet."

"Where's your ass been?" Zick replied.

"Asshole I have a life outside of getting shit faced with you guys."

I patted Klein on the shoulder. "That's too bad."

Ever difficult, he couldn't resist.

"I'm going to waste some fuckers at beer pong, I'll tell you that right now."

"Bro, I could put Bomber or Tee against you, or Dolvar's friend Billy, and I bet he could beat you too."     B-man said. Klein shook his hand, accepting a bet.

Johnny Klein was the character of characters. He was a hothead from Oregon, and we always wondered if it was a short fuse or a hidden substance issue that sparked his bursts of anger. He talked a lot of trash, which he could back up a fair amount of the time. To me, it always seemed like things were extreme with him, never "ok". Klein helped me dodge yet again something I needed to talk to B-man about but didn't have the wherewithal to start—the Melissa situation. As Klein took up all the oxygen in the group with his bombastic chatter, last call came, and Sarah rushed us to finish our drinks and settle up our tabs. Everyone at Greenies that night agreed to come to B-man and Dolvar's party on the upcoming Saturday. I paid little attention to the plans they were making for the party itself, but as far as I could tell, it was going to be the biggest event of the year.

In hindsight, it was fitting that the decision to throw a banger of a final party at Cape Henry House was decided over drinks at Greenies. The place wasn't simply iconic; it was simply the iconic drinking establishment.

# 15. "The Rat"

I went to the barracks that night and fell asleep rather quickly. At some point, I woke up to the sound of someone knocking on my door. I told them to give me a second, as I took a moment to come to. I found the light switch and put on my glasses, then some gym shorts. When I opened the door, standing in the corridor was B-man and Melissa! I flinched in their presence. They stood silently and glared at me as I remained shocked. Relief came when I jolted up out of my bed. It was a dream. More troubling was that I hadn't yet told B-man about the situation, and it seemed like the longer I put off telling him, the harder it got. I washed up and got ready for work; I felt dejected.

As I left my room and proceeded down the corridor for the quarterdeck, Casello sat outside of his room on his laptop. He looked up and smiled.

"I heard you're training up the newbies at the command well."

I stopped and faced him. "Thanks. One of them is practically self-taught. The others are good at following instruction."

"I heard that Senior Chief Beaumont selected you specifically to be their sponsor. Good sign for a promotion!"

I nodded. "I hope so. Thanks for the kind words."

He nodded back, and I waved as I continued onward. Just then, a thought came over me, and I sought Casello's personal advice. I stopped a little way down the corridor from him, then turned and faced him.

"Hey, Casello. I have hypothetical for you."

"Sure, what's up?"

"Okay, so let's say that you know someone that is 'kind of' seeing a girl, but you aren't sure…"

He interrupted. "Buddy, ask better questions, get better facts, or run for the fucking hills."

His answer rubbed me the wrong way, so I tried one more time.

"I hear you but for real, hear me out. Let's say you know someone, and they are in limbo with someone else, then out of nowhere they put a move on you."

Casello put his hand up. "Wait a minute. Are you macking on someone else's girl?"

I almost came unglued. He partly saw my hypothetical, but not from the angle I hoped. I got too deep into the topic with him to walk away, so I tried to clarify.

"She came on to, or macked on me. Literally in the next sentence after telling me she liked someone else." I said.

Casello perked up and set his laptop to his side. "Is she hot at least?"

I shook my head. "Dude. Not every guy is trying to score with every woman."

Casello stood up and approached, putting his hand on my shoulder.

"You're a sweetheart. I'm blushing. But for real, here's the scoop: If you don't care about the other dude, then do what you want. If the other dude is a friend or someone that matters to you, then address this to him. This ain't a soap opera, but you gotta take out the laundry before the laundry takes out you."

I appreciated his honest input. I thanked him, and we fist bumped. He wished me luck, and I let him get back to what he was doing. As I proceeded towards the quarterdeck, I passed by Wilky's room and could hear reggae playing and a faint smell of cologne or incense. I faced his door and smiled as I continued. When I reached the quarterdeck, I saw that the OOD was the First Class from a few weeks prior, the one Pickens was working with. I forgot his name, but I glanced over and saw the nameplate. It was Thompson. He looked up at me and I nodded to recognize him. Just before I reached the doors, he called out my name.

I shrieked, then slowly turned to face him. "Hi Thompson."

He signaled for me to approach the front desk.

"Pickens briefed me on you. I met you a few weeks ago as you may recall." he said.

I nodded.

"He tells me you are a con. That you like to stir up a ruckus and leave other people to face blame. You and your group like to disrupt."

I was in disbelief. Even when gone, Pickens still slung mud at me. For a split second I thought about simply telling Petty Officer Thompson that whatever Pickens said was untrue. Then my cynical side came out. Most important on my mind was how to talk to B-man about the Melissa situation. That Pickens spread lies, and I had to address them set me into a rage. At that moment, I went full-bore.

"I'm going to be perfectly honest with you. Pickens is a shit. Nobody likes him, and he spends all his time telling me why I suck at life. If I said hi to him, he mocks me, if I ignore him, he harasses me for not addressing a Second Class accordingly. I think he has small dick syndrome and honestly I don't care what he told you because it's bullshit." I said.

There was a chilling silence. *Drop the mic, Bosner!* I thought to myself. I could feel a smile grow on my face almost involuntarily. Thompson remained still, and cold faced. Then he smiled and laughed loudly. I laughed along with him, although I wasn't sure if the laughing was good or bad. He stood and smacked me on the back, then put his arm around me.

"Small dick syndrome? Nah, he's just a scrawny ass prick all around. Don't you worry about him. He complained about you, and I figured I would fill you in. He's finishing up tonight, then he transfers out." Thompson said.

I smirked with satisfaction. I didn't feel there was anything else for me to add to the conversation.

"Thanks Thompson, I appreciate it. Have a good one."

I exited the barracks and walked to Green Beater. I wasn't sure what to make of the contrasting conversations between Casello and Thompson, but I felt better. Plus, it was Friday! When I got to the command, there were trucks parked in front and crates were being unloaded. I knew they were likely supplies related to the upcoming det, and I figured things would be chaotic that night. When I entered the command, the chiefs were all converged at the front desk talking to the duty officer. They looked serious, but since I couldn't make out what they were discussing, I left them alone to avoid unwanted attention on myself.

When I entered the shop, everyone was sitting around. The day was going by slowly, but for night check it was a sign of a potentially ominous evening ahead; nights often began slowly, then on the backside of the shift a flurry of work would come in and we would work early into the morning trying to get everything up to par. I put away my jacket and got ready to go through the maintenance logs on the front counter. Zick approached me.

"Hey man. We have nothing going on tonight except for two wash jobs whenever the helos return."

"If that's all, then this shouldn't be too bad of a night." I said.

"They are gearing up for the det, and so now they are just getting the helos ready that are being sent out. As long as they don't break down, we should have a quiet run for the next few weeks." he replied.

I nodded with approval as he patted me on the back and headed into the hangar. McCord and Dolvar entered the shop talking about who they thought was going to win the Super Bowl. I shook my head and went out to do a quick check of the helos on the flight line. It was a nice afternoon, and a good time to catch up on minor tasks around the command such as making sure maintenance orders remained up to date, tools were in working condition, and that everyone's training file was organized in the shop cabinets. I became the go-to person in the shop for "tidiness" since I spent a few months the previous year doing such tasks when I injured my foot. I developed a stress fracture on my left foot from duty on the ship during the previous det. When we returned to shore, my foot was in a special boot and they rendered me unfit to work on the flight line. As the rest of the gang (and the shop) preferred working out on the flight line, nobody's feelings were hurt when I took up clerical duties. It even earned me the nickname "Secretary".

Sundown came, and most of us worked hard to find things to keep Chief from suspecting we had nothing to do. It was common knowledge among junior sailors that there wasn't a task a chief wouldn't order if they saw us wandering around bored. We cleaned the shop, and some of us did two or three checks on tools just to pass additional time. As it had been a quiet evening, we took a break together, convening in the shop as everyone sat around. Some told horror stories to Tompkins, Uller, Sadina, Franklin, and McCord who remained skeptical. After everyone ran out of tales to tell, they explained the existence of "The Rat", the shop's great mythical pastime. Sadina was not a believer of its code or even its existence, so Third Class Vincent, took it upon himself to explain.

"The Rat is an honor code which requires us to throw down if certain lines are crossed." he said.

Sadina didn't buy it. "That doesn't make sense. Sounds stupid."

Vincent pointed at another shipmate, Airman Apprentice Clearwater, and asked him if he would demonstrate The Rat. Clearwater agreed, and Vincent instructed him to go to the shop fridge and retrieve a small carton of milk off the top shelf.

Vincent continued to explain. "Sadina, that milk Clearwater has is mine. But Clearwater is a bastard and decides he's going to drink it himself."

Vincent nodded, signaling Clearwater to drink it. Once he did, Vincent pointed to the middle of the shop floor and yelled, "RAT!" Clearwater, trying not to spit up milk laughing, put the carton down on the shop counter and stepped up to the middle of the shop floor. Once both got into a grappling stance, they went at it. Sadina jumped back to avoid the tussle, clutching her face in disbelief. Vincent and Clearwater rolled around on the floor trying to pin one another and get the other to tap out. They twirled around until Clearwater broke out of Vincent's attempted arm lock and both got back to their feet. Clearwater tried grabbing Vincent's upper body, but was flung over, knocking the trash can to the floor. Everyone in the shop except Sadina and a few newbies roared with laughter.

The sound of the trash can striking the concrete floor rattled everybody's ears, then shortly after, the shop door flung open and Maintenance Chief stormed in. Everybody, except for Clearwater who laid on the floor, stood at attention.

"What in the hell is going on in here?" Maintenance Chief asked.

Everybody stood silent. The Maintenance Chief that night was Chief Ron Rogers. I don't recall where he was from, nor did I know much about him. He was a mostly fair minded chief, nowhere near as imposing as Senior. I knew Chief Rogers was aware of The Rat, and it was simply the noise level that prompted him to come into the shop.

"I know it's a quiet night, but you all know the damned drill. Get everything squared away so we can get these two helos washed up quickly once they land. Understood?" Chief said.

We nodded in agreement as he left. There was a brief silence, then everybody laughed again. Clearwater got to his feet and picked the trash can up, then he and Vincent shook hands.

Sadina stood in disbelief. "You are all crazy!"

We nodded and kept laughing. "Welcome to the shop!"

A bunch of us argued sporadically about our respective win-loss records on "The Rat", but nobody agreed on who had the best record. I, for example, had a 1-1 record. I beat Aldman, but lost to an aircrewman when I snatched a slice of pizza they ordered without first asking. The evening rolled into the night, and one of the other maintenance shops turned on music, blaring it into the hangar. It was rare that nights were slow at the command, but when they were, we took advantage of it. Some danced to the blaring tunes echoing through the hangar, others looked for tasks to undertake to keep the appearance of being busy. After a while, we divided the shop into two groups tasked with washing the helos upon their return. The only obstacle was to ensure that both aircraft had time to cool once they landed and shut down.

# 16. Always a Sailor

In quick fashion, the shop readied wash teams as well as two pairs to don cranial headgear and light wands to receive and park the helos upon landing. Soon thereafter, a rumble sounded in the distance and two approaching lights lit the sky. The flight line pairs ran out to "catch" the helos and direct them where to park. Luckily, because of the special nature of the evolution, the chiefs agreed to allow the pilots to land and park both helos near the hydrants so that our hoses and wash equipment could reach them. The new sailors were nervous as both helos landed and thundered slowly towards us, one in front of the other. Once they reached the wash location, the blades turned down, and the pilots gradually shut off the main, then auxiliary engines. After a few moments, both crews emerged from the helos as we stood by waiting for them to cool.

After the aircraft had cooled enough, the crews readied to clean them. Our gang divvied ourselves into our own team. With me was B-man, Dolvar, Zick, McCord, Klein, and a few others. Sammy, who worked in the main tool room (which was its own shop), helped us by getting the better hose. One hose—the one we got—came with a better nozzle that allowed for optimal water pressure. The tool room leadership insisted that all the command's wash hoses were the same, but our team knew otherwise. Luckily, nobody other than us figured that out. Our team worked out a system for washing the helos quickly and more thoroughly than others knew how. I always scrubbed and hosed the wheel wells and underside of the helo, B-man and Zick tackled the mid exterior and exhaust, and Dolvar and Klein got the interior. McCord, being as tall as he was, agreed to take the blades while the rest helped where needed.

Once we finished the wash jobs and they were inspected and approved, we towed the helos to designated parking spots on the flight line. In short, it required personnel at each side, as well as a person at the tail, a person in the cabin to operate the brakes, a person to operate a tow tractor, and a Plane Captain (many of us were Plane Captains) to direct the operation. The work was so routine that we could do it all like clockwork. When the gang was on the same team, we were all-stars, and much of the command knew it. As we moved and parked the helos where directed, Chief Rogers emerged from Maintenance Control with a big grin. He crossed his arms and bobbed his head with delight.

"Good job folks! Let's chain 'em down, get the hangar closed up, and get the hell outta here!" he cheered.

We finished up, checked in our gear, and before I knew it, I was on my way out to Green Beater. I saw B-man, Dolvar, and Zick heading out to the parking lot, they invited me to join them at Greenies, but I decided I was going to take it easy for the night—Friday was my only chance to get a break. As I drove to the barracks, I turned up the tunes especially loud. I was looking forward to a night of nothing, and I couldn't tell if there was a reason for it or if it was merely exhaustion from the past few weeks. As I parked, Wilky sat in his purple custom ride blaring music. I approached him as he rolled down his window.

"Whuttup!"

We fist bumped. I looked into the car and sitting in the passenger seat was Shanae.

"Man, I was jamming out in the car too." I said.

"It's Friday. What's your schedule?" he asked.

"Nothing. I'm going to chill in my room and get ready for the rest of the weekend."

Shanae laughed. "We will come by the party tomorrow. Bring your dance, Bosner!"

"Oh, yea give me a few drinks and it's on!"

"Maybe we will find Latisha and bring her with." Wilky said.

I gave him a look and waved goodbye as they both laughed and wished me a good night. As I entered the barracks to the quarterdeck, Anderson sat at the desk. Next to her dressed in civies was none other than Pickens. He was leaning against the front desk, talking poor Anderson's ear off. I frowned and rolled my eyes, but then he saw me.

"Oh, Bosner. It's Friday, and I'm done here!" he said.

"So sad to see you go. Why are you here now?"

"He was kind enough to stop by tonight to check on me. Wanted to make sure I knew all the ins and outs of watch on Friday night." Anderson said.

I looked at Pickens. He had no reason to be there. Anderson was plenty capable of being on her own as OOD.

"She's good to go, you are through." I said.

Pickens smirked and shook his head. He motioned Anderson to standby as he approached me.

"I see you're being rebellious. Have you been drinking?" he asked.

"No, and if I was, I wouldn't tell you. You are nobody."

Anderson's mouth opened as she covered it to hide her smile. Pickens stopped when we both stood toe to toe.

"It's Friday, you aren't doing anything. What, did your little pals ditch you?"

"No, ass. We're throwing a party tomorrow. Felt like going to bed early tonight."

"I bet I could out drink all of you anyway. Like I did when I saw you all at C.T. Slaters. Such a fine place, no wonder they asked you to leave!"

Anderson looked confused. "What?"

Pickens motioned back at her to let him continue. She giggled and shook her head.

"What is this crap? And C.T. Slaters sucks!" I said.

"I'm sure Blaine and Dolvar have to cover for you at the parties because you snooze the entire time. Total lightweights. All of you!"

At that point, I grew tired of dealing with Pickens' pointless attitude. He wasn't on duty, and he wasn't in uniform, so he wasn't worthy of being respected. As a result, I lost composure. I bit my lower lip, a sign that I was losing my temper. Suddenly, I grabbed Pickens by his shirt. He frowned, looking genuinely worried. Anderson stood but remained silent. I gazed at Pickens.

"Here, tell ya what. Bring your ass to the party tomorrow night. I'll let the gang know you are coming. Cape Henry Avenue. Bring your girlfriend so she can watch you get wasted before any of us." I said.

He brushed my arms off and stepped back, then swiped at his shirt as if I stained it or something. Then he looked at me and pointed.

"You got it. You don't scare me. I could've had you tonight, but since I'm leaving—"

I interrupted. "Spare me, you aren't on duty or in uniform and you're being a dickless fool. See you tomorrow. Or not."

I proceeded towards the corridor, waving at Anderson. "Have a great weekend!"

"Thanks, you too!" she replied, still smiling.

I walked down the corridor, feeling good about myself and not expecting to see Pickens again. As I walked by the laundry room, I noticed an unrecognizable person lip singing obnoxiously to 80s pop while loading clothes into the dryer. I proceeded onward, trying not to laugh. When I reached my room, I went straight to the fridge and got a snack, then to my room to dress in comfy clothes. I grabbed a book and laid on my bed to read and eat; that was the last thing I remembered.

The sound of a phone buzzing awoke me. I turned over to grab it and accidentally rolled over into my spilled half sandwich. I glanced at the number displayed; it was my grandparents. I answered.

"Hello?"

"It's your mother. Sweetheart, grandpa died."

I laid silently for a second as I digested the news.

"Oh…" I said.

I wasn't emotional, or even sad. My grandpa and I were close, but he had been ill for some time. All I could do was lay on my bed with the phone to my ear.

"He passed away early this morning, but he's in a better place." she said.

"I know. I'm glad he's not in any more pain. How's grandma?"

She hesitated. "Sad but relieved. She had to watch him suffer. It's over now."

I said little for the rest of the call, and I don't remember getting off the phone with my mom. I always coped with loss in a silent, numbing manner. For me, death to a loved one made for a time to remember, and to define how to proceed with life in honoring them. My grandpa wasn't just someone whose name I bore, he too served in the Navy as did my dad. I thought about everything I knew and remembered of him. I couldn't muster sadness, only a sense that I got to spend a lot of time with him when I was growing up, and that he in fact was ill for a long time. That he fought until the very end made me feel a sense of true peace about the matter. I put on some clothes and went for a drive.

I don't remember leaving the barracks or who the OOD was. Getting into Green Beater and leaving base also slipped my memory. I just drove. Eventually, I ended up at a dead end on the oceanfront, somewhere south of town. It was blustery out, but I got out of my car and hiked over the sand dunes to sit and watch the waves crest. A few people passed by; all of them wearing wind jackets with hoods up, concealing their faces. I sat on the sand with just casual clothes—sneakers, a pair of jeans, and a T-shirt—the cold didn't seem to register. I could only feel a gusting wind, and it didn't sound in my ears. All I heard was waves. The cresting, the gentle sounding rip tide, and then the cresting again.

My phone buzzed. It was B-man calling me, but I simply put the phone back in my pocket. A few more moments passed as I gazed out over the endless ocean horizon. Suddenly, a strange sense of comfort overcame me. A random crab sprinted across the wet sand into the restless ocean water, which made me smile. Above, seagulls glided almost gracefully with their wings spread as they relaxed against the wind to stay afloat. The natural scenes took me back to a memory of when I was growing up. My grandpa and I would go get burgers and fries from an old stand in my hometown. He would then drive us to a beach not far away where we would sit and watch the water. We would throw fries at the silly seagulls and watch them sprint to gobble them up. They were always so oblivious to everything except the fries it seemed, a simple memory, a simple joy. It was blustery and cold out—but not to them, nor me. That crabs continually danced their way into the water, and seagulls glided above, I could do nothing more than smile. I did so on the sand and watched waves while I remembered someone I loved. It was beautiful. No part of me was sad in the least; I jumped to my feet and ran back to the car.

Much like earlier, I couldn't remember where I drove, I only knew that I was doing so while speeding. Music blared from Green Beater with the windows down, and I sang obnoxiously. Drivers and pedestrians stared as I behaved erratically, but I didn't care. I was in a state of peace as I thought of my grandpa, and even my dad. Of both men, my most striking memory was of their content nature to keep their Navy experiences to themselves. Only after I joined did I hear their tales. I found it to be a great irony that the lingo and even the wild stories of sailors seem to never change even as generations come and go. It was many decades earlier when my grandpa had served; it was a few since my dad had served, but when grandpa passed, I realized something: once a sailor, always a sailor. I was ready to proceed with my life; grandpa would've wanted me to do that. On that Saturday, life was proceeding to Cape Henry House, and I would not miss it.

# 17. It Begins, Again

To make up for last weekend's party and Mission: Three Beers Standing in particular, I stopped at a grocery store and bought as many bags of chips and packs of hotdogs as I could hold. I figured we could grill hotdogs and save ourselves—particularly Sammy and myself—of the trouble of cutting through yards and leaping over fences while playing dodge-dog. It was still relatively early, only 1600 with daylight remaining, when I got to Cape Henry House. There were plenty of places to choose from for parking, but I felt like parking away from the house in case some jackass went out and vandalized cars. Once I parked, I cut through the front yard and leapt up the front steps, B-man and others were conversing loudly inside. I entered and raised the bags in my hands. Everybody in sight cheered.

"Got the replacements for last week's bullshit! Whaddya say?" I said.

"Sammy isn't here yet to share the joy!" Thomas replied.

For the second week in a row, Thomas looked sharp. In fact, he was the best dressed the previous week. Jokingly, I scoped him from head to toe.

"Thomas, I gotta be real with you. Why'd you look like shit the first time I met you?"

B-man laughed. "Bro, you just got here and you're already talking shit? Where the fuck is Bosner?"

Thomas stepped in front of B-man. "The first time I came here, B-man annoyed me into coming after I got back from driving across the country."

B-man glared at Thomas.

"Driving across country, in what? A dumpster?" I said.

"Ohhhh!"

Everyone's reply signaled an early start to the trash talk frenzy.

"Hopefully the Giants start as fast tomorrow as Bosner is right now." Dolvar said.

Lorrie approached and took the grocery bags.

"Here, let me take these and put them away before you fling stuff at people." she said.

"Oh yea, bro. I called you earlier. Can you spot a few bucks for the kegs? Bomber and Tee are going to bring two." B-man asked.

I gave him what I had in cash, then told them about grandpa passing away. Dolvar went to the fridge and chucked bottle beers at everyone as they sat in the living room. Amazingly, everyone caught theirs! I talked about the matter.

"I took a drive and I relaxed on the beach. I'm good. It's a sad thing but not so much when a person is old as hell and suffering. I mean, isn't that the goal in life? Make it to old age before you feel like shit and die?" I said.

Billy looked hard at thought. "Yea, I don't think most people have such a well-rounded view about it. Pretty fuckin awesome that you already do!"

Dolvar leaned over and hugged my head. "Clown. You're the biggest one. But we love you."

"I'm sure he was very proud of his grandson." Lorrie added.

Zick raised his beer to me. "Yea man, I mean you could go up to anyone and tell them a fact related to the town they are from. He had to have seen that in you too. The man is proud of you wherever he is!"

I raised mine.

"Bro, you talked about him a lot. You said he liked a good time. Has to be a good omen for tonight!"

In fact, my grandpa did like to have a good time. He, along with my dad, had a lot of wild stories. They were all good stories to hear, but not always with good details.

"Honestly, he talked about some of his exploits in the party world. He was a sailor too. Not sure if matching those is a good thing or not." I said.

"I mean, he didn't kill anyone or anything, did he?" Billy replied.

I shook my head. "No, nothing like that. Just chaotic stories of late nights and drinking."

"He means wild fights at parties, huh." Joanne said.

Everyone stopped and looked. Zick looked at her as though he was hoping she didn't say what she had.

"I think we met our quota for fighting. B-man put Dolvar through a wall, doesn't that count?" Thomas said.

"Bro, that was like a unicorn incident. Just don't fucking mess with me when I'm sleeping. That was our one fight. Probably good we got that out of the way so we can just have a bomb ass night."

Zick laughed. "Dude, nice rhyme."

B-man thought for a second, then smiled.

"Hey Zick, how about you go get us another round of beers?" Dolvar asked.

Zick gave him the middle finger salute, then proceeded towards the fridge.

"Beers rhymes with…" Lorrie paused and waited for us to respond.

"Jeers." I started.

She shook her head no.

"Leers." Joanne added.

Lorrie glanced at her and I.

"It's more obvious than those." she insisted.

B-man's head perked up. "Steers."

She looked disappointed.

"Clowns, it's QUEERS." Dolvar snapped.

Lorrie stood up. "You are all horrible!"

Zick, coming back from the kitchen with beers in his arms, said, "Deers."

"That's not even grammatically correct, Zick."

He bobbed his head towards Lorrie and winked.

"Fears." Billy added.

"Guys, come on… Thomas!! Please?"

Thomas looked a little unsure. Then his face lit up. "I got it!"

"Yes?" she asked.

"Seers!" Thomas blurted with a smile.

Lorrie smacked her hands on her legs and stomped off down the hallway before scowling, "Kill me now!"

"You said 'beer rhymes with…' and we gave you rhymes!" B-man said.

After a moment, Lorrie returned. Zick handed everyone a new beer, but Lorrie's sat alone on the table. He handed it to her.

"CHEERS. CHEERS. CHEERS!!! We're in a house that practically swims in beer and none of you can come up with the rhyme 'cheers!' God save us." she said.

Billy chuckled. "Hell, my next guess would've been 'Tears'."

Everybody laughed. Then Thomas asked a question I dreaded.

"Is Melissa coming out? It seemed like she bailed early last time."

The hair stood up on the back of my neck. I chickened out on talking to B-man about anything remotely close to Melissa. Making matters worse, B-man looked the most compelled when Thomas asked the question.

"I don't know. Haven't really heard from her. I think she's alive." he said.

Lorrie frowned at him. "She's alive, ass. But I'm not sure what she's been up to. I saw her online when I was using the messenger, she was hanging out with other friends. They know about the party."

"Hers or their loss if they don't come." Dolvar added.

Zick nodded. "More beer for us. Plus, Thayer is bringing some grill-able items."

Billy looked at him. "Grill-able items?"

"Bro, that kind of terminology worries me. Burgers, or steaks. Or burgers AND steaks sound a lot better. Hotdogs. Shit, bratwurst. Any specifics Zick?" B-man said.

Zick tried to reassure us. "Chill guys, Thayer's got this."

"Guys, I brought the hotdogs. I'm not sure if they will last. We might want to make them soon to make sure we at least get them."

B-man still looked concerned. "I mean Thayer loves to eat, but that guy would probably find a dead cat on the side of the road and then flop that on a grill and justify it. Grill-able…"

"You are being an ass today! Good thing I have some friends coming. They can drown your negative attitude out!" Lorrie said.

"I'm not negative! Just saying that—hey Bosner? Let's grill up them hotdogs."

B-man's broken train of thought made everybody laugh. I joined him outside so we could begin cooking. We lit the grill, then B-man took a phone call. Nervous, I worried that he was talking to Melissa, but I stood at the grill and tried not to show interest. I looked forward to the noise of the night to drown out my thoughts on the situation. I also thought about grandpa, and what he would've done. When I grew into an adult, the old man shared with me some of his adult stories, and I figured he would have an answer for me. Casello's advice was pretty good, but still, I thought if only I had a second opinion, maybe I wouldn't feel like such a wimp and fool.

In the back of my mind, I could imagine what grandpa would've said. Almost as though I was at his house and he was in his old rocking chair, I could envision him speaking:

> "...You gotta always treat women with respect no matter what. But, if ya run into a pain the ass, do just enough to get yourself out of the situation and keep her happy enough to go be a pain in the ass to somebody else!"

I laughed. B-man, in the yard still talking on the phone, looked at me. He finished up his phone conversation, although I paid little attention to what he was talking about. At that moment, I resolved myself to finally mention the Melissa situation to him. The time came to get it over with, especially because there was no telling what would happen IF Melissa did in fact show up to the party. B-man said,

"Bye" on the phone and hung up. As he returned to the grill and looked at me, I opened my mouth to speak of the loathed situation. Before a single word came out, a commotion sounded from inside the house. We looked through the sliding glass door and saw Bomber and Tee. B-man's eyes lit up as he headed inside. I took a second and swallowed some pride; I lost my only legit chance to speak up before the mayhem began.

I remained out at the grill, but I could hear Bomber's loud voice calling for help to grab the kegs. Along with Tee, the two stood at the front of the door, and behind them were more people. I saw two girls and a guy, but I didn't recognize them. I remained outside in the meantime to get the hotdogs started on the grill. The noise from inside was already loud, and yet the party itself really hadn't begun. I focused mostly on the task at hand, not looking inside and just trying to get myself ready for whatever the night would behold. The sliding glass door opened, and out came Bomber, Zick, Billy, and Sammy, who had just arrived. They were in pairs, lugging the kegs out to the patio by the grill.

"Hiding out here are ya!" Bomber said.

I took a sip of my beer. "Just getting the last of the bottle beer taste before I drink the foamy shit!"

They plopped the kegs behind me, near the picnic table and joined me by the grill. Sammy saw the hot dogs and laughed.

"OH MAN. Bonser cut through yards again!"

I raised the tongs and clanked them together. "Shit, if I did, it would've been a success this time around."

"I didn't see when you two hopped the fence back into the yard. You should do a reenactment!" Zick added.

Bomber slapped me on the back. "No Zick, not until Bosner here does a couple keg stands. When Tee comes out, we will break him in!"

Just then, McCord stepped out the sliding glass door with a woman.

"Aight boys, where's them kegs!" he greeted.

Zick approached him and they fist bumped. "Glad you made it out!"

"Damn right! By the way, this is my wife, Julie."

Julie was tall, almost my height.

"Pleasure to meet you. You are both tall!" I said.

Bomber shook both of their hands. "Heard good things about you, McCord! Pleasure to meet you, Julie!"

Julie smiled. "He likes wrenching on machines. That's for sure!"

As Zick enjoyed talking about cars, the rest normally just listened and learned. We weren't really up to his level of knowledge on the subject which made McCord a perfect companion in that respect. After everyone greeting one another, Zick and McCord walked off talking about a rebuild on something or other. Bomber got cups, and I began taking the hotdogs off the grill. Knowing that the crowd was going to get bigger and with our drunken appetites, there was little doubt in my mind that what I brought was nothing more than an appetizer. *Thayer better come through,* I thought to myself.

"This is a big party." Julie said.

I laughed. "This isn't even close to what we're expecting."

"I saw you got two kegs. Hopefully your expectations aren't too high."

"Nobody is even drunk yet. Once that happens, then you can decide." Sammy said.

"Jason and I don't party too much anymore. We will probably leave before it gets too wild."

As I headed into the house with the plate of hotdogs, I faced her and winked.

"Well Julie, for your sake, I hope you do too."

Inside, Bomber was holding a bag of red cups, but appeared to have become distracted by a conversation with Thomas and a few others. I put the plate of hotdogs on the kitchen counter, then went to get napkins. Lorrie approached, and whispered into my ear.

"Let me get one of the hotdogs. I'm starving. Didn't want anyone to know." she said.

"Go for it. I'm getting napkins and some condiments."

Dolvar saw the hotdogs sitting on the counter and announced loudly that there was food. Lorrie and I angrily glared at him. He walked up, patted me on the back and grabbed a hotdog. Billy and a few others followed suit, I already had lost track of how many people were at the house. From my perspective, it looked as though everyone and their damned cousin received an invitation! With the situation looking hopeless, I quickly got napkins and condiments then jumped in to get a hotdog before they were all gone. When I grabbed one, there were already 13 or 14 missing! Before I even took a bite of mine, I was shoved and dropped it.

"Bosner, you weasel! Going to get food before you say hi? Who does that!" A voice called out.

I turned and saw that it was Tee. She looked at the floor, having noticed that I dropped the hotdog. Angrily, I grabbed it.

"10 second rule, damnit." I said.

Tee laughed. "Is this practice for something? Blowing on it and going plain?"

I had not planned on being callous so early in the evening, but I couldn't resist at that point. As I chewed, I made a gagging noise. Tee frowned.

"Oh I hate you!"

She grabbed her mouth and bolted outside.

Bomber laughed. "You devil, you! Finish up and get your butt out here for the keg stand."

I shook my head as I continued eating. Bomber pointed at me, then proceeded out the sliding glass door.

"Suckers can start first sometimes." he said.

I finished eating, but instead of going straight outside, I sat on the couch for a moment with

Joanne and Lorrie. Almost everyone went out back to the kegs, but there were a few people sitting in the living room. It turned out that the people remaining inside were Lorrie's friends, two of whom were men. Five people Lorrie knew showed up to the party, and unbeknownst to me, she and B-man were mutually friends with the two guys. One was a tall, well-built Latino named Ortiz, the other was average in nearly every detail except for the curiously pink button-up shirt he was wearing; his name was Marcus. Along with Ortiz and Marcus were three females who were exclusively Lorrie's friends. The three ladies were Vicky, Lisa, and Yolanda, but they were mostly interested in themselves, so I took their cues accordingly. I turned my attention to Joanne.

"Did you eat?" I asked.

"No, I figure I will pass out sooner if I don't."

"Hopefully you don't get a hangover!" Lorrie said.

"You don't want to miss the fun!" I added.

Joanne smiled. "At this place, I don't think that's possible."

Just then, the front door opened, and in came Wilky and Shanae. They looked around, then saw me sitting on the couch.

"What up!" Wilky greeted.

I got up, and we bro hugged.

"Not much man, it's early so we have some time to bullshit before the ruckus!"

Shanae hugged me. "What ruckus? You attempting to dance?"

"Give me some cognac and I'll burn down the place dancing!" I joked.

I hadn't noticed that Wilky was carrying two brown bags, and after I made the joke, he lifted them up and smiled. *Spoke too soon, idiot,* I thought to myself. I shook my head, but that just made Wilky and Shanae laugh. I directed them into the kitchen to put away the booze, then introduced them to Joanne, Lorrie, and the others. Everyone but Lorrie's girlfriends greeted them, they smirked and went back to texting on their phones and gossiping amongst themselves. Wilky looked around the house, then remarked that the party seemed more "chill" than the last one. Before I could warn him it was likely to get rowdy soon, a chant of my name roared from out back. He and Shanae looked shocked, Joanne and Lorrie waved at me while everyone else just stared in confusion.

I stood up from the couch and looked out the sliding glass door. Everyone outside was yelling for me. I knew it was for the keg stand, and my attempts to play deaf failed since I stood and reacted to their chants. I remained standing in place for a moment before Wilky nudged me to go out. To make matters worse, Bomber opened the sliding glass door and waved for me to come out. I bowed my head before getting up and going outside. Wilky came with me while the rest wished me luck. When I stepped outside the door, I saw that the tap was on the keg, and everyone was standing around waving for me to be "number one" for the night. Wilky patted me on the back, then walked over and greeted B-man. Tee grabbed the collar of my shirt and waved for others to grab me and put me in the stand position. As I put my lips on the nozzle and they pumped the tap, I could see through the sliding glass door into the house. Upside down, I saw the front door open, and Pickens entered with his girlfriend.

# 18. Piss-kens

Seeing Pickens come to the party made me lose what little composure I had to even get a chug in while doing the keg stand. As soon as the cold brew touched my lips, I already failed. Distracted, I was lucky to get "two seconds" into the chugging before the beer shot out my nose and I choked. Everyone booed, and when they put me back on my feet, I turned to enter the house and see Pickens. Before I could, he came straight for the sliding glass door while his girlfriend stayed in with the others at the couches. I stood at the keg while everybody laughed at my epic failure as the opening keg stand act. Pickens came out to the patio.

"See? Here I am, so now you have to pay up!" he said.

"Pickens?" Sammy replied.

Ironically, Pickens' comment made the moment even more awkward.

"Hi. You came, but pay you for what? I didn't make a bet, I just told you to come if you dared." I said.

"Well, you're gonna have to pay me once I out drink you!"

I wasn't the most polished drinker of the gang, but I felt confident that I could beat Pickens tit for tat. Even better, I remembered he told me that ALL of my friends were "lightweights".

"Hey Pickens, you think you could out drink any of us?" I asked.

Everyone stopped and faced him. He became nervous.

"Yea, I sure can!" he said.

I smiled and watched Dolvar interject.

"Out drink us? Out drink ME?"

Pickens appeared to realize he may have gotten himself in too deep with his arrogance. He proudly held firm in his boast, however.

"Let's just start, and we will see who wins!"

Everyone laughed and patted Dolvar. B-man, with a glaring smile, began adjusting his hat. It was his way of showing supreme confidence.

"Bro, you have no chance. No fucking chance."

"Yea? Yea? I don't think you've seen me when I'm kicking ass!" Pickens replied.

Tee approached us. "Boys, what's the bet?"

Dolvar walked between Tee and Pickens. "Hey fucker, here we go: Winner pisses on the fucking loser. Got it?"

Everybody remained silent as Dolvar gazed at Pickens. He bobbed a bit, his eyes wandering. He finally drew out his hand to shake with Dolvar. "Got it!"

"High stakes are the BEST stakes!" Tee shouted towards sky.

Bomber put his arm around her. "This is a going to be fun."

B-man continued to glare at Pickens. "Bro. No fucking chance."

"Yea, kinda like the Giants tomorrow!" Sammy said.

B-man turned and faced him as they got into a conversation about the Super Bowl.

Wilky looked at me. "Bruh I told you, he looks up to you guys. You 'gon break him tonight."

"But he got himself into this shit. He's gotta learn! Now, let's get you some good shit." I said.

Wilky patted me on the back and we both went inside. I took a shot of cognac with him out of respect, then we went to the couches where the girls sat as they chatted up a storm. We sat down as Shanae told everyone about my "exploits" at the club.

"...and then Bosner put on some crazy moves I never seen before. That place was going wild as shit over it!" she continued.

"Hey, hey, he got himself a big, beautiful mocha too! He got game, it's weird ass game, but he got it!" Wilky added.

Everybody laughed except for Ortiz, who stared at me and slowly shook his head. I got the impression that the big guy saw me as though I was a cartoon or something. At that moment, B-man, Bomber, and Tee came inside and gathered around the table. They began getting cups and preparing for beer pong as B-man called for Lorrie, kissing her through the air. She stood up smiling and put both hands over her heart.

As she walked over to join the others at the beer pong table, the front door opened and in came Ms. Highlights with her two friends—the three of them had reached hang around status at Cape Henry House. She saw me and said "hi". Marcus seemed to take a liking to her, and he immediately jumped in and began attempting to woo her. At some point, Marcus and his pink shirt looked at me and asked how my butt was doing. Ms. Highlights had cracked him. All eyes were again on me, ominously. I attempted to explain, but to no avail. Wilky got up and walked into the kitchen. He came back with two shots. Cognac, again. I tried to stall.

"Nah, take it. Enjoy the night. Bruh, don't forget, you're a good man. They dish at you because it's all they got." he said.

I smiled and put my arm around him.

"Fuck it. Bottoms up!"

As I took the shot and winced, Zick and McCord came in through the front door. The two were rambling on about cars, continuing their motor romance. After a moment, Joanne threw a couch pillow, hitting Zick in the head. He flinched, then turned and saw that it was Joanne. She beckoned him with her index finger. Zick hastily ended his conversation with McCord, confusing him for a moment, but then he saw Joanne and realized Zick was about to be busy. He smiled and nodded, then walked into the kitchen area.

"I didn't forget you!" Zick said to her.

She smiled. "I don't care. You're mine now. Come."

The two got up. Holding hands, they ran out the front door.

"Be back in a bit!" he said.

Where they were going, we didn't know; what they were going to be doing, we had no doubt. The door slammed shut behind them.

"Getting the love on. It's good for the soul." Shanae said.

Everyone sitting around at the couches chatted for a bit, then Shanae looked over at Pickens' girlfriend. She was silent compared to Lorrie's three ditzy girlfriends. Shanae attempted to introduce herself.

"Oh, don't worry about that." Pickens' girlfriend responded.

Her response particularly irritated me.

"No. For real, what's your name?" I asked.

Wilky sat next to me, pretending not to hear the conversation.

"Listen, I'm not with carrot top. He just buys me meals for me hanging out with him. He made me come here for appearances." she explained.

Wilky, Shanae, and I all looked at each other, unable to come up with a response. The girl was so rude, so callous, that I felt bad for Pickens. He was much more desperate than I realized. Shanae looked angry, but I gave her a look, implying her not to start a fight. In my mind, it was too early for fighting, although a cat fight at Cape Henry House would've been notable. Wilky and Shanae flirted around as I sat and sipped my beer. After a little while, Klein arrived. He looked angry, but he usually did.

"Alright bitches, I'm here!!!!!"

Some in the house heard him and waved. Others nodded. Klein looked over and saw me. He nodded, and I nodded back.

"What's the bracket? Who's up next?" he asked.

"Beer pong? I don't think there's a bracket. It's just free play. They just started." I replied.

He shook his head and mumbled something as he walked in towards the kitchen. Wilky and Shanae gathered their things and got ready to leave. Shanae wanted some quality time with him, or at least that's what I gathered from her gestures. I walked with them out to their car. Just before they left, I remembered they left their liquor in the house. When I brought that to their attention, they continued to get into the car. Wilky looked at me with a smile.

"It's yours, dog. It will help you with your inside game, and the dancing."

I smiled and waved to them as they left. Before I turned around to go back inside, I could hear a car speeding down the street from the other direction. As it neared the house, it came screeching up, honking its horn, then swerving into the spot

that Wilky had just vacated. I stood there with no
idea who it was, but then the driver's side door
swung open and out came Souza. He looked
especially excited.

"Souza, what's up!"

We both hugged, and I noticed a strong smell
of alcohol.

"Aye, Bosner! I'm late, but I made it."

"Where did you come from?"

"Oh, yea, that's a long story, but I'm here
now. Let's get drunk!"

I walked with him up to the house, and as we
got to the door, Ms. Highlights came out with
Marcus. Souza's eyes lit up.

"Hey, it's you again! Whaddya say we head in
and dance or something." he said.

Ms. Highlights rolled her eyes and grabbed
Marcus' hand.

"Get lost. I'm with someone." she said.

"That was quick." I replied.

Souza smirked at her and then went inside. I
continued to stand there for a second, looking at
Marcus. Something about him struck me as odd, and
I was certain it wasn't just the pink shirt, or that he
seemed to have hooked up with a girl whose name I
still didn't know.

"Bosner? Hello?? You can go now!" Ms.
Highlights said.

"Sheesh, I'm out of here!"

When I got inside, Souza was already on the
couch talking to Pickens' girl, who I referred to as

219

"Nameless". I saw no point in trying to talk to Souza at that point, because I wasn't a cock block, and I didn't want him to think I was interested in a girl I had absolutely no interest in. Zick and Joanne came into the living room from the pass out room, which I found odd because they both went out the front door earlier and I never saw them come back in. There was no way into the pass out room except through the kitchen. Zick had a beaming smile, and Joanne looked equally satisfied.

"You did your thing in the pass out room? I saw you go outside." I said.

"An old hat trick Bosner. Let's get a drink!" Zick replied.

He tugged Joanne with him towards the sliding glass door and I followed them. As we walked towards the door, Klein stood at the side of the beer pong table giving everyone hell; B-man, Lorrie, Bomber, and Tee were still going at it, and both were down to two cups each.

"Fuckers. If I was playing, I would've already won! Damnit you are slow. I'm getting old sitting here waiting." Klein said.

As I reached the sliding glass door, Tee grabbed him by the collar of his shirt. I had the door halfway open but stopped to watch the clash.

"Klein, I will break you over my knee if you don't shut the fuck up!" she replied.

He stood there, with Tee still holding him by the shirt. Slowly, he broke into a smile.

"Tee! There ya go. Good spirit. I'm pulling for you and Bomber! Yea, I love it!" he cheered.

I shook my head and proceeded out back. Billy just finished doing a keg stand while Dolvar was sitting at the picnic table laughing with Thomas and some other partygoers about Pickens. I asked Dolvar where Pickens was at, and with his head he tilted left towards the side of the house. I looked, and there stood Pickens, facing away, taking a piss. He was swaying left and right, clearly drunk. Dolvar was grinning as everyone else in his group giggled and watched the demise of Pickens.

"Dude. Already? Did you go shot for shot with him?" I asked.

Thomas laughed. "Dolvar did two to Pickens' one. This is hilarious!"

"Fucking clown. He's such a clown that he's not even a clown… I don't know what he is."

I walked over to Pickens as he finished his business.

"Pickens. Are you okay?"

He swung around, zipper still down, facing me with a drunken glare; eyes shot.

"I'm always okay. I'm wasting Dolvar. It's not even close. Look at him."

He pointed at Dolvar as he sat at the table laughing excessively with an entourage.

"He's so drunk he can't stop laughing. I'm going to win… for once!" Pickens continued.

I honestly felt bad. I was hardly drunk myself, and I really disliked Pickens, but him trying to take on the epic drinker of our group was sad. At that moment, something in me drove me to help Pickens out. I decided I was going to hide him so Dolvar couldn't win. I put my arm around Pickens and guided him towards the sliding glass door. As we passed Dolvar and the group, I gestured behind Pickens' to the group, "he's wasted!!!" to give us cover as I tried to hook him up. I knew I couldn't put Pickens in the pass out room, so I began brainstorming. When we entered the house, Bomber and Tee had just beaten B-man and Lorrie at beer pong, and it looked like B-man was going to smack Klein because of all the trash talk. Klein was looking around for a partner, but I was busy guiding Pickens through.

When we passed the beer pong table to the living room, I saw that Souza and Nameless weren't there, but Pickens was so far gone that he didn't seem to notice. I finally decided I would put him in Penley and Anne's room. I figured that nobody would look in there, nor would they disturb the room, unless of course a random couple did. We walked down the hallway, and then Pickens oddly opened up.

"I'm single, Bosner. That girl isn't mine. I tried, but I had to bribe her to come out." he confessed.

"Oh yea? I had no idea!" I said.

"How do you do it?"

We came upon Penley and Anne's bedroom door, then we stopped.

"Do what?" I replied.

He pushed off, then swayed drunkenly before putting his hand on the back of his neck.

"I talk a lot of shit, but I don't know how to get lucky."

I almost laughed. I actually thought Pickens had at least rounded the bases. Luckily, I was still sober enough to play it cool for Pickens' sake.

"Pickens, you try too hard. That never works. You just have to let things flow, and when you do that, you'll find her."

Just then, we heard laughter, and Pickens leaned to the left to see around the hallway corner towards the living room. Zick and Joanne ran into the house in a playful mood, enjoying the night as the inseparable couple of the party.

"Like that. Zick does it so well. And then you. You wake up with love on your neck and shoulder. I want that!"

I patted him on the chest. "Pickens, if you weren't such a dick, then you could probably roll with us and you'd get to have drunken, reckless fun and love. Maybe another time. It's time for you to get rest."

He looked hopeful, but luckily, he was transferring to another duty station, so the fancy talk was just patchwork for a fool. I opened the door to Penley and Anne's room and saw the bed. At that moment, I had an epiphany; it may be best to put Pickens on the other side of the bed up against the wall. I figured if I did that, and Dolvar came looking, he would check the room and see an empty bed and Pickens would be off the hook. Plus, Pickens was so sloppy drunk that he wouldn't have known if I put him on a bed or out on the street. I walked him past the bed to the wall, softly letting him down and laying him on the floor. I tried not to laugh out loud as I got to my feet and walked out. Pickens snored.

*Hey, I tried,* I thought to myself.

I left the room and returned to the party. B-man was in the kitchen with Lorrie, and it looked like they were getting frisky. I was happy; she was a good girl, and I preferred my best friend be with her than Melissa. I also hoped that I would never have to bring that name up again. In my mind, I was hoping I could just sweep the issue under the rug. I then turned my focus to the party at large. Klein had recruited Sammy as his beer pong partner, but they were losing to Bomber and Tee five cups to two. I tuned Klein's voice out because he was just too annoying to listen too, but his body language and flapping jaws made me laugh. I felt bad for Sammy. For fun, I walked into the pass out room and saw two bodies on the floor. I wasn't very drunk yet, and it comforted me in knowing that I wouldn't be the first one down.

Before I left the pass out room, I heard clinging and laughter coming from the laundry area. As the wall separating the laundry nook from the pass out room had an enormous hole in it, I peeked through to see if I could tell who was back there. I saw someone sitting up on the dryer unit, but nothing more. Curious, I walked around and saw Souza playing with Nameless, both flinched when I walked around the corner.

"Having fun?"

"Bosner! AGAIN!?" Souza shouted.

At first, I didn't get the reference, but then I remembered the pool tables at Greenies. Nameless looked flustered and fondled her pants. From where I stood, I saw nothing. Based on her reaction, it was clear she rearranged her clothing so Souza could please her. I put my hand in front of my face to hide my vision and apologized. I walked away as I could hear Nameless moan in satisfaction to Souza. Back in the living room, Zick and Joanne were getting ready to sing karaoke, Ms. Highlights and Marcus were heading out back, and Sammy was yelling at Klein for being so damned annoying that it distracted them from winning. Bomber and Tee taunted Klein, and when B-man refused to return for another round so soon, Klein stayed at the table to play a rematch. He pointed at me.

"Bosner, get your ass over here we are going to whoop Bomber and Tee!"

I hesitated, but Bomber and Tee waved me over as they laughed. Pride was at stake, and at that point I knew I had no choice.

"Fine. But one request… shut the hell up and let me just play. Got it?" I said.

Klein nodded and began resetting the cups. B-man grabbed a pitcher to fill with beer. Likely sensing my reluctance to be involved with beer pong, Tee walked up to me and patted me on the back.

"Give me a fact, Jack!" she said.

"Did you know I ripped ass by the door over there and nobody noticed?"

She frowned, and then Bomber tipped his cup to me. "Splendid!"

"Yea… yea… Just make sure you rip ass on the fucking table so we can win, alright?" Klein said.

Bomber and Tee looked at each other, wondering where the conversation was going to go next. Just then,    B-man returned with the pitcher and began filling the cups while Lorrie remained in the kitchen. She clapped and cheered for Klein and I. B-man patted me on the head, then stood with Lorrie. Tee pointed at me, then flexed her arms. Bomber threw first, the ball sank it into our nose cup. Klein barked obscenities while I shook my head. Tee shot and sank the ball into our upper right cup. Klein slapped the table, while I mumbled hopelessly.

Bomber and Tee kept the pong balls because of making both of their shots. Just as Bomber released the ball, someone came storming down the hallway towards the living room. The noise seemed to distract Bomber as his shot missed, and the ball bounced off the rim of our center cup and landed on the floor at the foot of the hallway. Pickens came stumbling out and stepped on the it. He then stopped and looked around the room.

"Pickens, you shit!" Bomber yelled.

In a drowsy, drunken state, he swayed around and looked into the kitchen at us.

"I'm hungry. Who wants tacos!"

Zick and Joanne continued playing karaoke, B-man and Lorrie stood in the kitchen laughing at Pickens' ineptitude, Klein stood silent for once, and Bomber and Tee stood angrily because of the disruption of their beer pong dominance. I shook my head and approached Pickens.

"Come on. I was trying to help you out, asshole."

I walked Pickens away from the kitchen and beer pong table. "If you won't sleep where I put you then you are on your own." I added.

"Tacos. Tacos now!" he replied.

Klein, Bomber, and Tee ordered me back to the table, but before I walked away from Pickens, Thayer stormed into the party.

"I'm here, food is here, the night can start! Who wants to help me bring all the grub in!"

Everyone looked happy, then Pickens stumbled up to Thayer.

"Tacos!"

Thayer looked at him, perplexed. "Uh, no. Steaks, brats, shrimp!!"

Pickens patted Thayer on the chest and then proceeded out the front door. Thayer looked back at him and then asked for one more volunteer. Sammy walked in from out back, and everybody at the table made him go. Klein pulled me back to the table, and then Tee prepared to make her shot. She missed.

Klein looked at me, and then Bomber and Tee looked at each other; we had life! Lorrie clapped, and B-man muttered about how Klein and I could be lucky enough to not get humiliated. Klein took his shot and hit the back left cup. We applauded, and then I took my shot; I made the nose cup! Bomber and Tee looked confused as B-man patted me on the head.

"Bro, I don't know what's going on, but roll with it!"

"I plan on it!" I replied.

Klein missed his shot, but unlike Bomber, noise didn't distract me when I took mine. As I cocked my hand back to fling the ball, Thayer and Sammy came in with bags and bags of food. Thayer was rambling about being ready to cook and eat, but I still took my shot, and it made the upper right cup. B-man and Lorrie shouted in support, and Bomber and Tee looked at us with disgust. Thayer and Sammy went out back with the food to relight the grill, and Klein and I continued our game. We exchanged shots for a time, and then the game drew to a tie, each of us having one cup left. At that point, B-man and Lorrie were standing at the side of the table as dedicated spectators. Zick and Joanne continued singing karaoke. Thomas and Billy came inside, and so did a bunch of others. Ms. Highlights and Marcus stood behind Bomber and Tee, and then I became distracted.

*That damned pink shirt!* I thought to myself.

Everyone was standing at the table quietly except for the karaoke duo. With only one cup left for each team, the stakes were high. It was our turn. Klein took the first shot; it was a hit! Everyone except for Bomber and Tee applauded. At that moment, I felt invincible. It was as if fate came to the rescue and I was going to sink the double whammy that finally put Bomber and Tee out of their misery. The normally jealous B-man was looking hopeful that Klein and I could pull it off. Thomas and Billy were fist pumping in our favor, Lorrie looked excited. Ms. Highlights looked compelled, but then there was Marcus and his pink shirt. I cocked my hand back and felt a perfect touch on the ball; I had the perfect angle, the perfect release. But there was a pink shirt across the way! The ball glided to the far left and didn't even contact the table. Bomber and Tee received redemption shots; everyone was going wild.

Klein continued to glare at me, but I pretended not to notice; I screwed up royally. Marcus and his annoying pink shirt had distracted me again, and I just couldn't understand. Bomber tossed his ball, and it went straight into the cup. Because of the redemption rule, all Tee had to do was make the cup as well, and they would cast us off into "Loserville". By now, everyone gave up on Klein and me, and they were cheering for Tee. She looked fearless; there was simply no way she was going to miss the shot. She didn't. The room, with Zick and Joanne's singing, filled with roars of drunken excitement over the night's most unlikely tight game. I felt bad, and Klein wouldn't let me hear the end of it.

"Son of a motherfucker! Bosner, I knew you would fuck it all up! What was that shot at the end? What, did you jack off in the bathroom before we started and your jizz dried the fuck up on the last throw? Terrible. Fuck!"

Oddly, I felt good. Klein's meltdown was enjoyable. Bomber and Tee kissed, then Bomber winked at me and went outside, presumably for a victory keg stand, or maybe a simple beer. Tee pointed at me and again flexed her arms. I nodded.

"Good game, damnit!" I said.

B-man and Lorrie told me I played "a helluva game". I believed them, since I was lousy at beer pong and playing it to the wire was fine by me. There had been no team rules set up on beer pong, so nobody knew who was going to play next—the alcohol probably had something to do with that. B-man insisted on playing again, but Lorrie hesitated. People coming in and out from the back carried the smell of whatever Thayer was grilling up. Whatever it was, it smelled delicious, so I went outside and see for myself. Dolvar was standing at the grill with Thayer, and by now he was clearly drunk. With him though, getting drunk didn't indicate how many more drinks he could handle; in fact, we never figured out just how much that was. Ms. Highlights and Marcus came outside to have a smoke, and at that point I decided I was going to figure out what Ms. Highlights' name was once and for all.

"What's your name, seriously?"

She laughed and puffed on her cigarette. "Bosner. Don't worry about it."

Frustrated, I looked at Marcus. "What's her name?"

He opened his mouth, then she backhanded him in the chest.

"Bosner is Bosner, and we are who we are. Got it?" she said.

"This is weird shit. I'm here all the time and you won't even tell me who you are!"

She smiled and took another puff off her cigarette. Marcus held her hand, and I begrudgingly walked away.

"Bye Bosner." she said.

Thayer, Dolvar, Sammy, and others were standing near the grill, so I joined them.

"Thanks for bringing chow, buddy. What's on the menu?"

Holding the tongs, Thayer faced me. Sammy lifted the lid on the grill.

"London Broil steaks on now, shrimp in a bit." Thayer said.

"That's it? Those are like, the cheapest!" I replied.

Thayer gave me a mean look. "I brought 'grill-ables' didn't I? Prick…"

"Yea, I guess I can cut you a little slack." I said.

We stood at the grill in silence for a moment before Bomber and Tee came from around the side of the house, immediately calling out my name. I turned to face them, and Tee motioned for me to do a keg stand. As usual, I hesitated. Sammy reminded me I did better than him at beer pong, but since I muffed my last toss so badly, I had to make up for it by doing a keg stand. Bomber and Tee stood there nodding. I felt had. I grumpily agreed to do it, again. Bomber and Tee readied the tap and held me up with the help of Sammy. Amazingly, I did an eight second keg stand! When they put me down, everyone was impressed. I did exceedingly well at beer pong earlier, and I did much better than usual at the keg stand—my second one of the night at that!

# 19. Brawling Drama

McCord and Julie, whom I barely saw throughout the night, stepped outside to let everyone know they were leaving. Everyone wished them well, and some exchanged contact information with them; McCord had undoubtedly become part of the gang. I vividly remember the two leaving, because of what McCord told me when I asked him why they were leaving so early. Instead of a typical, "I'm-a-married-guy" answer, he said something that I never forgot, and what set off some of the wildest chain of events I can ever recall.

"Great that you came out, and great to meet your wife, Julie." I said.

Julie smiled and nodded.

"Thanks. Yea, you know buddy it's that time. I can feel it." McCord ominously said.

"What do you mean?" I asked, as Julie walked back inside.

McCord put his hand on my shoulder. "Well, you know. Parties are fun. I love to drink, but there's always that point at a party when a man knows things are going to go south. You'll be fine, this is where you belong. Enjoy it!"

He patted me and gave everyone a glancing wave. We waved back, and he went inside. I thought for a second about what he said, but it didn't really seem to register outside of the fact that I knew he was older than most of us and, of course, he was a married man. I let the thought pass by quickly, and then I stood with Thayer, Dolvar, and Sammy at the grill. Just then, B-man poked his head out the door and looked at me.

"Bosner! Get in here bro, you're my beer pong partner!"

Bomber and Tee cheered me on, and everybody thought it was a good idea.

"This is your night, Bosner! You'll get 'em this time!" Tee said.

I nodded at B-man, then entered the house. Zick and Joanne remained in the living room singing their hearts out. They looked great. On the couches were Souza and Nameless. *Souza, you're such a sleaze,* I thought to myself. They singled Billy and Thomas up at the beer pong table, our apparent challengers. Lorrie stood near B-man as a cheerleader. Klein stood with Lorrie's girlfriends watching, as did a handful of others I didn't know. Ms. Highlights and Marcus came inside just after me and watched from a distance. I lined up square with B-man at the beer pong table.

"Okay, Bosner. B-man is counting on you." Billy said.

"It's okay if you suck to start though, luck always runs out!" Thomas added.

I wasn't having it. "Ha ha yea yea… just throw the damned ball."

Thomas threw first, the ball bounced off the nose cup and onto the floor. I thanked Ortiz for picking it up and handing it to me. Billy took his shot and made it in the rear center cup. He and Thomas hi-fived while B-man cursed. Lorrie patted B-man on the back for good luck, and then he took his shot. He drilled it in the front left cup. He and I fist bumped, then it was my turn. Just like the beginning of my previous game, the front door opened as I took my shot, but when it dropped into the nose cup, nobody seemed to care, except for me. Besides seeing the front door open through my peripheral vision, I paid no attention to who came into the house. I faced the cups bragging about my great shot, but after a moment I noticed everyone continued looking towards the front. When I finally looked, I realized why.

At the front door was Melissa. Two guys and a girl accompanied her, all unrecognizable. Lorrie ran up to Melissa to hug her and the two shared words, but I couldn't hear with Zick and Joanne singing. Melissa reluctantly hugged Lorrie and after a brief exchange, the two started towards the beer pong table. Melissa's friends walked closely behind her. They didn't fit the demeanor of anyone else at the party. Lorrie walked back to B-man and Melissa approached me, her brown eyes pierced through my soul! She didn't appear mad, but the blankness in her expression was bad enough. My knees trembled, and it seemed as if she knew it.

"Bosner." she said.

Her tone and complexion were off, she appeared drunk or under the influence of something.

"What's up. How have you been?" I replied.

She continued towards me until our noses almost touched. I was completely unsure of what to expect. Zick and Joanne continued singing, but I tuned it out to where it was almost like it was just a murmur.

"You didn't fucking come get me." Melissa said.

Initially, I didn't know what she was talking about, but then I figured she was upset because I didn't make a move after she left the previous weekend. B-man walked up and stood at the side of Melissa and me.

"What is this?" he asked.

She looked at B-man with an eerie smile. Lorrie stood behind B-man as Melissa's friends remained behind her.

"Your friend is a fucking pussy, Blaine." Melissa said.

He looked puzzled, and understandably so. I felt so numb that I couldn't even open my mouth to tell him what she was talking about.

"Hey, watch it. I don't know what the fuck this is, but you can't just come walking in here starting shit like this."

"I'm saying that your friend is a fucking pussy."

She faced me again.

"Melissa, what in the hell is up?" I asked.

While facing me, she pushed B-man back with her left hand. She then leaned into me, grabbing my crotch and kissing me. For a second, I froze, unable to react. Lorrie yelled something, and then B-man as well. I stumbled backwards, completely dumbstruck. Finally, I came to and pushed Melissa back.

"What in the fuck is this! What is wrong with you!" I said.

She stepped back, then gave the meanest glare. After a second, she faced B-man.

"I wanted you, fucker. You wouldn't let me in, and so I was going to teach your bitch friend some things and make you see. He's too much of a pussy, and you're a fucking prick. I hate you!"

In a flash, she slapped B-man across the face, and then before he could react, she lunged at him with her fingers digging into his neck. Lorrie and I jumped in to restrain Melissa, but everything became a blur. B-man pushed off her, then her three accomplices pounced. The fight was on!

There were groans, growls, screams, and other noises. Maybe the worst was the sound of breaking objects, glass in particular. There were sounds of fists hitting flesh, breaking furniture, splashing, tearing of clothes, even a ringing noise—I think the latter was just my own ears ringing from the melee. When Melissa's accomplices lunged at B-man, he grabbed one guy by the neck while the other guy and girl tried bringing him down. I tried to hold Melissa back, but the grappling mass that was B-man and the other three people fell into both of us and we ended up on the floor. Lorrie went after the girl accomplice, as they screamed and tugged at each other's hair. The beer pong table flew into the air and beer spilled over everybody. Ortiz grabbed one guy off      B-man and flung him into the corner of the room nearest to the pass out room door.

The sliding glass door flew open and people from outside piled in. Souza jumped in on the mob that formed around Ortiz and Melissa's accomplice. I quickly rose to my feet, but after taking a step, I slid on spilled beer from the beer pong table. I tried to stay upright, but somebody shoved me from behind and I tripped over someone, falling to my stomach. Melissa continued to scream as she hurled party cups, glasses, and anything else she could find on the kitchen counters at me. Then Lorrie ran in and a tussle between the two ensued. Everybody in sight was fighting! Partiers that I didn't know and hadn't seen began throwing anything and everything! A state of total chaos reigned in the house. I finally got back to my feet and in an almost possessed way, I scoped the kitchen and living room as though time had stopped.

I stood at the foot of the kitchen, behind me was Lorrie and Melissa pulling hair and clawing at each other on the linoleum, which was now soaked in beer, and riddled with broken glass and crushed party cups. To my left near the sliding glass door was Dolvar, who just punched another guy square in the face; they were falling backwards into the legs of the upside-down beer pong table. Billy was at the edge of the kitchen counter; he smashed a red party cup in someone's face as they tried to grab a glass and fling its contents at him. Thomas stood nearby. He horse-collared someone who lunged at Dolvar from behind. Thayer ran up to the sliding glass door, saw what was happening, then stayed outside, precariously guarding the grill.

In front of me near the doorway to the pass out room was Bomber and Tee, they restrained people who were trying to get into the fight. Next to them at the corner of the wall was a pile of people, where I saw Souza and Ortiz. They were grabbing shirt collars, throwing punches, and cursing like hell. I couldn't tell how many people were in the pile, and I wasn't sure if the people at the bottom of it would survive! Ms. Highlights was trying to pull people off the pile, while Marcus stood with an unlit cigarette in his mouth and threw random punches at random people.

To my right was Sammy, who had somebody in a backwards chokehold. B-man, on his feet, brawled with one of Melissa's male accomplices. The two were at the edge of the kitchen linoleum, exchanging blows. The lone female accomplice was back on her feet as well, but she bolted for the front door, holding her face. Klein and another guy were throwing haymakers at each other and mostly missing until the two tripped over the beer pong table. Nameless bolted out the front door, screaming for Pickens, whom I hadn't seen for a while. Then, most notable of all, was Zick and Joanne. The two were holding the microphones, standing on the couches, facing the massive brawl and singing passionately as though an audience roared in approval. The entire scene was absolutely surreal!

The brief window in which I scoped the epic party brawl faded back into reality for me when someone thumped me in the back of my head. The blow wasn't painful, but I saw a flash, and when I turned around, a tall guy stood with fists clinched as though he was preparing to put me out of my misery. Luckily, he swung as I ducked and grabbed his extended arm, flinging him onto the upside-down beer pong table. The sound of the guy slamming onto the plastic underside of the table was incredibly loud. He remained down, grabbing his back and moaning.

As best as I could tell, the gang was holding its own against all the other belligerents. Now free from fighting, I ran to Bomber and Tee to help restrain people. A can of beer nearly struck the three of us, we dodged it as it exploded against the wall. We looked in the direction where it came from and only one person in the vicinity wasn't engaged in the melee. I charged at him, grabbing him by the collar of his shirt. I spun him around to push him towards the sliding glass door, but he tripped over someone trying to get up from the beer drenched floor and we both fell.

"Fucker!" he said.

I held him down. "You're the fucker."

I slowly let him up, then he pushed off. "You need to leave, now. Get your friends and go."

"I'm Bosner, this is my friend's place, asshole."

He spit blood onto the linoleum. "You're a bitch ass!"

Just then, someone grabbed the guy from behind. It was Dolvar. When he resisted, Sammy jumped in. They pinned him down, he finally stopped fighting back. He got up, fixed the collar of his shirt, then went to the unraveling pileup in the corner to find his other friends. Things slowed down. B-man had the last accomplice in a headlock, and with Klein, the two aggressively walked the guy to the front door and shoved him out of the house. Some people left as Lorrie and Melissa, still in the kitchen, stopped fighting. Melissa bawled. Lorrie pinned her up against the drawers in the kitchen by the sink and questioned her about her actions. She wiped tears from her eyes and tried to clear her throat.

"Everyone here hates me. All I did was try to be good to everybody. Blaine doesn't want me, and Bosner doesn't want me either."

B-man approached the two as people throughout the house continued to get up, gather themselves, and leave.

"Blaine is all about the good time. He doesn't go any further than sleeping in the same bed! And Bosner, what in the fuck is this talk about him?" Lorrie asked her.

Standing there in a bit of shock, I could almost feel B-man glaring at me. I continued to face Lorrie and Melissa, but B-man's eyes were practically burning my cheek.

"He seemed lonely." Melissa said.

I opened my mouth to speak, but Lorrie waved at me to remain silent.

"…so I gave myself to him. Blaine couldn't care less. Either way, Bosner didn't like it." Melissa continued.

Lorrie faced me, and I once again opened my mouth to speak. Before I could get any words out, B-man shoved me.

"Bro, what is this shit? What the fuck is Melissa talking about?"

I put my hands out to try calming him. "B-man, listen. Nothing happened, I didn't let it."

He shoved me again. "What, so if I'm not officially with someone you think it's cool to just pounce?"

He tried to push me again. I had enough, so I grabbed his arms and ran him back towards the wall next to the sliding glass door.

"Cut this shit out! Nothing happened!" I said.

B-man grabbed me by my shirt near the shoulders and repulsed me. We both stood for a moment staring at each other. Bomber and Tee approached us both, poised to break up the next fight. Everything quieted down in the house, and most people had either stepped outside or left altogether. Lorrie approached B-man and I as Melissa remained in the kitchen, leaning up against the drawers. She quit sobbing and stood looking at us as we continued to stare each other down.

"Bro, why didn't you tell me? Melissa is crazy, sure. But you're better than that."

I flailed my hands. "That's where I fucked up. I didn't know what to say, or how to say it."

In an odd moment, Zick yelled into the mic at people as they left.

"Yea that's right fuckers. Leave. Don't fuck with us. This is our house! Thank you, thank you very much!" he rambled.

Joanne followed on the other mic. "Yep, what he said. Fuck off!"

Everyone forgot about the predicament between     B-man and I momentarily and marveled at Zick and Joanne. After a second, B-man faced Melissa.

"I'm not into you. I'm sorry, you're cool, but that's why I wouldn't go all in." he said.

She stared back at him as she wiped lingering tears from her eyes. Everyone stood on edge, unsure of what would happen next. Ortiz approached her, and at his height he was looking down at her face.

"You need to leave. It's probably best if you and your friends don't come back." he said.

We looked at him with a level of surprise. Melissa slightly nodded and walked towards the front door.

"I'm into you, honey!" a random dude called out.

Without facing him, she reached out and gave a middle finger as she continued out the front door. Ortiz stared at her with focus until she closed the door and was out of sight. After a moment or two, Bomber and Tee flipped the beer pong table back over. B-man, Lorrie, and I started cleaning up the mess. We did so in silence. I grabbed a broom and dustpan and began sweeping up broken glass. At that point, Zick and Joanne joined us, mopping up where I swept. The initial survey of the damage revealed broken glass, a little blood, puddles of beer on the floor, and cracked drywall in the corner where the brawling pileup had ensued. Among us, there was minimal injury; just a few bruises, some pulled hair, but no blood!

# 20. Seeing Pink

A few partiers remained at the house with the gang. I still wasn't very drunk, but that may have resulted from adrenaline from the fight. Dolvar lobbied everyone to cheer up and began passing out cups of beer. Bomber and Tee waved him off and made rounds to say goodbye. We thanked them for their help in calming down the fight and helping to clean up. As they left, people relaxed and commingled again, but I noticed Lorrie seemed distant. Her face was plain, and she looked as though she was deep in thought. I could only wonder why, but the unpleasant exchange between B-man and myself was the first thing that came to my mind. The melee damaged the beer pong table, the middle section bowed inward. We tried to straighten it out, but it was beyond repair. B-man set his cup of beer on the midsection of the table to gauge just how bowed inward it was. The beer in his cup sat mostly on one side, showing the unlevel nature. We laughed.

"Still isn't as bad as the ship." he said.

I smiled. "Nope. Sure isn't."

"How the hell do we follow up all that shit that just went down?" Billy asked.

Ortiz handed him a beer. "Drink more."

"If you assholes didn't bust the beer pong table we could still play, and I would whoop your asses!" Klein said.

Dolvar patted him on the back. "You lost. A lot."

Klein muttered to himself. Just then, the strangest thing happened. Out of nowhere, Ms. Highlights and Marcus walked up to the table where we stood and drank. Klein looked at them as his drunken foolishness completely took over.

"You fucked this whole thing up. I should be playing beer pong right now and you just sit there like all this shit is okay!"

Ms. Highlights looked startled. "Excuse me?"

The rest of us stood there, unsure of where Klein's outburst was going. Marcus looked at Klein and pointed at himself. Klein nodded.

"That's right motherfucker I'm talking to you. Pink shirted bitch."

B-man approached Klein. "Bro, we just got out of a fight. Chill."

Klein couldn't help himself. He was prepared to blame anyone he saw fit for how the night unfolded. As     B-man tried to grab him from behind, he lunged towards Marcus. In an almost graceful fashion, Marcus threw a perfect punch at Klein's face. The sound of the contact was clean. Klein fell backwards to the floor, holding his nose and crying. We looked at Marcus as we all stood speechless.

"Come on baby. Let's go." Marcus said as he took Ms. Highlights' hand.

They walked towards the front door, Marcus raised his cup and we raised ours. The two left. Klein remained on the floor, holding his face. I laughed more than anyone else; all night I kept looking at Marcus because of the oddity of his pink shirt. I never figured out why I was so fixated on something so random and obscure, but Klein's completely erratic behavior towards Marcus seemed to vindicate my suspicion. Lorrie got a paper towel and handed it to Klein, getting his attention. He got to his feet and looked at all of us, his eyes red and filled with tears. We tried not to laugh any more than we already had.

"I'm good. He tricked me!" Klein insisted.

We booed at him in response, and he slowly regained his composure. The night finally appeared calm! The TV continued to play karaoke tunes, but neither Zick nor Joanne sang. They became enamored with each other, showing their mutual affections on the couch. Lorrie still seemed detached, and Thomas began asking about partiers and where they went, and when. Ortiz gathered his things and left, but before doing so B-man and I thanked him for his help.      B-man offered him honorary status at future parties. After we said our goodbyes, Dolvar resumed trying to recount exactly when certain people came and left, and then Pickens' name came up. As I heard his name mentioned, I thought about where I put him, but then I remembered he left the house when Thayer arrived.

I chose not to tell Dolvar because I didn't want Pickens to suffer his destined fate if found.

It compelled Dolvar to find Pickens, and he started by searching the pass out room. He wasn't in there, and when Dolvar walked into B-man's room, he discovered someone passed out on the floor faced down. He woke the person up and ordered them to the pass out room. I followed Dolvar down the hall towards Penley and Anne's room. I was confident there was nobody in there. To my surprise, when Dolvar stormed in, there were screams. The room was dark, and the light that beamed in from the hallway revealed a woman, and another person who I couldn't recognize. For a split second, I thought maybe Pickens had returned to the room and was making love, but it was Souza and Nameless. Dolvar and I laughed.

"You fuckers always cock block! Damnit!" Souza snapped as he and Nameless ran to the bathroom.

Dolvar and I stood at the entrance to the bedroom for a moment, then Souza and Nameless hurried out of the bathroom, partially dressed. The two bolted into the living room and left. As they left, Souza ranted, "I know a place where we can go and not be intruded on!"

Dolvar looked confused. "So, Souza stole Pickens' girl?"

"I guess so. The bastard must've left the party sad or something."

The two of us walked into the living room. By now, everybody was eating Thayer's grill-ables. He did a good job on the grill and made the cheap London broils better than expected. I felt a buzz finally, and as I finished the steak,  B-man asked me to join him out front for a smoke. I normally didn't smoke, but occasionally during a party (particularly after heavy drinking) I partook with him. We walked out front and stood at the top of the steps, then lit up.

"Bro, did all that shit really happen?"

I took a puff. "Man, I told you. I didn't want to—"

"Nah bro, I'm talking about the fight. All that crazy shit that happened in there!"

"I'm still wondering if it was a nightmare, a dream, or a bad trip." I replied.

"There was some blood in there, but not from us. This place is sacred or something!" B-man said.

We both shared a laugh and fist bumped, then Lorrie came out. She reached towards B-man, gesturing for a cigarette. He handed his to her.

"How are you doing?" I asked.

She smirked and nodded as B-man put his arm around her.

"Lorrie, all that shit in there. I don't know what's going on. That all came out of nowhere." he said.

She tensed up. "No, it didn't. I don't think you meant any harm, but she didn't just create whatever the fuck that was in there."

B-man tried to respond, but she took one more puff off the cigarette and handed it back to him before returning inside. B-man faced the door for a moment, shaking his head.

"I don't know what the hell…"

It was pretty clear to me what was going on. I finally decided I had to speak up.

"Lorrie wants you. If I were you, I would go for it."

He stared at me like he was going to say something back, but before the conversation could continue, we both heard snoring from beyond the porch railing. B-man and I both looked in the direction it came from. Beyond the railing was a bush, but it was too dark to see beneath it where the source of the snoring came from. We both went down the steps to the bushes and kneeled to see who it was. To our shock, it was Pickens!

"Get the fuck outta here!" B-man said.

I laughed at first, but then tried to keep my voice down. We both reached down to grab him.

"Damn, he's freezing. Glad he's still alive. I wonder how long he's been out here." I said.

"Bro, he's been here awhile, I think since Thayer came."

I patted Pickens on the cheek to revive him.

"This boy…I tried to protect him but he set himself up for failure." I said.

Pickens wouldn't wake up, so we tried to prop him up using our shoulders and walk him back into the house. At the foot of the steps, the front door opened and out came Lorrie with her jacket on and her purse in hand. Distracted, B-man relaxed his shoulder, I almost dropped Pickens.

"Lorrie, are you leaving?" he asked.

"Blaine, the house is fairly cleaned up. I'm ready to go. I'll see you later."

Lorrie reached the sidewalk and began walking off into the dark as B-man followed her. I stood there trying to keep Pickens upright for a moment before sitting him up against the side of the steps. I followed the two. B-man pleaded with Lorrie to come back as both of them walked down the street. I felt partly responsible for the ordeal since it was my reluctance to speak up about Melissa that led to most of the tension. I ran past the two and stopped them.

"Lorrie, will you talk for a minute? That whole thing with Melissa is a big misunderstanding, I promise!" I said.

She glared into my eyes, and I could see tears forming in hers. B-man tried putting his arm around her, but she pulled it off. He tried to explain.

"Lorrie, I'm not into Melissa and I never—"

"She was just a cozy pal or something Blaine, I get it!"

He opened his mouth, but only one word came out. "I…"

"You what, Blaine?"

"I…" he repeated.

"You're a trip! Have a good fucking night!"

At that moment, I took matters into my own hands.

"You two, will you stop this bullshit and figure out whatever the hell it is you both want?" I asked.

They both faced me. I let my feelings rest on my sleeve. "Yea, I'm talking to you both. Lorrie—B-man isn't the best at explaining his feelings, but he sure as fuck wasn't interested in Melissa. That her and I even got into whatever the fuck you want to call it, that's reality. The reality that    B-man wouldn't show her interest! You know who he shows an interest in? You! B-man—Lorrie put up with Melissa being close to you and stuck around anyway… why you lolly-gagged until now, I don't know, but here's your chance!"

I almost impressed myself with the candor, but then the house we stood in front of lit up and the front door opened. A neighbor stared, and I knew I needed to return to Pickens. For a long second, I glared at both B-man and Lorrie.

"You two have it. Everyone sees, except for the two of you. Figure it out. I'm heading back in." I finished.

I swiftly walked back towards the house, leaving    B-man and Lorrie on the dark street. To my horror, as I approached the house, I saw someone standing above Pickens. It was Dolvar! His pants were unzipped and was preparing to win his bet. I ran full speed to stop him, but he started peeing, some of it landing on Pickens' slumped shoulder. I grabbed Dolvar to pull him away.

"Dolvar, no! You win. It's all good. You got him on the shoulder a little. That's good enough!"

Heavily intoxicated, he pushed off and stumbled backwards. "A bet's a fucking bet!"

"Sure is! You won, you also got him. Now turn and piss over there!" I ordered.

He obliged. Then, I saw B-man slowly walking towards the house from the street with his head lowered. Lorrie was nowhere to be found. I nudged Dolvar to go back into the house, then I approached B-man.

"She called a friend to come get her and told me to leave…" he said.

We both stood briefly on the front lawn.

"Its been a long night. Give her a little space and time." I replied.

"I like her. I wasn't trying to hook up with either of them. Things just happened, but Lorrie is the one."

I patted him on the back and then signaled for him to help me get Pickens in the house. I did my best to avoid contacting the piss-soaked section of Pickens' shoulder.     B-man begrudgingly helped, and as we slugged Pickens inside, Dolvar barked aloud. He was holding two cups of beer and gesturing to everyone inside that he won the bet. They laughed, and I tried to seem pleased even though I felt bad. B-man and I laid him in the pass out room and then joined everyone. Nobody mentioned Lorrie leaving, it was understood that it wasn't on the best of terms. Zick was feeling bold and began giving out shots of whiskey to those willing to take them. I was one of the willing.

I had two shots of whiskey, and after being prompted to talk about the history of the Roman Empire by Billy, I rambled into a blur. Everyone but B-man seemed entertained by my incessantly drunk rambling. He was neither upset nor sad, just blank faced. Dolvar, still proud of winning his bet, tried doing a handstand. Once vertical, he fell going the other way and slammed onto the coffee table. He seemed okay, and luckily there was no glass to worry about. Thomas tried singing karaoke, but he couldn't figure out how to connect the microphone; Zick and Joanne were too busy with each other to tell him how. I continued rambling, I think, but to whom and about what, I don't remember. Eventually, I went to get some water, but after blinking, everything went dark.

# 21. Johnny's for Klein

A car sped by on the street and somewhere in the house a tune played. I opened my eyes to the usual morning light, always blinding and unpleasant. I tried clearing my throat, but I gave out a relentless cough. To my surprise, I was partially sitting up. With my eyes finally open and able to see, I found myself still in the living room, propped up on a wall. The tune was the TV, someone had turned the volume down low, but the karaoke music continued to play. My left eye hurt, and when I touched that area, it was tender and sore. Zick and Joanne were on the couch with a blanket. Dolvar was lying face down on the hard floor at the foot of the TV entertainment center. I got to my feet and stumbled down the hallway towards the bathroom.

I took a long piss, then went to the sink to run some water over my face. I put my hands under the faucet and patted it gently. When I looked into the mirror, I saw I had a black eye! I couldn't remember getting a black eye, but it explained the tender pain. After cleaning up, I returned to the living room. Klein crept out of the pass out room looking terrible. He had bruising around his nose and his eyes still looked rough; I wasn't sure how much of that was from drinking and how much was from crying.

"Bosner. What happened?" he asked.

"You got punched out by a guy in a pink shirt." Zick answered.

"Thanks a lot, fucker."

Zick raised his arm from the covers and gave a middle finger salute. Klein shook his head, then looked back at me.

"What happened to you? Pink guy attack both of us?"

"No. They left, and I was fine last time I remembered. I don't know what happened." I said.

Joanne poked her head out from the covers.

"Someone's girlfriend punched you because you passed out with your eyes open." she replied.

Klein and I looked at her, then each other. We fist bumped.

"Great, I get  hit by a pink shirted asshole, and you get punched by a girl for sleeping with your eyes open."

I looked out the sliding glass door to assess the damage. One keg was lying on its side, the other remained upright and presumably had beer left in it. Looking at the kegs made me thirsty, so I got an unused cup and poured water from the kitchen sink. Dolvar mumbled from the floor, then rose to his feet. He stretched and went charging towards the closet. He flung the door open and then a commotion sounded. Klein and I ran to the closet entrance, and inside Dolvar and Sammy wrestled.

"Asshole, I didn't forget what you did!" Dolvar yelled.

"I told you if you fuck with me, I'd whoop you!" Sammy replied.

Klein entered the closet to break the two up. "What are you wusses whining about?"

"I was just messing with Sammy."

"I was relaxing on the floor out there, and Dolvar kept trying to give me a wet willy. I laid him out and slept in here because it's more comfortable!"

*God, the things that happen AFTER I black out!* I thought to myself.

"Bring that shit out here, ladies!" Klein taunted.

The two finally stopped quarreling and slowly emerged from the closet. Once out, Dolvar glared at Sammy, then they fist bumped.

"Good one. Clown."

Zick and Joanne went out back for a smoke break, and I checked on B-man. My last recollection of him was not good. There was laughter at the end of the night, except for him. I knocked on his bedroom door but heard nothing. I slowly opened it and peered in. Laying atop of the covers with his arms behind his head staring at the ceiling, B-man was wide awake.

"Did you sleep at all?"

"Bro, last night…"

I entered the room. "Is over with. Today is the Super Bowl! The Giants!"

He smiled bleakly. "I know. I'm excited. Just bummed about the other shit."

Dolvar entered and jumped on B-man. "The Giants! The Giants! They are going to…"

"Lose!" Sammy interrupted.

Dolvar leapt off the air mattress and ran after him.  B-man laughed as I reached out to pull him up.

"Get your ass up! Today we are going to focus on good shit!" I said.

We both entered the living room.

"Breakfast beers for anyone?" he asked.

I shook my head. "Oh no. Let's get some grub and worry about beer later."

Thomas and Billy emerged from the pass out room followed by a few others. One was a random girl who approached me. I didn't recall seeing her the night before. She looked closely at my face.

"You were creepy last night." she said.

"I don't even know or remember you. When did you get here?"

She patted me on the cheek and gathered her belongings. A guy came out of the pass out room and held her.

"Babe, is that the guy you punched?"

"Creepy for falling asleep? Really?" I said.

The guy shook his head. "I'm sorry that happened. Apparently, your eyes were open as you snored, and that bugged her out."

"And who are you?" I asked.

He smiled as we shook hands. "I'm Ray, but you can call me 'Bisbee'. This is my fiancé, Linda. I'm a friend of    B-man's but GO PATRIOTS!"

B-man gave him the middle finger salute as I remained confused.

"Great. I'm always hurting when I wake up at this place." I said.

Bisbee looked at me awkwardly. "I don't follow?"

Zick laughed. "Bosner is just grumpy because he always wakes up hurting. Last week, his ass hurt."

There was some laughter, but not from me. "No, that was two weeks ago!"

Linda appeared confused as well. "Um, okay?"

Just then, Pickens emerged from the pass out room. Everybody cheered as he waved for us to quiet down.

"My head… oh God, and why is my shoulder wet? What's that smell?"

We looked at Dolvar, who was grinning from ear to ear. I approached Pickens and almost put my arm around him before remembering what the wetness was from. I got him a cup of water and asked him if he had a ride home. Bisbee and Linda offered to give Pickens a ride on the condition that he wash his shirt to rid it of the nasty odor. We settled on duct taping the area of his shoulder that was wet. Our blissful attitude kept Pickens from realizing his pee drenched shoulder, and he was too hungover to realize why we insisted on duct taping it. Thankfully, it was good enough for Bisbee and Linda to give him a ride. As the couple and Pickens made their way to the door, his head bobbed up.

"Wait! The bet! Who won—"

We waved, and in unison, said, "Later Pickens!"

As the front door closed and the three walked to the curb and entered the couple's car, we laughed. After getting another cup of water and sitting next to Zick and Joanne, I scoped the living room and kitchen. The inward bowing beer pong table and the damaged dry wall in the corner between the entryway to the pass out room served as reminders of the wild previous night.

"You know, it's amazing how we seem to get away with what we do in this house and the place is still intact." I said.

"Did anybody here get bloody?" Joanne asked.

Amazingly, we all looked at each other and the answer was no.

"Magical place, this is." Thomas said.

"Bro, the weekend isn't over yet. Super Bowl!!!"

We all cheered.

"Yea man, so what's the deal? Are we watching it here?" I asked.

"What do you think?" Dolvar said.

Billy twirled an empty party cup on the table.

"I think you need cable or satellite to tune in. Last time I checked, you have neither." he said.

Nobody thought to ask B-man or Dolvar if they installed cable or anything. Since I had been coming over, we always watched DVDs or simply played music. Before I could even say anything, I looked at B-man and saw his face turn glum.

"I'll call and see if I can get it now."

"Good luck with that. It's Sunday and trying to get cable on the same day? Yea, Bosner has a better chance of getting slugged in the other eye for sleeping with one open." Thomas said as he winked at me.

B-man dialed up the cable company on his phone and walked into his room.

"So, how would your grandpa rate this weekend so far?" Billy asked.

I grinned. I believed he would laugh at what happened. Craziest of all, the party already featured drinking, music, stupid fights, and drama. I couldn't see it getting any wilder.

"I never expected this weekend to be boring. If he was here, I doubt he would either." I replied.

Thayer emerged from the pass out room and gave out a loud yawn. He walked to the fridge and pulled out a foil covered plate containing leftovers. He plopped the plate next to the sink and with his bare hands began eating a cold steak.

"Thayer, really? You know we could always do Johnny's!" Joanne said.

With a mouth full of food, Thayer turned and nodded. "Let's do that too!"

"Is there anyone else left in the pass out room?" I asked.

Zick got up from the couch and walked into the room. He came back out and nodded. "There's a girl in there."

"Oh, that's Tina!" Thayer announced.

We stared at him.

"She liked the food." he added.

Dolvar laughed. "That's better than her liking Bosner sleeping with his eyes open."

"Hey asshole, another girl did!" I replied.

"That was Linda, right? Her man's name was Bisbee, I believe?" Thayer added.

"Good memory, when did they show up? My eye remembers better than my brain does…"

Thomas laughed. "They got here late. You were rambling to Bisbee about the fall of Rome, but he was more interested in talking about the Super Bowl."

Dolvar raised his fist. "GO GIANTS."

"Anyway." Thomas continued. "He gave up on you when you changed topics to the Coliseum."

"It pays to stay awake!" Billy said.

Thayer had other things on his mind. "Bisbee told me he liked Carolina style barbeque."

"Thayer, is there anything you like more than food?" Thomas asked.

"Tina is good."

Joanne perked up. "You and Tina, last night?"

Thayer smiled and nodded. "Well, food is good, but there are exceptions."

B-man came out of his room and finished up his conversation on the phone. It didn't sound like it was going well. He angrily hung up and announced that cable was not an option.

"What is this bullshit about not being able to install cable today!" he lamented.

Billy threw a party cup at him. "Why did you wait until just now to get it installed?"

"We work hard all week, and when we get home we're tired. It's not like we have time to call these damned people to get things like cable set up." Dolvar said.

"You work all week, and then get off and get shit faced. Yea, busy life man." Thomas replied.

Dolvar playfully pushed him.

"Maybe satellite?" I suggested.

B-man looked up at me with an angry glare. "Maybe breakfast instead?"

Joanne nodded with approval, and Thayer seconded. Just then, Tina walked out of the pass out room. As she was the last person up, everybody cheered. She waved us off as she approached Thayer and hugged him. Tina looked to be Thayer's perfect match. She was tall like Thayer, and voluptuous. Even better, Tina had an SUV, which meant if she came with us to breakfast, one of us didn't have to drive. Unfortunately, B-man called dibs on riding with someone before I could, and the group as usual looked to me to be a driver. Everybody gathered themselves, everyone but Sammy, Klein, and B-man rode in Tina's SUV. As Tina drove off for Johnny's with most of the group, I went to Green Beater and cleaned out the back seat. I watched      B-man closely to see how he was holding up. I was certain that the only way for him to enjoy anything was if his beloved Giants won the Super Bowl.

"A big bacon cheeseburger sounds really fucking good right about now." he said.

Klein tapped me on the shoulder. "So what is this place, a chain?"

"No, it's some diner that Lorrie turned us on to."

"Just get the big bacon cheeseburger, it's the best!" Sammy said.

We agreed. Klein sat back in the seat and looked unsure.

"So, B-man. Are you gonna be okay today?" I asked.

"Bro, I'm okay… just wish last night ended up a little different."

"Join the club! I got clocked!" Klein interjected.

Sammy laughed. "You had it coming. You went full dick mode on that Marcus dude."

"Shit, I got punched for sleeping…"

"Bro, it was spooky! Who sleeps with their eyes open?"

I shook my head. "Now I have to deal with all the stares."

"What happened to Lorrie? Like, she was at the party, and then she wasn't." Klein asked.

We were silent, then B-man looked over at me. Klein assumed I did something.

"I tried to calm shit down after the Melissa fiasco. Took a lot out of everyone including Lorrie." I explained.

Klein's eyes opened wide. "Dude, for real… were you messing around with Melissa? That fight was wicked last night!"

Sammy gestured at him to drop the topic.

I put my hand up. "It's okay Sammy." I looked into the rearview mirror at Klein. "I didn't mess with Melissa. She's just wild and when she doesn't get her way she tries to play with other people."

Klein scoffed. "Dude, she's hot. I would've—"

B-man turned and faced him. He stopped.

"Listen, that's not how I roll. I hope she's okay and I hope Lorrie gets over the ordeal. The whole thing was a stupid mess. The rest of the night was good. I have a black eye to prove it!" I said.

We arrived at Johnny's and I parked next to Tina's SUV. The rest of the gang was already inside and seated when the four of us entered, Connie was chatting with them. When she saw the rest of us walk in, she walked up and hugged us each. We introduced her to Klein, and then we took the booth just behind the rest of the group. Connie ran coffee out to us, except for B-man who got a soda instead.

she asked us how we were doing, but before any of us responded, she saw my eye.

"Oh lord, what did you get into?"

Klein, Sammy, and B-man laughed. "He got into a fight with a girl."

She gave a flustered look.

"What they meant was that I fell asleep with my eyes open, and a girl punched me to see if I was alive." I said.

She smiled. "Ah, honey, you gotta watch out for that. They'll getcha every time!"

We looked at each other and nodded with approval. she asked us for our order. We got what we knew was the best thing on Johnny's limited menu. Klein looked up and down the menu.

"Okay, so for real. What's good here?" he asked.

Connie, chewing gum, smiled and took a step back. Everyone faced him.

"The Big Bacon Cheeseburger!"

Other patrons and even the cooks looked at our group and nodded.

"Oookay... Big bacon cheeseburger, please?"

Connie remained standing over the table. Klein looked flustered.

"He'll take that with fries and a pickle slice." I finished.

Connie smiled and nodded. "Coming right up, honey."

We sat at the booth quiet for a moment, then Thayer faced B-man from the other booth.

"So, what exactly happened last night?"

"What do you think? Where the hell were you?" Sammy said.

B-man faced him back. "Bro, where were you for real? Out freeloading off the grill?"

Thayer scoffed and smiled.

"He was freeloading on me, assholes." Tina replied.

Thayer flinched suddenly as we heard a hand smacking him below the table. Everyone sighed. I filled the two new love birds in on what happened the night before. I explained to them how the fighting started with Melissa and her group showing up and so on and so forth. We asked him for details on how he was "freeloading on Tina" from outside in the cold. They provided an interesting story of using the picnic table, and how they almost knocked the grill over while getting frisky to the melee that was going on in the house. It almost sounded unreal, but most of what happened the night before was unreal to us all, so whether or not it was true, we rolled with it.

The food eventually arrived, and just like the rest of us had, Klein looked in awe at the large and very affordable big bacon cheeseburger that sat on the plate before him. He took the first bite and seemed to enjoy it. We enjoyed our respective big bacon cheeseburgers, fries, and pickle slices. Thayer ordered an extra side of fries to go, as usual, but that time he claimed he needed the calorie intake to offset what he was going to burn when he and Tina "faced off" later that day. Once we finished up, we asked for the check, and      B-man invited Connie over for the Super Bowl party.

"I'm married, boys." she said.

We stood up to stretch and gather our things, then she returned with the check.

"But I don't see him except maybe twice a month, I know about two of his girlfriends, and the kids are out of house. So, maybe I'll stop in." she continued.

We nodded and then scrounged up the cash in our pockets to put on the table as our tip. I saw a few $20 bills in the pile and figured we met our standards. We bunched back up in the same vehicles and headed back to Cape Henry House. There was nothing but small talk on the way back, but Sammy and Klein got into a flatulence contest in the back seat so for the first time, I allowed smoking in the car to offset the stench. B-man lit up, and I turned up the tunes to focus on things other than the awful smells.

# 22. Boobs, Booze, and Ball!

We got to the house first, and I parked out front nearest to the front door. When we entered, Lorrie stood in the kitchen while the rest of us stood in an awkward silence. She bought a large plant in a pot and placed it in the corner to conceal the damaged drywall.

"Hi boys!" she greeted.

It shocked me to see her, and I nudged B-man to get him to approach. Sammy and Klein waved at her.

"Where's Melissa?" Klein asked.

B-man approached Lorrie. "I don't care."

The two embraced, then B-man took her hand and led her to his room. Sammy, Klein, and I looked at each other and shrugged. I looked out front and saw that the rest of the gang had arrived. I sought Dolvar to discuss the situation with the Super Bowl. He was out front with Zick, Joanne, and Thomas, cracking jokes.

"So, what should we do for the game?" I asked.

"Ask B-man, clown."

"Yea, uh he's busy for a bit. We need to figure something out."

"Busy with what?" Zick asked.

"He's just busy."

I realized they were unaware that Lorrie was in the house.

"Never mind. He invited Connie over for a party we can't have if we don't have the Super Bowl on here."

"Do you have an antenna setup, by chance?" Thomas asked.

Dolvar perked up. "Actually, Penley has one in his room!"

He ran into the house as Zick, Joanne, Thomas, and I remained outside.

"Fuck it. Let's get a beer." Zick said.

We went inside and proceeded to the back patio where Thayer, Tina, and Billy already were. They got some beer out of the second keg as I gathered cups to get beers for the rest. We stood around sipping beers and gossiping about the mayhem of the night before. After a bit, Zick and I peered into the house to see just what Dolvar was up to on the TV. He seemed to struggle to get the antenna to work. Zick and I went inside to see if we could help him. He stood staring at the TV and the antenna atop of it; the channels were all fuzzy. Zick reached for the antenna and began playing with its position to see if he could get better reception. When he held it over his head at a certain angle, the picture came in mildly better, but was still not good.

Dolvar and I stood back while Zick went into electrician mode. He put the antenna down and went blazing through cabinets and drawers in the kitchen.

"What are you doing?" Dolvar asked.

Zick continued rummaging. "Looking for extra wiring. Do you have any by chance?"

"Mad scientist Zick?" I joked.

He continued speeding through the cabinets and drawers.

"Penley might have some in his room. He likes to dabble in electrical shit." Dolvar added.

Zick finished looking in the kitchen, dejected. "I don't want to go through his stuff… that's not right."

Dolvar patted him on the shoulder. "I'll look. We are already on their shit list and I'm not missing this game."

Zick and I got our beers and sat on the couches. He pulled his shirt back, revealing some love marks on his shoulder from Joanne, and I recounted my battle wounds from a few weeks prior. We laughed about it for a minute, then heard B-man and Lorrie doing stuff in the bedroom. Dolvar hurried down the hall with a wad of wires. He was so focused on the TV situation that he didn't know what Zick or I were talking about when we mentioned the bedroom sounds. Dolvar asked us about how to use the wires. As far as I could tell, we hooked up the antenna and still didn't get good enough reception. Zick had other plans, however, as he returned to the kitchen drawers and retrieved electrical tape. He explained he was going to splice the wiring and lace it so he could run it outside, hoping to find a height location where the antenna itself could deliver a good signal. Dolvar and I stood there confused, but hopeful. Zick had Dolvar hold the wire on one end from the TV as he took the other end and ran out back. I followed him.

Zick went out back with one end of the mysterious wire and the antenna console. I followed him through the yard while everyone on the patio wondered what we were doing. They all convened at the fence by a telephone pole as Zick began climbing. At that point, he held the antenna console in one hand, hugging the telephone pole with the other, and biting onto the wire and electrical tape. I remained confused about what exactly was going on.

"Geez Zick, if you like gymnastics you could've stayed at the Rec Center on base!" Sammy joked.

"Why is he up there doing that when he's not even a Giants fan?" Billy asked.

I looked at Joanne. "Can't say I've ever seen Zick climbing around like this before. Have you?"

"Only on cars." she replied.

Everyone watched and waited for Zick to say something. He was hell bent on getting the antenna set up. Finally, he finished what he was doing and climbed back down the telephone pole. He used the wire to wrap around the pole and hold the antenna console below the insulators and wires. I wasn't sure exactly what I was looking at; I don't think anyone else did either. Zick walked through the group and back into the house. He was quiet and determined. We followed him into the house to the TV, where he took the other end of the wire that Dolvar held and connected it behind the console. Sure enough, the channel came in pretty good! We clapped and whistled. Unfortunately, it was the wrong channel, and it was the only channel that came in. Zick tried to rearrange the wiring, but to no avail. He snapped, smacking his fist on the wall. Dolvar was sympathetic. We now knew we had to go somewhere to watch the game.

Zick went outside to drink his beer, smoke, and relax. We talked for a bit, then he dismantled the elaborate setup he constructed. We went out back and watched Zick climb back up the telephone pole to dismantle his concoction. At that point, B-man and Lorrie emerged from the house. Most of the gang didn't realize she returned so they stared and smiled.

"What the fuck did we miss?" Lorrie asked.

She was holding B-man's hand as they came outside, both wearing Giants gear.

"Oi!" Dolvar called out.

B-man looked like a million bucks. He patted Dolvar on the head, then looked at the telephone pole.

"For real bro, what the hell did we miss?"

Zick finished unfastening his wire setup and climbed down.

"Zick wanted to show off his mad gymnastic skills." I joked.

"Sorry guys, I tried. We're going to have to go somewhere to watch the game." Zick said.

Lorrie smiled. "You're such a sweetheart. Blaine or Dolvar should've gotten their asses up there. This is their game."

"It's America's game!" Thomas added, as Lorrie stuck her tongue out at him.

"We have time guys, let's have another beer and figure out where we are going to watch it." I said.

Thayer nodded. "Time for a snack too."

He walked back to the picnic table where his container of fries sat; everybody scoffed. We refilled our cups with beer and went inside. Everyone sat in the living room in silence. There was a feeling of rejection about the game not being available at the house. We brainstormed places we could go to watch the game. The primary concern was we were too late to go anywhere and get good seating.

"Greenies is always the fallback." Zick said.

"Bro, Greenies is good for everything except a Giants Super Bowl. Greenies has the worst TVs."

"What about C.T. Slaters?" Billy added.

Lorrie shook her head. "We kinda got kicked out of that place."

"What about that wing joint? Bill's Buffalo whatever?" Sammy said.

"That place is impossible to get into, even on a regular Sunday." Dolvar replied.

Joanne, sensing the dejection, cracked a joke. "We can sit here and have Bosner tell us the history of the Super Bowl. That should cover the length of the game."

Even I laughed at the idea. B-man got a brief kick out of it, but then went back to sulking. Lorrie held his arm and whispered words of comfort into his ear.

"You two shacked up quick." Tina said.

B-man looked at her, smiling. "Buy me a plant to cover some shit broken in my house and you get special treatment."

Lorrie pushed off, then punched him in the arm.

"Focus, people... what are our options for this game?" Dolvar said.

Everyone seemed spent on ideas, then Thomas stood up. "Let me make a phone call. I might have an idea."

Thomas went outside to make the call. Everyone remained in the living room except for Billy and I; we went out back to get everyone a refill of beer. We returned and sat back down on the couches while everyone looked out front at Thomas, who was pacing back and forth on the phone. Finally, he returned.

"Alright people. We're going to E.Z. Girlz."

Everyone stared at him.

"Bro, Sunday funday is one thing, but Giants in the Super Bowl is another."

"Exactly. We are going to watch it there!" Thomas replied.

We looked at each other.

"Explain." Lorrie said.

Zick smiled. "Boobs, booze, and ball. I like it."

Joanne playfully pushed him.

"I second that!" Klein added.

B-man wasn't having it. "Get the fuck out of here. That place? Like, it's too small to even hold a big screen TV, let alone a couple of Giants fans!"

"Hey, I go in there for their 'Thirsty Thursday' specials. Not too bad of a place." Billy said.

"I bet if they had 'Feasty Friday' Thayer would be all up in that shit." I joked.

Thayer's face lit up. "Damn straight!"

"Guys! Focus." Lorrie said.

"I have connections. It's a good setup for the game and they don't have many people. $20 for all you can eat, and drinks are half off. Shit, beers are already like $3 on a normal day." Thomas explained.

Thayer stood up, rudely pulling Tina up with him. "I like it. Let's do it. Let's do it now!"

Zick looked up at Thayer. "Okay, chill. There will be plenty of food and drinks, I'm sure."

Lorrie looked at B-man. "Hun, that sounds pretty good to me. Plus, you'll get to see plenty of boobs either way."

"Okay, so the choices are a Bosner history lesson here, or—" Joanne paused.

Sammy enthusiastically interrupted. "Boobs, booze, and ball!!!"

Klein repeated him, then Thomas, Billy, and me. Before I knew it, everyone was on their feet stomping and chanting the three easiest words in a male's vocabulary.      B-man capped off the chant as he and Dolvar chest bumped.

"Fuck it, boobs, booze, and ball! GO GIANTS!"

A decision finally came, and as always, they appointed me as a driver. Dolvar ran into his closet and emerged fully dressed in Giants gear. Thayer agreed to drive Tina's SUV so she could drink. We gathered whatever we thought we needed and got into the two vehicles. The drive to E.Z. Girlz wasn't too long, but it was a seedy-looking place on the other side of town. Some of us saw Billy and Thomas in a new light, knowing they frequented there. The rest of us were familiar with the venue— but it didn't seem exciting under normal circumstances. When we got into Green Beater, Sammy sat up front, and in the back seat was Billy, B-man, and Lorrie.

The drive to E.Z. Girlz was typical. Sammy did his best to annoy B-man about the game, and who was going to win. The rest of us just sat in the car enjoying their hostile back and forth. B-man was more than just a fan, he was passionate about the New York Giants. In my experiences watching games with him, he didn't handle losses well or trash talk from other fans. I was hoping for a Giants' win simply because they were as big of an underdog as any team entering the championship.

Once on the freeway, I mistakenly took the wrong exit; Thayer followed me, and we both pulled into a gas station. I took advantage of the mistake to top off the fuel in Green Beater. As I pumped, two homeless looking men standing in front of the store saw B-man and Lorrie sitting in the back seat sporting Giants gear. They began rooting.    B-man, feeling ever so boastful, got out of the car and walked up to the men. They shook hands and discussed the game and the potential outcomes. I finished filling up while Thayer and company stayed parked behind us. Dolvar ran out of the SUV to use the bathroom, so I walked up and stood with B-man. We talked to the men about the game, then as Dolvar returned we finished up our conversation. The men wished B-man and Dolvar good luck. Then we got back in the vehicles and were off.

Since I had gotten off at the wrong exit, I had to take two extra left turns and then drive an additional mile on a freeway access road to get to E.Z. Girlz. When I pulled into the club parking lot, it reminded me of how obscure E.Z. Girlz was. The building was a small brick and mortar shop-like structure with a large blinking sign that flashed "E.Z." then "Girlz" in tandem above the entrance. The few parking spaces in front closest to the front door were unavailable, so we parked on the side of the building by a pair of dumpsters. B-man was anxious, but the rest of us remained hopeful that we would have a good time. Thayer parked to the left of us, and his group quickly exited the SUV, showing much more enthusiasm than everyone who rode with me. Lorrie continued to try cheering B-man up. As we walked around the side of the building to the front entrance, he shook his head.

"I'm going to pretend that watching the game here is good luck. Don't any of you start…"

Sammy and Thomas walked behind the rest of us and snickered.

# 23. E.Z. Win

As we entered the club, there was a narrow corridor lined with plank board walls. A large bouncer stood at the doorway on the other end that led to the clubroom. The smell of perfume and the sound of a loud bass was immediately noticeable. We approached the bouncer slowly. He was tall, with facial piercings and a notable afro dyed in a variety of colors, the lighting made it hard to distinguish them. The bouncer put his hand out, signaling us to stop.

"Okay kids. You know the drill."

Dolvar and Billy stood at the front of the group. They both looked back at Thomas, who nudged his way to the front.

"Hey, I'm a friend of Randy's. Brought my peeps here to catch the game. We brought cash."

The bouncer stared at him for a minute. "Cool. I still need to see I.D. Your peeps look like they just got outta diapers."

We got out our IDs and stacked them in the bouncer's hand. He thumbed through them and handed them back as we walked into the clubroom, single file. The clubroom wasn't large, to the left was a bar with a projection screen draped down the middle. There was an older man sitting at the edge of the bar sipping on a shot of liquor and bottle of beer, then a large man sitting in the middle facing the screen. He sported a Patriots jersey. Straight ahead was a dance floor with poles and lowered seating for customers. To the right was a wall with three doors, presumably for private sessions with the strippers. In front of the three doors was a fold-out table lined with chips, dip, and finger foods. To our immediate right was another table with two strippers wearing tight tank tops revealing their upper body features. The music was blaring, so it was hard to hear them. I was the fourth person in line within our group, and I saw as everyone paid them cash for a wristband.

"Twenty, sweetheart!" One yelled into my ear.

She had jet black hair and glitter lipstick on. I had to maintain my composure. I handed her two $10 bills. "Yep! Here you are!"

As I walked into the middle of the clubroom, B-man and Dolvar gathered at the bar facing the projection screen. The pre-game coverage of the game had begun. The large Patriots fan tapped B-man on the shoulder and the two struck up a conversation. Dolvar soon gravitated towards the them and joined in. I couldn't hear what they discussed because of the loud music, but they appeared to be getting along. Thayer went straight for the food while Billy and Klein stood at the end of the bar looking to order a drink, Tina was just behind them looking at Thayer. Sammy and Lorrie stood next to me. We simply looked around to scope out the odd layout of the club.

"I thought this place would be worse than this!" Sammy said.

I laughed. "What can I say? Thomas got us the hook up!"

I realized I didn't see him in the club, nor did I see Zick and Joanne. In that moment, I let it go, figuring they were using the bathroom or something. Lorrie stepped up to the bar and spoke with B-man, Dolvar, and the Patriots fan. The dark-haired dancer remained seated at the table by the doorway. She looked at me and waved; I realized I was staring at her. I waved back and tried to act busy. Thayer was loading a plate with food, and I followed suit.

"Thayer! Did Thomas, Zick, or Joanne go back outside?" I asked.

"Thomas? He came in here. He was in front of me!"

I turned and faced the bar and screen; to the left at the edge of the bar where Billy and Klein were standing, a man, woman, and then Thomas came out of a back door. The woman looked like she was a stripper that happened to be tending the bar. Billy, Klein, and Tina placed drink orders while Thomas stood with the man. The two walked towards me, then Thomas introduced us. His name was Randy, the owner of the establishment. He was a bit overweight, my height, with slick back hair, and he wore an ugly light blue button up. We shook hands as he welcomed me to E.Z. Girlz.

"Hey man, thanks for having us! We didn't have anywhere else to catch the game!" Thomas said.

Randy laughed, revealing a few gold teeth. "Shit, this was our first go. Never did an event for the Super Bowl. Dead so far. Hopefully it picks up! Just glad you came; this is a decent sized group!"

He patted Thomas and I on the shoulder and walked around the bar as the bartender readied orders. Randy pulled out a microphone from behind the bar and made an announcement.

"Hey everybody, listen up! Thanks for coming out, and big shout out to Thomas and company! We hope for a good game tonight, and for everyone here now, first drink is on me! Lydia, pour 'em and shore 'em! Oh, and there's food! Looks like one of you found it!"

Everybody looked at Thayer, who turned around upon hearing Randy's jab. Facing the bar and everyone else, he waved as we laughed. The old guy seated by Billy and Klein raised his shot glass and whistled. Lydia winked at me as I placed an order for a beer. She slid it to me. *I ain't that easy!* I thought to myself. Dolvar and B-man stayed glued to the projection screen and were jawing in friendly fashion with the Patriots fan. Lorrie sat next to B-man, who remained standing. I walked back to the table of food and got a plate of chips, dip, vegetables, ham slices, and cheese. Kickoff began, then the loud music changed over to loud audio of the game. Thayer and I remained standing for the time being, then Sammy joined us.

The club remained mostly quiet as far as attendance throughout the first quarter of the Super Bowl, but just after the second quarter started, people began arriving. By then, B-man and Dolvar took seats near Lorrie and the Patriots fan. Billy and Klein sat at the lowered customer seats near the stage and faced the projection screen. Thomas continued to talk with Randy and a few of the strippers. I realized Thomas was a sort of fixture at E.Z. Girlz. Thayer, Sammy, and I joked about Thomas' VIP type status at the obscure stripper joint, then a patron approached us. He seemed to have an eye for me.

"Aye. You!" The patron said.

Sammy and Thayer tried to hide their laughter and stepped away. I tried briefly to pretend that I didn't notice the strange patron, an older man slightly shorter than me, with dreadlocks and sporting a bright yellow shirt that bore a black skull wearing a pink top hat. From my peripheral vision, I could tell that Sammy and Thayer were beside themselves with laughter, but I took one for the team and engaged with the man.

"What's up!"

"I don't got no money for you. Aliza ran off with my stuff. It'll be a few weeks before I can get the green to you!" he said.

The man smelled so strongly of pot that I wondered if he slept in a batch. He certainly seemed high. Sammy and Thayer slapped the bar, laughing at the scene. Their behavior annoyed me, but then my ego took over and I played things off. I reached out to slap the man's hand.

"Oh, it's all good hoss! We got the game on, having some drinks and some grub. Aliza can fuck off tonight, man." I said.

He bobbed his head and hugged me. "That's wassup!"

I got the man a beer while he approached the table to get food. It looked like he arrived with a group of three people, but they sat at the bar watching the game. As I ordered the beers from Lydia, I approached the trio. When I got close, they noticed me.

"Is that your pal?" I asked, pointing at the man.

The trio, two men and a woman, nodded.

"What's up with him? He seems a bit dazed…"

The game audio was loud, so one man leaned towards me. "He's been dazed since 1994! That's Maurice. Nice fella. Don't mind him."

"What, did he have too many cookies? He's rambling to me about 'Aliza'."

The woman laughed. "Boy, he be talkin 'bout Aliza, but his boo was 'Alita'. Don't tell him that though."

I took their cue, and I brought the beer to Maurice. Sammy and Thayer looked confused, as I struck up a conversation with Maurice and his friends. They both approached him and I at the buffet table as I handed him his beer.

"Who's your friend, Bosner?" Thayer asked.

I looked at Maurice and put my hand out to slap his. "This is Maurice. Aliza's man!"

Sammy and Thayer stood there and nodded at him.

"Yea, she left me man. I love that woman."

"Smells like you love green too." Sammy said.

"Nice shirt." Thayer added.

Just then, the club erupted with cheers and some boos. The Giants scored a touchdown. B-man jumped out of his seat, knocking it over, and slapped Lorrie's hand, then Dolvar's. Lydia snapped her fingers at him and motioned to him to calm down and pick up the barstool. He pulled his cap down and then went around the club, slapping hands with everyone who would. I hugged him when he came over to the buffet table.

"Aye, brother. Go New York!" Maurice said.

B-man slapped his hand. "Yea baby! GIANTS!"

"Why'd they change uniforms?" Maurice asked.

We looked at him strangely.

"Who's uniforms?" Thayer said.

B-man chugged the rest of his beer. Maurice pointed at the screen as it showed the Giants players hurrying back on to the field to kick off.

"New York! Them boys used to wear green!" he said.

"Nah bro, you're thinking of the Jets. These are the New York Football Giants! Catch you in a bit!"

B-man ran back to his stool and resumed watching the game. Just then, Zick and Joanne entered the club. They both looked tired and sweaty, but Zick had an ecstatic look on his face. I waved at them to join us in the back by the table.

"Got a workout in, did ya?" Thayer said.

Zick wiped sweat off his forehead. "Yea man. Joanne didn't really care to watch the game."

"I'm a Green Bay fan. I'm still not happy they lost to New York." she added.

Zick kissed her on the cheek. "She wanted to blow off some steam. I helped her out."

"Like where?" Sammy asked.

Zick smiled and pointed at Thayer. "Dumbass here didn't lock the doors on the SUV."

"Man, let me tell you. Aliza and I used to always make love in the back seat. If I got her up on the door just right... man, I'm just sayin." Maurice said.

Joanne and Zick looked at him. "Who—"

I introduced them quickly to avoid any runaround conversations. "This is Maurice. Aliza is his girl. Here, I'll get us some beers."

I went back up to the bar as Maurice put his arm around Zick and started off about Aliza. I stood by Dolvar, B-man, and Lorrie to wave Lydia down.

"Lorrie, how are these two doing?" I said.

B-man and Dolvar continued to argue with the Patriots fan.

"So far so good. The game is close. I hope they win so Blaine isn't filthy later." she replied.

"Ah don't worry. If they win, we're getting fucked up. If they lose…"

"We're getting fucked up!" Lorrie added as we both hi-fived.

Lydia came down and took my order. I ordered six beers, and she signaled a stripper to bring them over to us. I returned to the buffet table and jumped back into the conversation. Maurice and Zick were talking about cars, and Joanne stood beside him with her arms crossed.

"Beers coming!" I said.

She smirked. "I guess it's better that he talks to guys about cars than ladies about titties."

Joanne no sooner spoke, and the stripper brought a tray with the beers. I winked at her, then smiled at Joanne as she shook her head. Everyone grabbed a beer; I tilted my bottle to cheers with Joanne.

"Hey, you two are the best people in here. Don't forget that." I said.

Joanne smiled, and then I jumped back into the senseless chatter with the boys. Halftime came, and the game was pleasantly close. Some strippers began bringing out shooters, and at that point I began ordering water. Because of the close score, I paid closer attention to the second half of the game. Lorrie remained with B-man, but Tina found her way to the back by the food where she conversed with Joanne. More people arrived at the club, and while the place wasn't a packed house, it was livelier than when we arrived. I caught a glance of Randy running out from the back room to speak with the strippers, and I could tell that we satisfied him with the turnout. I felt good for Thomas' sake; we certainly helped him on that night!

Before I knew it, the game was winding down, and the Patriots had possession of the ball. Most of us huddled around Dolvar, Lorrie, B-man, and the Patriots fan, glued to the screen. In a flash, the Patriots drove down the field and scored a touchdown. The Patriots fan jumped out of his seat and began gesturing to everyone in the club.

"THAT'S RIGHT CROWN 'EM NOW!" he barked.

B-man ducked his head as he clinched his fists and smacked them on the bar. Lorrie put her hand on his back, but he was inconsolable. Dolvar threw his hat on the floor. He and B-man nudged their way through the group to the back near the buffet table. The Patriots fan, now seated, swiveled in the stool and faced us in the back. He continued to cross his arms and bob his head in a mocking style. I looked back at the screen and saw there was just over two minutes left in the game; it was Giants' ball. Something came over me, and I impulsively felt the need to cheer B-man and Dolvar up. As I talked to them, Dolvar put his hand up and walked back to the bar. B-man, however, stood and looked at me as I spoke.

"Damnit, you complained all season about the Giants. Look at where they are! They are in the Super Bowl, at the end of the game with a chance to win!"

I grabbed B-man and turned him to face the screen and walked him back towards the bar. We watched as the Giants meagerly moved the ball towards the 50-yard line, the Patriots fan continued making cheap remarks.

"Give it to us now. It's over. This is all just a waste of time. Gave us a good run, but this is the Patriots' year!"

Lorrie leaned over the bar and faced the Patriots fan. "It's not over yet."

The situation looked ugly for New York; they were in a difficult 4th down situation, but they converted for a 1st down. I grew frustrated with the Giants' hard style, but then came one of the most memorable football plays ever. B-man, still looking dejected, and the rest of us, watched as a 3rd down came and the Giants snapped the ball. The quarterback scrambled around, and it didn't appear there was anywhere for him to throw. We leaned into the bar, and the Patriots fan stood up and clapped. Amazingly, as the Patriots defenders got hands on the quarterback, he tugged his way out of what looked like a sure sack. The whole club seemed to hold its breath. The Giants quarterback then threw a ridiculous throw across his body to midfield.

A Giants receiver somehow trapped the ball between his hands and his helmet—a catch that made no sense except it was legal!

"That is some whack shit." The Patriots fan said.

The club was in an uproar over the ridiculous completion. I fist bumped B-man in the chest. "See! They aren't done yet! I told you!"

I had no idea what was going to happen, but I figured I would roll with the pep talk I gave B-man. Maurice walked up behind us and commented on the game while B-man remained glued to the screen. After a few insignificant plays, the quarterback dropped back and lobbed an almost unchallenged completion to the corner of the end-zone. The Giants' score sent the club into a frenzy. The Patriots fan bowed his head, with his forehead hitting the bar and his hands covering the back of his neck. B-man bear hugged me and threw me back. I fell backwards to the floor as Lydia yelled at him; what she said, I couldn't hear. I almost had the wind knocked out of me, but I got back to my feet and hugged B-man. Dolvar hugged Lorrie. Everyone was boisterous. Maurice stood and rambled incessantly.

There were only seconds left in the game, but even the Patriots fan knew the gig was up. A brutal sack of the Patriots quarterback by Giants defenders sealed the deal, the Giants won, 17-14. The dim lights grew dimmer, and then the music came back on. A strobe light began pulsating throughout the clubroom, and it was even harder to hear. The strippers folded the tables up and cleared the food. Thayer quickly grabbed one more plate before they took it away. Lorrie leaned towards me.

"…glad they won!" she said.

The club was so loud, I hardly heard Lorrie, but I knew what she said. Lydia ran beers out to everyone, and since I sobered up, I agreed to have one more in celebration. At that point, I wasn't sure who was paying for what, but I knew I was good to drive, and Thayer feasted enough that he likely had a keg-level tolerance. Tears of joy and drunkenness ran down B-man's cheeks. Lorrie grabbed him and they embraced. Dolvar talked trash to the Patriots fan who now looked completely dejected, but he finally mustered the energy to shake Dolvar's hand.

After about ten minutes, B-man began making rounds, talking to anyone as best he could. I could see that he was yelling to be heard over the blaring music, but I wasn't sure if anyone he was talking to could understand him. People whistled, and then I looked as strippers came out from the back door at the end of the bar. Five emerged, two of them gave us the wrist bands at the entrance earlier; they proceeded to the dance floor. Dolvar took notice along with the rest of us, the exception being B-man who was still rambling about the Super Bowl.

"I gotta hope the Giants win more often, it seems to be the one thing that keeps Blaine off of other women." Lorrie joked.

My eyes returned to the dark-haired stripper I took a liking to earlier. Now only wearing a G string, her hair, lips, and boobs had me captivated. I nodded to acknowledge Lorrie's joke, but she saw where my attention was and walked off. I felt a nudge on my right shoulder, and when I turned to look, Dolvar stood there with a wad of dollar bills in his grasp. He tried handing them to me, but I hesitated. He nodded and nudged me to take them, so I did.

Klein, who I hardly spoke to at all, approached.

"He's handing everybody greenbacks. Fuck it. Let's shower the babes!" he said.

Lorrie stood with her arms crossed, smiling and shaking her head. I lost track of B-man, but Klein, Sammy, and Dolvar stood with me.

"Make it rain baby!" Sammy yelled.

Before I ran dollars out of my hands towards the strippers, Randy walked from behind the bar onto the dance floor whispering something into the strippers' ears, one by one. They stopped their routine and stood straight up before proceeding back around the bar to the back room. We booed. Randy put his hand out for us to quiet down, and then he signaled Lydia to turn down the music. The strobe lights stopped, and the lights came back on. There was a brief silence, and then the bouncer entered the clubroom from the hallway. For a moment I thought we were about to get thrown out. I thought that maybe the money Dolvar was handing out was dirty or something. Everyone appeared confused.

"Alright everybody! We are closing up early tonight!" Randy announced.

Some in the crowd booed. Klein, Sammy, Thayer, and I looked at one another. Randy waved at everybody to quiet down again.

"Come join us at… hey B-guy?"

Randy looked around the club, then B-man put his hand up.

"It's B-man!" he yelled.

"B-man! We are going to B-man's to celebrate the championship and enjoy the ladies!" Randy finished.

I was completely shocked. I looked at B-man, who seemed completely dazed and simply full of football glory and alcohol. Randy returned to the bar area and instructed Lydia to settle everyone's tabs. The Patriots fan put down cash for his tab and left with his head lowered. Maurice and the trio that accompanied him approached me to ask for directions to "B-man's club". I wasn't sure how to answer, or if I should've at all. Luckily, Dolvar walked up beside me and answered on my behalf. He told them to follow the cars leaving the club— everyone at the club was coming over to the house, except for the Patriots fan.

It turned out that between B-man's big mouth and Thomas playing up his reputation, the two inadvertently convinced Randy to bring his show to Cape Henry House. I never found out what they said, or how Randy thought we had a club of our own, but when the patrons and strippers at E.Z. Girlz agreed to come with, the deal was sealed.

# 24. Cape Henry House

# Forever

I'm not entirely sure who rode with who, but on the ride back to the house, I knew Klein, Sammy, Zick, and Joanne road in Green Beater. They too were unsure how the boys pulled off the feat of bringing a strip club to the house. The four chatted amongst themselves as I drove. There were eight vehicles in our entourage heading to Cape Henry House.

 The most memorable moment of the drive came when we reached the intersection at Cape Henry Avenue near the familiar railroad tracks. As the line of cars turned, music blaring, a person on the street side walking a dog gazed at the spectacle. For the first time, it appeared as though the neighbors in each of the houses lining both sides of the street pulled back their curtains and peered out their windows at a motorcade of partiers, sports fans, sailors, beautiful women, you name it. It was as if they all peeked to pay homage to the encore of one of the wildest party weekends ever. Rock blared from Green Beater as heavy bass thumped from other vehicles, some with rims gleaming as they turned onto the street. The image of being in a music video came to mind. The moment didn't pass me by; I soaked it all in!

I parked in front of the house as everyone tried to find which one was party central. Thayer parked just behind me, and then the rest of the vehicles following us realized where to park. Tina, B-man, Lorrie, Dolvar, and Billy emerged from the SUV. Somewhere from just down the street came Thomas with Randy and two strippers. B-man drunkenly ran up to me.

"Bro, let's get the living room set up!"

"You know it!" I replied.

As we bolted up the steps to the front door, B-man looked up, pointing to the sky.

"GIANTS! YEA BABY!"

We took the beer pong table and folded it up as best we could, leaning it up against the wall in the pass out room. When we came back into the living room, everyone started entering the house. B-man and Dolvar ran into the bedroom, sliding out two four-cube organizer shelves. They stood them in the middle of the room between the TV and couches before deciding to lay them on their sides. I slid the coffee table away from the couches as people began sitting down. Dolvar stood still for a moment before he had another idea. He ran out to the back, snapping his fingers and calling for help; I went with him.

We went out back to the picnic table where the two kegs remained, the empty one remained laying on its side. He shook the other one in the tub of melted ice water and nodded that there was still beer in it. He signaled me to the side of the house where a large board of plywood leaned up on the exterior in the dark. Sammy followed us, and Dolvar directed him to get more help to bring the keg into the kitchen. Dolvar and I grabbed the board and carried it into the house. Once inside, Dolvar directed me to help him lay it over the two four-cube shelves. Finally, I realized what we were doing; we were making a platform for the strippers to dance on! B-man talked to Thomas and Randy as Billy and Sammy slogged the keg into the kitchen. Maurice and his friends walked through the front door and quickly saw what we were doing, one of them helped us center the board atop the shelves. The strippers applauded as Dolvar leapt onto the makeshift dance platform and jumped up and down to prove its sturdiness.

I got a cup of beer from the keg, and to my surprise it was still cold and not the least bit flat! Zick played with the TV, getting the music set up, and before long a strobe light flashed on as well. The strippers proceeded down the hallway to the bathroom to get ready. We handed out cups of beer to Maurice, his friends, and everyone else within sight. Thayer and Tina went into the kitchen and got leftover dip out of the fridge while everyone else got situated. Luckily for me, my favorite stripper came out, and she waved promiscuously at me as she entered the living room. I simply smiled back. With only the sink light in the kitchen on, Cape Henry House became an after-hour strip club. Dolvar handed me another stack of dollar bills, I took them without hesitation. He patted me on the side of my arm, smiling. Lorrie stood by the front door, shaking her head. I approached her.

"This took on a life of its own!" I said.

"It sure has."

"What do you think?"

She leaned towards me as the music was loud. "Blaine is on cloud nine. This is great. Let's enjoy it!"

I nodded. Billy had a cup of beer in his hand and was bobbing his head to the tunes. Thomas sat at the end of the couch by the front door, Joanne sat next to him as Zick got cups of beer before sitting next to her. Klein pumped his fist and yelled at the ceiling. Thayer stood at the side of the dance platform holding Tina, both enjoyed the tunes. Sammy came up from behind and slapped me on the back as I watched the strippers dance.

"OH MAN." he barked.

Maurice waved at me to sit with him and his group on the adjacent couch.

"What is this club?" he asked.

I grinned. "This is Cape Henry House!"

He smiled and nodded. "Good joint. Wish I would've found this place before!"

One of Maurice's friends pulled out a cigar and lit up. I motioned to him to smoke outside, but Dolvar nudged me on the back and told me to let him be. Beer in hand, I sat back and enjoyed the show; I was in awe of the moment. My stripper swerved her hips and ran her hands over her breasts and down her sides. Her eyes were closed at first, but when her hands reached her hips, she stood upright and opened them. She gazed at me; her eyes pulled in me. I handed her a wad of bills in my hand and she took them as she tucked them into her G-string. The other stripper, blonde with hints of glitter on her cheeks, was dancing closely to Maurice's friends, and on the other side Zick, Joanne, and Thomas looked at me as my favorite captivated me. She reached for my hands, and as I stood, she leaned towards me.

"And who are you, baby?" she asked.

"I'm into you. That's who I am."

"What happened to your eye?"

I laughed. "Oh, just a wake-up test gone wrong."

She was mostly fair skinned with a mild tan; I could only wonder if she was possibly Latina or Asian. She continued smiling at me.

"I'm Tonya."

In the background, people clapped and chanted my name. It wasn't exactly my first rodeo, but never had I been at a friend's house and had a stripper in my grasp! I let the moment be great, and I kept my face close to Tonya's bosom as she continued dancing. The moment seemed to last just long enough, and then a new tune blared. Tonya stepped off the platform and proceeded back down the hallway to the bathroom. I remained standing in place. Billy nudged me.

"Dude, go get her!" he said.

"I'm good, buddy. Pinch me!"

One of the other strippers off to the side stepped up onto the platform, and I grabbed Billy and sat him down in my place on the couch. I went to the keg for another beer, where B-man and Lorrie stood.

"Bro, you were in it!"

I looked at them both, a smile still attached.

"Bosner, you're too cute!" Lorrie said.

I stood with them and chugged my beer.

"You should've seen him in Guam!" B-man added.

"Man, this is almost better than that!" I replied.

Just then, the front door opened. Connie entered, carrying a rack of beer. She scoped the room and looked dumbstruck by the sight of strippers and loud music. I approached her.

"Honey, what is this!" she asked.

Still smiling, I took the rack of beer from her.

"Glad you could make it! A little late for the Super Bowl, don't ya think?"

She patted me on the chest and laughed. "I had to work late and take care of some other things. Glad I came though, this looks wonderful!"

The gang noticed Connie, and they gave her a hearty welcome.

"You all are for real! I had no idea!" she said.

B-man and Lorrie approached her, I walked over to Klein who stood at the doorway to the pass out room watching the entire spectacle. People threw money at the strippers. The tunes were beating, and everyone seemed happy. Dolvar began dancing with the blonde stripper. Maurice and his friends cheered and whistled.

"Man, I should've come to your parties sooner!" Klein said.

"Woulda, coulda, shoulda! Asshole!"

Tonya emerged from the bathroom in tight black dress and walked into the kitchen. I fist bumped Klein, then poured a cup of beer and handed it to her. She took it.

"So, tell me about yourself." she said.

"I'm Bosner. Welcome to Cape Henry House!"

She sipped the beer. "Bosner?"

"In these parts, that's what we roll with."

"You are cute, Bosner, but that eye. I'm sorry, darling."

"Eh, it happens." I replied.

"Are you military?"

"Oh yea. Well, most of us are. We keep things calm. Just beer and loud music. And strippers!"

Tonya laughed and took another sip of beer before running her hand down my arm to my hand. I handed her what cash I had left. She then approached Billy and Maurice to talk to them. I knew well that she had a routine, but I didn't care. The weekend was too wild to let formalities get in the way. Strangely, the night brought a lot of things to mind. I reflected on the three weeks of mayhem that took place at Cape Henry House. With all the music and noise going on around me, I eventually looked into the kitchen by the fridge and stared at the wall. It was as though Maria, and even my dad and grandpa were standing there holding cups of beer and giving cheers. I suppose such a vision was odd, but the events at the house over the course of those three weeks made anything look sensible. Everything was great. I simply bobbed my head to the music. The night was sublime.

"Good way to say 'fuck you' to this place, what do you think?" B-man said.

"What do you mean?" Connie asked.

Lorrie leaned in and kissed B-man, who then embraced her. Connie smiled.

"Some of the guys are shipping off, and we are closing up shop after tonight." I explained.

"Huh? Deploying and leaving the area?"

"Some of the guys are moving out of here, and some of them are deploying for a few months. Don't worry, you'll see us around still!" I said.

She put her arm around me. "Oh, good. I'd miss you guys otherwise!"

One of Maurice's friends got up and walked past us towards the sliding glass door. I followed him. Outside, he sat up on the picnic table, resting his feet on the bench seats. I stood across from him.

"Helluva place." he said.

"Thanks."

He pulled out a dime bag and gestured to me. I put my hand out and shook my head.

"Oh no. We don't do that stuff."

"Cops?"

I laughed. "No. We're the other ones."

"Ah. I was Gulf War. Just a handyman now."

"Thank you for your service, hoss." I said.

We fist bumped, and I stood there for a moment before returning inside. Everyone continued to enjoy themselves, but then the front door swung open; it was Penley and Anne! As they stood at the entrance, I stood straight up and looked around. Nobody seemed to notice them. Penley at first looked appalled, but he then covered his face to hide his expression, one of laughter. Anne was simply beside herself, practically unable to put her thoughts together into words or sound. Thomas remained seated on the couch closest to the door, enjoying the atmosphere, but he eventually turned and saw the two. He jumped to his feet, presumably to explain what was going on. Penley put his hand out to stop Thomas in his tracks. I intervened. I approached Anne, who remained standing at the doorway with everyone but Thomas and I still oblivious.

"You two are back early!" I said.

She gazed into my eyes and appeared to be in a state of mind beyond anger. "What is this?"

"Come with me, let's talk." I replied.

I tried walking her towards the hallway, but she remained in the living room by the front door.

"What in the fuck! What is this! Why are you all…!?" Anne gasped.

"Now, listen, I can—"

Penley put his hand out and interrupted me. "Go back out there. Right. Fucking. Now."

I hastily nodded and walked away. I got another cup of beer and tried to pretend everything was good. Lorrie approached me and gestured towards Penley and Anne. I nodded, and then she attempted to talk to them. I stood in the living room and watched what I knew was the last of the show for the night. The tunes continued beating, and the strobe light continued to flash. Zick and Joanne looked oblivious as they remained on the couch. Billy stepped away, Connie took his place on the couch and chatted with Maurice. His one friend appeared to be outside still, but the other guy and the girl remained seated on the couch enjoying the show.

B-man nudged my arm. "Bro, did Penley and Anne just get back?"

"Yea, I think the show's almost up."

He scoffed and stormed towards the two. I flinched, knowing the house was about to erupt. A moment or two passed, and then Anne gave off an awful scream. Everybody, including the strippers, stopped and looked. Someone shut off the music, then Anne stormed through the living room to the hallway entrance.

"What in the fuck is this! Who are you people! Why are you in my house!"

Randy, standing by the door watching the show, flinched. "Hey, who is this broad?"

I approached him, hoping to keep him calm. "Yo, sorry bud. These are the other roomies."

"Huh?"

The whole situation was a mess, it was almost funny.

"Yea. I think the show is over. Sorry man." I said.

The strippers looked at Anne. Anne stood, surveilling the living room and kitchen. She looked out the sliding glass door and screamed again. When I looked, I saw Maurice's friend blowing clouds of smoke.

"Who the fuck are these people! Why are you doing this!"

Randy walked towards her. "Yo, lady, what's the deal?"

"Randy, it's cool. Let's get everybody out of here. Thomas will fill you in. Sorry." I said.

Penley stood in the living room. "Show's up everyone. Please leave now!"

Everyone but the gang got up and began gathering their belongings. Randy called for Thomas, and the two went out the front door. I thought for a minute that Thomas was in real trouble. I ran outside as the two stood on the front lawn. Randy turned and faced me.

"Yo, this doesn't concern you!"

"No, whatever is up, it's okay we can resolve this." I replied.

Thomas waved at me to go inside, but I refused. Randy ran up the steps and got into my face.

"This isn't your beef, motherfucker. There won't be any trouble if you get your ass back inside. Got it?" he said.

I looked at Thomas. He nodded. "Go back in. It's okay, I got this."

Then, I heeded. As I walked inside, Connie approached the door, holding Maurice's hand.

"Hey honey, nice party. I'm going to roll with Maurice. See you at Johnny's sometime!"

I patted her arm and shook Maurice's hand. "Thanks for coming out. Catch you later."

Maurice's friends were on their way out the door as well, so I asked them about he and Connie. The girl laughed and insisted that Maurice was just a "baked baby boomer" and wouldn't hurt a fly. I shook the guys' hands as they walked out the door, then the woman handed me a card.

"You boys should come our way sometime; I can see you like to party."

"Thanks." I replied.

"Nice shiner, too."

"Sleeping with your eyes open does it every time!" I joked.

I took her card, which had the name "Monica" accompanied by a phone number. She smiled back at me as she continued with the guys, I waved at them, then walked inside. Three of the strippers, including Tonya, had their jackets on and purses in hand. Tonya kissed her palm and then touched my check. I briefly smiled as she bid me farewell. "See you around, baby."

Lorrie, B-man, and Penley stood in the kitchen. They seemed calm, as did everyone else who now sat on the couches. Anne stormed out of the hallway back into the living room. She looked around and saw the beer-stained floors, scuff marks on the countertops, and missing items from the kitchen cabinets. Thankfully, we cleaned up any blood stains the night before. The sight of the plant in the wall's corner prompted her to examine it, she realized it was covering damaged drywall. In the pass out room, she saw the damaged beer pong table folded up against the back wall. After she screamed again, Penley walked in to console her. B-man looked at the plant in the corner and thanked Lorrie before kissing her.

Anne stormed out of the pass out room, past the kitchen and living room, and back down the hallway. Soon, we heard her in the bedroom.

"Who the fuck was in my bed!" she screamed.

Penley proceeded to the hallway and faced B-man, Lorrie and I, he silently laughed. We heard the bedroom door close, then angry voices as the two argued. After a few moments, the door opened as did another one; Anne gave off yet another scream. Out of the hallway, the fourth stripper ran out, covering her naked breasts as she bolted out the front door. Dolvar emerged from the hallway shortly after with a beaming smile.

"Alexis is nice." he said.

B-man's eyes bugged out. "Bro, you're a dog."

Once all the guests left, we stood around in the living room in an icy silence. It was as if everyone reached the same conclusion: a wild, last weekend at Cape Henry House went down in proverbial flames. Dolvar took it upon himself to hand out cups of beer to everyone as we remained silent. Finally, Zick broke the silence and laughed. We looked at him.

"Pretty kick ass weekend. Music, fights, beer, Super Bowl, strippers dancing at the house. Throw in Bosner's black eye, and some of us are going on det!" he said.

With Zick's remark, I realized that Penley and Anne coming home early just made the night—and the weekend—more memorable.

"How would your grandpa rate this?" Billy asked.

I smirked. "Ah, he's somewhere saluting."

"How did Dolvar pull that shit off with the stripper? I didn't even notice when he took her in the back!" Klein said.

Dolvar smiled. "It's an old trick I'll show you sometime once you lose your virginity."

"OH MAN." Sammy barked.

"I think you're talking about Bosner." Klein added.

"First it was a sore ass, then a shiner this weekend. Bosner, you're off to a terrible start!" Thomas added.

I laughed. "Hey, hey. I had some neck wounds a few weeks back. I'm getting there!"

B-man raised his cup. "Bro, the New York Giants are Super Bowl Champs!!!! Drink up!"

Everyone raised their cups and chugged. We stood around joking and drinking to the night that ended abruptly, then Penley emerged from the back and stood silently at the hallway entrance. He broke out in another silent laugh, then helped himself to a cup of beer.

"Man, you guys outdid yourselves with this one. We'll talk tomorrow." he said.

"These guys like to party. Didn't you consider that before getting into this arrangement?" Joanne asked.

Everybody looked at Penley, who raised his cup to her. "Good one."

As he walked back down the hallway to his room, he stopped and turned around. "Oh yea, congrats B-man and Dolvar on the Super Bowl win."

"NEW YORK GIANTS!" B-man and Dolvar yelled.

Penley smiled. "AND! B-man, we got a fight to wage."

"Ten years later." Billy added.

"Pass out room! Fight!" Zick yelled.

B-man and Penley stood face to face. Without saying another word, the two stepped into the pass out room; we followed suit. Lorrie turned on the lights, and then the two grappled. Penley shoved B-

man back towards the massive hole in the drywall.
Just before falling through, B-man overpowered
Penley and drove him back the other direction. The
two tripped and fell to the floor, still grappled up.
We laughed and cheered as they grunted and cussed.
Anne stormed into the room, but Sammy and Zick
stood in front of her and explained that the fight was
purely mutual from a previous agreement.
Distressed, she swiftly left and went back to her
room.

The grappling and tumbling between B-man
and Penley continued for a minute or two before B-
man drove Penley over a box in the corner. Falling
awkwardly over the box, Penley grabbed his back
and tapped out. We clapped and laughed, but it was
a disappointment that the fight ended because of an
awkward fall and not a pin. After making sure that
Penley was okay, B-man pulled him up, and the two
bro hugged. We returned to the living room and
Penley drank one more beer with us as he told us
about his weekend with Anne; it was nowhere near
as remarkable as our weekend had been. Once
Penley went to his room, B-man vented about the
living situation having deteriorated. We ultimately
convinced him that in all fairness, the few weeks at
the house were not sustainable from then on.

I got drunk not long after Penley went back to
his room, and I attempted to tell the gang about my
trip with Wilky and Shanae, and the "voluptuous"
Latisha. I got everyone laughing especially hard
about the ordeal, but I'm not sure if it was because

of the actual story, or because of how I told it—in my drunken signature fashion. Thomas told a story about an ex-girlfriend, but I was too woozy to gather any of what he was saying. I remembered something about "pontoon boat" and "no protection" but coming from Thomas it could've been as likely that he was talking about life vests as it was about condoms. At some point not long after, B-man grabbed me and walked me into the pass out room. I mumbled, "How 'bout them Giants" then everything went dark.

# 25. A Gang's Hurrah

The sound of a helicopter flying overhead was the first thing I noticed. I opened my eyes to that ever so unwelcome light that comes after a weekend of partying. Reality returned, or just Monday. Vision blurred, I quickly checked my phone to see what time it was, and luckily it was only Noon. Sluggishly, I got to my feet, gathered my belongings, and walked into the kitchen. Nobody was in the living room, and then I looked back in the pass out room. The place was empty! For a moment, a thought ran through my mind that maybe the weekend was a dream. When I saw "New York Giants Super Bowl Champs" written in permanent marker on the fridge, I realized there was nothing fake about the weekend. The makeshift dance platform remained set up in the living room as well. I smiled and shook my head as I left the house and got into Green Beater.

On my way back to base, I turned up the stereo and sang at the top of my lungs. I felt good, and as I approached the base gate, I had a smile on my face. At the gate, the sentry glared at me oddly as I presented my military ID.

"Good afternoon. Is everything okay?" the sentry asked.

"Um, yes, how are you?" I replied.

"I don't have a black eye."

*Shit,* I thought to myself.

The sentry looked closely at my ID. "Were you in an altercation, Petty Officer Bosner?"

"Was tired from work. Fell asleep with my eyes open. Someone wanted to check and see if I was alive. Turns out that I am."

The sentry smiled. "Yea, that'll getcha every time. Carry on."

Signaled to proceed, I drove down the main base road towards the barracks. I parked and quickly headed inside. On the quarterdeck was Thompson. I tried to hurry past him towards my room, but he stopped me.

"Your eye. Do I even want to know what happened?"

"Nope. Probably not." I replied.

He stared at me like the sentry had, then shook his head and waved me off. I gave him a nod and proceeded down the corridor towards my room. Music jammed in Wilky's room, and true to form, Casello sat in the hallway with his laptop. We both waved at each other, but he said nothing about my eye. Once in my room, I changed out of my battered clothes and took a long, hot shower. I shaved, and then I tried putting a warm, damp cloth over my face to ease the bruising around my eye. It didn't seem to help nearly enough, so I finally resolved to deal with whatever reaction it might garner once I arrived at the command. I took too much time getting ready for work, mainly due to my facial situation. I hurried out of my room and down the corridor towards the quarterdeck. Anderson was at the front desk, and she quickly noticed my eye.

"Bosner, goodness what happened!?"

I wanted to hurry past her and head straight to the parking lot, but she was always kind and I felt like I owed her at least a vague explanation.

"It's not what it looks like. I slept with my eyes open apparently, and it scared someone."

She shook her head. "It's bad, my dear. I have something that will help though."

She grabbed her purse, pulled out a vile of makeup, and tossed it to me. I looked at it, then at Anderson. She nodded.

"Don't worry, I'm a lady. I have plenty of it. Dab a little over the bruising."

"Thanks!"

I hurried out the door to Green Beater. I sped out of the parking lot and down the road to the command. Once I parked, I looked into the rearview mirror and quickly applied some of the facial makeup over the bruising. Amazingly, it worked to perfection! I gave off a laugh of approval as I got out and headed into the command. I arrived with two minutes to spare; so far, the day was a success. When I entered the shop, B-man approached me. I was the only guest who stayed at the house the night before, as everyone else went home or back to their barracks. McCord came into the shop sipping on a cup of coffee. He told B-man and I that Senior wanted to see us as well as Dolvar and Zick. The LPOs had not yet entered the shop, so McCord's news prompted B-man to walk both of us with him out behind the hangar.

"Bro. How does Senior know about the party?"

McCord shook his head. "Hey man, I heard about the fight after I left. I didn't say shit."

I patted him on the chest. "Yea, you called it without calling it."

"Dolvar rode with me today, but I haven't seen him since we got here. I hope he didn't squeal." B-man said.

"I don't think he would. Who knows, maybe Melissa reported it." I replied.

B-man was flustered.

"Bro, everything is good. I mean it was a wild incident, but we got up from it and everything. I don't know why the command would be involved."

McCord did his best to comfort him.

"Hey, hey. Take it easy. Who knows why he wants to see us? If it's about the party, I'll do the talking. Nothing happened when my wife and I were there. That's the doggone truth."

Just then, the back door to the shop swung open.

"Hey, come in. Senior Chief Beaumont is looking for you guys." Sadina said.

318

We looked at each other, then reentered the shop. Standing in the main doorway to the hangar was Senior, looking sharp and clean cut as always. The military creases in his khaki shirt and trousers were razor sharp, his ribbon rack almost seemed to gleam. The sight of him made us nervous. He waved at B-man, McCord, and I to follow him as the rest of the shop looked at us with curiosity. Once we entered the hangar, Zick, Dolvar, and Sammy were standing there waiting. Senior glanced at us and then signaled to follow him towards Maintenance Control. We looked at each other, confused about what was going on. B-man slowly shook his head, as he was certain that the past weekend was about to be laid plain to us. I had my concerns, as well.

"So boys, how was your weekend? How about that Super Bowl?" Senior asked.

We looked at each other. None of us wanted to respond. Then McCord did. "It was good Senior. Really good. Yes, the Giants pulled off a great upset!"

He smiled. "Blaine, Dolvar. You two are Giants fans, correct?"

The two looked at each other and nodded. "Yes, Senior."

We followed him into the doorway to the main corridor of the command. We turned left and entered Maintenance Control. Once there, he looked into one of the vacant offices and signaled us to enter. He waved at Sammy to close the door behind him. Senior took a seat at the desk as the six of us stood there, in our coveralls, at attention.

"At ease, boys."

We relaxed, and then he began twirling a pen between his fingers.

"Okay. So, on Friday night, Chief Rogers was running the show. He had your shop break up into teams to do the wash jobs on the two helos we are prepping for this upcoming det." he said.

We slowly nodded.

"You all worked on one together. Aircraft #218. Correct?" he continued.

There was a mutually awkward feeling among the six of us. Nobody answered. He grinned.

"It's okay. Nod your heads. I have some good news: Skipper came in this weekend with the Wing Commander. Totally impromptu visit. They boarded both helos just to check them out. Yours was outstanding. The Wing Commander remarked how clean it was."

I felt a sigh of relief. I think we all did. Getting accolades from the Skipper was good enough, getting them from the Wing Commander was epic! Life as a sailor was best when those two were pleased with work output.

"See you all tomorrow. Damned good job." Senior said.

We thanked him, then Zick asked about the others that helped us on the wash job. Senior smiled and told us that they needed personnel for a temporary assignment to the Supply Depot. He added they didn't want to "give up the best in the shop" so they sent the others. We bobbed our heads and took our cue to hit the locker room. As we got to the doorway of the main corridor, Senior stopped us.

"Hey, you know some of you are going to be gone for a bit on this det. Don't forget to treat yourselves out and celebrate!"

*Oh… if he only knew*, I thought to myself.

Everyone nodded and continued towards the locker room. Once we entered and the door closed behind us, we shouted and hi-fived. McCord asked if it was normal to get out early, and Dolvar gave one of his typically snide replies, "Of course, clown." As we changed into our civies, Sammy asked about plans for that evening.

"Lorrie's off today, bro. Gonna spend the evening with her and pack. I'm goin on det!!!"

We all fist bumped with B-man.

"That stripper, Alexis, I got her number. I'm going to call her up for a sequel." Dolvar said.

We laughed and replied, "She's gonna cost you!"

Sammy looked at Zick. "Whaddya say? Seafood buffet at Dodge's Pier?"

"Joanne gets off in a little bit. I think we are going to catch a movie and relax."

"OH MAN."

"Bro, those two are the gold standard! Three weeks at that house and they end up as the great couple of the bunch!"

Zick blushed. "Thayer invited her. I just sang."

B-man put out his fist. "To the great pair that met at the great house."

"Cape Henry House!" I added.

We all fist bumped again. Then Sammy looked at McCord.

"Sorry Sammy. You know me, just going home to the wife. Old guy here."

In a sarcastic fashion, Sammy grabbed me by my shirt. "Bosner! Bosner! Seafood buffet!"

"I'll pass. Gotta unwind. Had a doozy of a weekend, or three."

Sammy looked disappointed at first, but then he smiled. Once back in our civies, we exited the locker room out the back and walked together towards the parking lot.

"I mean, that house and those parties. I guess a break would be nice, huh?" Sammy said.

"Bro, how the fuck did the cops not get called? How did we not get hurt?"

"Hey asshole, I got a black eye!" I said.

"And you covered it well. Who helped you clean it up? I know that wasn't all you." Zick said.

"Girl at the quarterdeck in my barracks."

"Yea but bro, you got that randomly. It wasn't fight related. How the fuck does that happen?"

"And Klein, what about him?" I asked.

B-man laughed. "If you get punched by someone wearing pink and cry, you are in your own category."

The rest of us laughed.

"Ya'll best not act up away from that house. Seems like that house was your sweet spot." McCord said.

Sammy put out his hand. "I cut this pretty good."

"Clown... but that wasn't from the house, that was from playing dodge-dog on private property."

"No, no. He was wounded in action!" I said.

Everybody called out, "Mission: Three Beers Standing."

"That's right." I said.

We stood in a circle in the parking lot. Wilky drove by in his purple custom ride and waved as he honked. We waved back. At that point, I sent everybody off.

"Alright boys... McCord, enjoy your day with the wife. B-man, enjoy Lorrie, finally. Dolvar, save your damned money. Zick, keep rocking with Joanne. And Sammy, enjoy the buffet. I'm going rogue!"

We bro hugged and then I started for Green Beater as they all walked towards their vehicles. As I opened the door, B-man whistled and got everyone to look towards him.

"Bosner! Tell Latisha we all said hi!"

"Ooooooooooo!"

I gave a crude salute as I got into Green Beater. I wasn't sure what I was going to do that afternoon, so I started towards the barracks. Once at the parking lot, something came over me and I pulled back out onto the road to exit base. I turned the stereo up and zoned out into my thoughts about what transpired. From a regular Friday night and Saturday morning at the command three weeks back, I thought about the vortex that was Cape Henry House. Deployments and dets always warranted stories worth telling when we returned to shore, but never was there a place or an experience quite like the one we had during those three weeks in 2008.

With few exceptions, much of the gang remains in contact to this day. We get together periodically and laugh at the memories. Everyone agrees on one thing wholeheartedly; through sore butts on front steps to bruised egos of fragile women, through wasted trips for food and drink to strippers at a house turned club, the experiences only strengthened the camaraderie of the gang at Cape Henry House.

As I drove Green Beater off base on that Monday in February 2008, I wondered if the gang's last hurrah was on the horizon. As it would turn out, the gang's hurrah over the course of those three weeks was anything but the last. In fact, it would prove to be stronger in the days, weeks, months, and years that followed. Time proved it.

# *Bonus Inning*

While I drove through town, music still blaring, I developed a craving for a deli sandwich. I remembered some shipmates at the command talking about a new chain of stores that featured touchscreen technology for made-to-order sandwiches. One of the aircrewman told a bunch of us in the shop that they ordered a "Philly-cheesesteak-pizza-au jus", and that the touchscreen combinations for sandwiches was almost endless! The thought made me even more hungry, so I set off to find a location. After some time, as I continued to blare music and act a fool in Green Beater, I found one with a "grand opening" banner flailing in the breeze. I almost missed the turn, so I sharply swung the wheel, making Green Beater screech. As I barely made the turn into the establishment's parking lot, I parked on the side of the building, hoping to avoid stares.

When I entered the place, I could smell the newness of the interior. There was a circular counter where the cashiers and registers were, then to the back right was the deli section. There, I saw a glass countertop lined with touch screens; the servers were beyond the countertop preparing orders. I never been to a place quite like it before, and thankfully the touch screens were user friendly. I ordered an Italian-style sub with olives, pickles, lettuce, tomato, onions, extra meat and cheese, and spicy mayonnaise. A numbered ticket printed from just below the touch screen as I finished placing my order. The setup was impressive, and I knew I would likely return. I stood there briefly before looking around—that's when the day went in a new direction.

As I stood waiting, a particular person caught my eye. To my left, also with a ticket in hand, was a familiar looking female. She had dark hair, a nose piercing, and a small birthmark on her right cheek. We both stared for an extended period and greeted one another. *Who are you...* I thought to myself. There was a quiet, awkward moment, but we continued looking at one another. She had hazel eyes, but I didn't recall that about her from before. In fact, my memory was leading me to believe I met her at a club or something. She was certainly not at the club in downtown when I was with Wilky and Shanae. She definitely wasn't at E.Z. Girlz, nor was she from Greenies. Finally, I thought she may have been one of Ms. Highlights' friends, but I was certain that I didn't see her at Cape Henry House.

"I swear I know you." she said.

"Yes, you look familiar." I replied.

"Are you in my art group?"

"I don't think so."

She continued to smile, but with a hint of frustration. I likely did the same, but my mind raced to recall where I knew her from. Finally, a glimpse came into my mind of her trying to talk to us somewhere. I was with the gang, and we had a hard time hearing her. *Bam! You're the C.T. Slater's girl*, I thought to myself. I covered my chin, then slightly pointed towards her.

"You work at C.T. Slaters, right?" I asked.

She laughed. "Oh, you know what? You were with the Giants fans weren't you!"

"Yea, uh... we left the bar on bad terms."

"Honestly, I would've preferred you guys stayed. The couple that we seated there after you was terrible." she said.

"I know them. The guy's name is Pickens."

She shook her head. "Yea, he complained about everything on the menu. Actually, his girlfriend did, but she made him do the talking."

The servers called "Number 17", which was the girl's ticket number. She walked to the counter, retrieved her order, then returned.

"So, I'm Kelly. Since you obviously forgot."

I stared carelessly into her eyes. "I'm Bosner. Since you probably never knew."

She looked down at the floor, then back at me. "So, about C.T. Slaters. I kinda left there, and I'm not going back."

"Oh, I'm sorry to hear that!"

"It's okay. I didn't care for that place, really."

"We didn't either." I joked.

She giggled as I continued to stare at her. At that moment, the servers called "Number 18", but I remained fixated on Kelly. A moment passed, and they called the number again.

"Uh, I think that's you?"

I blushed. "Oh! Yes. Thank you."

I retrieved my sandwich and walked back to her.

"What are you up to?" she asked.

"Nothing really. Off work for the day. Just this sandwich I guess."

There was a genuine attraction, and it was practically screaming at me. I could almost imagine her strangling me to make sure I realized she was showing me interest.

"Oh… okay… I'm not really doing anything either." she replied.

*Bosner old boy. Here's your cue,* I thought to myself. A surge of nervousness in my mind gave way to confidence.

"Wanna do that together?" I asked.

"Okay."

Her face lit up. It was a wonderful sight. We walked side by side to the register where I paid for both of our orders. After that, we proceeded outside.

"So, Bosner. You must be military. Tell me about your first name."

"About that…"

We both sat down on a bench facing the street. The weather was delightfully mild, and the sun beamed through gaps in the mostly cloudy skies.

# CAPE HENRY HOUSE

As Kelly and I talked, I smiled uncontrollably. As I best remember, only one word came to mind, *SCORE!*

Made in the USA
Monee, IL
07 December 2021

84004694R00198